"I will do my best for my chi
in this matter of my remarri
Miss Somerton, you may rely o
I am more than conscious tha
depend on me—indeed, I wo
give my life for any of then

What on earth had possessed him to say
something so dramatic? *Blame it on the midnight
madness.* Serena made a little smothered sound.
Dominic raised his eyebrows at her, daring her to
comment.

She shook her head. "It's time I returned to my
chamber." She bent over and kissed Louisa's
forehead. The way she smoothed a lock of his
daughter's hair reminded Dominic of Emily. For
one moment, he found himself wanting that
touch on his own hair, that tenderness directed
at him.

No.

Yet instinctively, he drew closer, and as Serena
straightened, she bumped into him. Dominic
grasped her arms to steady her. Immediately, he
released her.

They stood, staring at each other.

"Good night," she blurted. And almost ran from
the room.

Books by Abby Gaines

Love Inspired Historical

*The Earl's Mistaken Bride
*The Governess and Mr. Granville

*The Parson's Daughters

ABBY GAINES

wrote her first romance novel as a teenager, only to have it promptly rejected. A flirtation with a science fiction novel never really got off the ground, so Abby put aside her writing ambitions as she went to college, then began her working life at IBM. When she and her husband had their first baby, Abby worked from home as a freelance business journalist…and soon after that the urge to write romance resurfaced. It was another five long years before Abby sold her first novel to Harlequin Superromance in 2006.

Abby lives with her husband and children—and a labradoodle and a cat—in a house with enough stairs to keep her semifit and a sun-filled office with a sea view that provides inspiration for the funny, tender romances she loves to write. Visit her at www.abbygaines.com.

The Governess and Mr. Granville

ABBY GAINES

Love Inspired

Recycling programs for this product may not exist in your area.

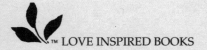

™ LOVE INSPIRED BOOKS

ISBN-13: 978-0-373-82932-3

THE GOVERNESS AND MR. GRANVILLE

Copyright © 2012 by Abby Gaines

www.LoveInspiredBooks.com

Printed in U.S.A.

Forget the former things; do not dwell on the past.
See, I am doing a new thing!
—*Isaiah* 43:18–19

For Bridget Latham

With love and best wishes for your new life with Darrell

Chapter One

Woodbridge Hall, Leicestershire, England, 1816

Dominic Granville seldom troubled himself with the running of his household. He had a spinster sister and a host of servants to take care of that. Besides, he had plenty to occupy him, between his land and its tenants.

Oh, yes, and his children.

His assumption that things would continue very much as they had for the past five years had proved correct. Until today.

Until he'd opened the letter newly arrived from London, fixed with a seal of aristocracy that he remembered from his school days at Eton, but hadn't had much occasion to see since.

Blast.

Dominic reread the letter, penned in a firm, elegant hand. It said exactly what he thought it had on his first reading.

He tugged the bellpull behind his desk. While he waited for his butler, he scrutinized the letter a third time. *How inconvenient.*

"Sir?" Molson had a habit of materializing silently; somehow he'd opened the library door without Dominic noticing.

Over the years, Dominic had mastered the art of hiding his start of surprise, so now he looked up calmly.

"Is Miss Somerton in the schoolroom?" he asked.

"I believe, sir, Miss Somerton and the children are—" Molson hesitated "—in pursuit of lepidoptera."

"Chasing butterflies?" Dominic said blankly. "Why?"

"Miss Somerton felt it was an occupation Masters Thomas and William should practice, sir. I believe she called it a lesson in nature sciences."

"What about the girls?" Dominic asked. "Shouldn't they be stitching something?"

"Misses Hester, Charlotte and Louisa are also pursuing lepidoptera."

Dominic frowned. In the past three weeks alone, he'd had to send word to the governess that shrieking outside the library window wasn't acceptable. That allowing the children to drink lemonade in the billiard room—which, technically, was forbidden territory—left a sticky residue everywhere. Both times, instead of contrition, her response had been to invite him to *play* with the children. Extraordinary.

When he'd found her timing the children as they slid down the banisters, his instinct had been to dismiss her on the spot. For his sister's sake—Marianne had hired the woman, and would be distressed at having to replace her—he'd constrained his reaction to the delivery of a stern lecture about safe pursuits.

Maybe today's letter was timely, after all. "Send Miss Somerton to me as soon as they come inside," he ordered.

"Certainly, sir." Molson's confiding tone said he knew just why Dominic needed to see the governess. The butler glided from the room.

Dominic wondered if he was the last to hear the news. He seldom traveled to London these days, and didn't read the society pages of the newspaper. Unlike his butler, apparently. He presumed Marianne hadn't—

A scream from outside the library brought him to his feet. He strode to the door and flung it open.

The entrance hall teemed with people—all five of Dominic's children, Molson and a footman on his hands and knees, grimacing as he groped behind the oak chest that had been in the family since Elizabethan days. A maid stood pressed against the wall, her hand over her mouth: she must be the screamer. The last participant in this pandemonium was the governess, Miss Serena Somerton, who was patting the maid's shoulder.

"There, there, Alice," she soothed. "It was only a lizard. It couldn't possibly harm you."

Which told Dominic all he needed to know. "Thomas," he barked.

Silence fell, sudden and absolute.

Eleven-year-old Thomas stepped forward. "Yes, Papa?"

His twin sister, Hester, younger by thirty minutes, slipped her hand into his. Whatever trouble Thomas was in, Hetty would insist on sharing it. Which made it dashed hard for Dominic to discipline his son.

"Did you bring a lizard inside, Thomas?" he asked.

"Yes, Papa, but it was one I'd never seen before, and it was bright green and it looked right at me."

"It's very beautiful," Hetty said loyally.

The younger girls, Charlotte and Louisa, nodded.

"Only, it escaped," Thomas explained, as if Dominic might not have guessed.

Dominic rolled his eyes. "Did I not expressly forbid the bringing inside of wildlife because of the pain and inconvenience the household suffers when it escapes, as it invariably does? If my dogs can live outside, so can your lizard."

A flicker of agreement crossed the face of Gregory, the

footman, who was straining to reach farther behind the chest. Seven-year-old William sucked in a tiny breath—either in awe at his brother's daring to disobey, or in fear of the consequences.

"Yes, sir," Thomas said. "I'm very sorry."

With a tiny jerk of his head, Dominic indicated the maid, still being thoroughly shoulder-patted by Miss Somerton.

"I'm very sorry, Alice," Thomas said.

"I didn't mind at all, Master Thomas," the maid lied brazenly, eyeing Dominic as if he was about to take a switch to his son's behind. "Like you said, it was very pretty."

Thomas flashed her the charming smile that, more often than not, got him off the hook.

What discipline would Miss Serena Somerton employ against this offense? Dominic wondered. He turned his attention to the governess. Goodness, she looked as if she'd been dragged backward through a bush.

An assortment of leaves and twigs clung to the skirt of her pale gray dress. Her bonnet was decidedly askew, and although Dominic was no expert on fashion, he was fairly certain the blond tresses curled on her shoulders were meant to be *inside* the bonnet.

And she had a smudge on her nose.

The urge to restore order, to reach out with a handkerchief and wipe away that smudge, was almost overwhelming. But of course, he couldn't do that.

"Children, could you all please go to the schoolroom immediately." The governess belatedly recalled her duties. "We will sketch some of the butterflies we observed." She held up a hand to forestall Thomas's protest. "I'm sure that when Gregory finds Captain Emerald—" Captain Emerald must be the lizard "—he will take him outside."

"You'll put him somewhere safe, Gregory, won't you?" Thomas pleaded.

"Yes, Master Thomas," the footman said through gritted teeth.

Dominic suspected Gregory considered the safest place for the lizard to be under the heel of his shoe.

"Miss Somerton, may I see you in the library?" Dominic asked, as the children traipsed upstairs in a semiorderly manner.

"Certainly, Mr. Granville." She took a step toward him as she began untying the strings of her bonnet, the brim of which had an unmistakable dent.

"I suppose you'll want to tidy yourself first," Dominic said.

She looked surprised, but said agreeably, "As you wish." She lifted the bonnet from her head.

Alice shrieked; Molson made an exclamation, quickly muffled.

Miss Somerton turned to stare at them. "What's wrong?"

"It appears, Miss Somerton, you have a lizard on your head," Dominic said.

The green creature (emerald was a gross exaggeration) perched motionless, as if moving might reveal its location to people who hadn't noticed it.

Dominic braced himself for the governess to fall into a faint; he would be obligated to catch her.

Instead, she stilled, not in panic, but in cautious relief. "Isn't that just like a lizard?" she said. "I didn't even feel it, the stealthy little creature!" She beamed at the butler. "Rather like you, Mr. Molson."

So she, too, found the butler's ability to materialize out of nowhere disconcerting? Molson appeared to take being compared to a lizard as a compliment; his countenance retained its butlerish impassivity, but his eyes twinkled. Had Dominic observed his butler's eyes twinkling before?

"I don't suppose you have a jar you could put over Captain Emerald, Mr. Granville?" Miss Somerton asked.

"No, Miss Somerton, I do not carry a jar on my person for the purpose of trapping lizards on young ladies' heads." Dominic stepped closer. "But if you remain still, I hope to pluck it from your hair. With your permission."

It seemed to take her a moment to realize he was asking for that permission.

She smiled suddenly, but carefully, so as not to move her head. "Pluck away, Mr. Granville, please."

Her blue eyes were alight with humor. Dominic found himself grinning in return; the situation was quite absurd.

Though Miss Somerton was of above average height, he still looked down on her hair, which was, he noted objectively, a color the poets called flaxen. He lowered his fingers in a pincer movement and grabbed the lizard.

"Ha!" he murmured under his breath.

"Am I to assume from your cry of triumph, Mr. Granville, that you have Captain Emerald in your grasp?" Miss Somerton asked. "And that I am therefore free to move?"

"I have the creature, yes, but one of its feet has become tangled in your hair." Dominic was suddenly aware he was closer than he'd ever been before to his children's governess—and that he was touching her hair. Chaperoned by a butler, a footman and a housemaid, to be sure, but still... He wasn't sure if this morning's letter made the proximity more or less acceptable. "May I, er, attempt to extract it?"

"That would be an excellent idea." She encouraged him in much the same tone she used with Thomas.

Which had the effect of removing any impropriety—which was good—but at the same time relegated her employer to the status of one of her charges.

Dominic narrowed his eyes and applied himself to his

task. "By the way, I wouldn't describe my earlier reaction as a cry of triumph, Miss Somerton."

"My mistake," she said demurely.

"You might hear such a cry from me in, say, the hunting field," he continued, "but I scarcely think capturing a lizard is worthy of acclaim."

"Slaughtering a large animal is a far more admirable achievement," she said.

Dominic paused in his untangling to meet her eyes. They were wide and innocent.

He wasn't fooled. No wonder his children were running wild! Their governess valued chasing butterflies and lizards above the academic and sporting pursuits essential to the life of an English country gentleman.

Dominic freed the lizard at last and took a relieved step back. "Gregory, could you take this and deal with it as you see fit?"

"Yes, sir," the footman said with grim pleasure.

"Oh, Gregory, no," Miss Somerton protested. "You wouldn't harm one of God's creatures, would you?"

Gregory looked uncertain at this invocation of the deity. "It's a pest, miss. And it frightened Alice," he added virtuously.

"Only for a moment," the maid said. A quelling look from Molson sent her hurrying toward the kitchen.

"Gregory…" Miss Somerton clasped her hands in front of her and gave the man a look so beseeching, Dominic was amazed the servant didn't melt into submission. "I realize you've been grossly inconvenienced by Captain—by this lizard. It definitely does not deserve your mercy. But Thomas is anxious to have it as a pet."

When Gregory scowled at the mention of Thomas, she added quickly, "Hetty is, too. I'm pleading with you, for Hetty's sake, to leave it in the stables. In a jar. With a few twigs and leaves for comfort. And maybe a fly or two—the common lizard eats invertebrates, so any insect will do. A worm would be wonderful, if you happen to come across one."

As her list of demands grew more unreasonable, Dominic almost laughed. Clever of her to include the blameless Hetty in her plea for a reprieve for the lizard.

And plea it was, since strictly speaking she couldn't order Gregory to do anything. It was an awkward situation for Miss Somerton, Dominic knew. Since she was neither a member of the family nor a guest, she had no authority over the servants. But her status was unquestionably above Gregory's... even more now than it had been.

"Unfortunately, miss, Mr. Molson would need to excuse me from my duties for me to perform such tasks." Gregory directed a hopeful glance at the butler, clearly wanting permission to be denied.

"You may do as Miss Somerton asks, Gregory," Molson said, and the footman departed in reluctant possession of one green lizard.

"I shall tell Thomas—and Hetty—the good news," Miss Somerton declared.

"The library first, if you please," Dominic said, deliberately forgetting his suggestion that she tidy herself. If he waited for the governess to comport herself in a more orderly fashion, he would be here until midnight.

After Molson had relieved Serena of her dented bonnet, she preceded Mr. Granville into the library. She was conscious of him behind her, conscious of his innate authority and, also, something she feared was disapproval.

Perhaps he'd learned of one of those *incidents* that she'd decided wasn't serious enough to report to him. In her opinion, the children were so courteous and well-behaved, few infractions were that serious.

Dominic Granville waved her to a seat. "Miss Somerton, you probably know why I wish to talk to you—"

"About Thomas going away to school?" she asked hopefully. "As I see it—"

"Not that." He frowned as he settled into the studded leather chair on the other side of the oak desk. "Obviously, Thomas will start at Eton in September, just as I did, and my father did before me."

Oh, dear. That frown...she could think of only one incident that might cause such a reaction. "I should have made Charlotte confess to you herself—please don't blame her for my error. But, Mr. Granville—" she leaned forward in her seat "—if Cook has *dared* call Charlotte a thief again, when she was acting *purely* out of Christian compassion, I...I—" She sputtered, outrage on Charlotte's behalf causing words to fail her...but not for long. "I hope you will tell that evil woman she has overstepped the mark!"

Mr. Granville rubbed his right temple. "It seems to me, Miss Somerton, that calling my cook evil might be 'overstepping the mark.'"

"I apologize, sir." She ignored the skeptical rise of one dark eyebrow. "However, Charlotte is the kindest—"

"What did she steal?" he demanded.

"A leg of lamb," Serena admitted. "Technically, *half* a leg—we ate at least half of it for dinner on Sunday, you'll remember."

Mr. Granville began rubbing his left temple, as well as his right. "If she was hungry, why did she not ask for food?"

"She gave it to a beggar who came to the kitchen door. Mr. Granville, he looked *starving!*" Just thinking about the poor man brought tears to Serena's eyes. "Cook turned him away, without so much as a crust."

"That was wrong of her." Mr. Granville had a reputa-

tion for giving to those in need, which encouraged Serena
to hope for mercy.

"*Very* wrong," she agreed. "Charlotte was in the kitchen
at the time, and she took matters into her own hands. She
grabbed the meat and ran after the man."

Mr. Granville winced, doubtless at the thought of his nine-
year-old daughter chasing a vagrant across his property.

"I agree, it wasn't the most ladylike conduct," Serena reflected. "But her sense of compassion is most commendable."

"Did you punish Charlotte?" he asked.

"For giving to someone in need?" she said, shocked.

"She took the meat without permission."

Serena bit down on a heated defense of her charge. "I told
her she should have come to me, and I would have negoti-
ated with Cook."

"That's not sufficient," he said.

Serena had had very little conversation with her employer.
She took her instructions, such as they were, from his sister, who'd hired her. But she knew he wouldn't welcome the
kind of robust debate that prevailed in the rectory at Piper's
Mead, her parents' home. A pang of homesickness for her
family stabbed her. She managed a stiff, "I apologize, sir."

"Two apologies in the space of half a minute," he observed. "It may interest you to know the second was no more
convincing than the first."

Serena tried to look interested. The shaking of Mr. Granville's head suggested she'd failed.

"Miss Somerton, deplorable though my daughter's behavior is, that's not why I summoned you."

She opened her mouth; he held up a hand. "No, please, I
don't want to hear confessions of any more of my children's
escapades, or your inability to discipline them. I have received a letter from the Earl of Spenford." He picked up a
sheet of paper and waved it at her.

"Oh," she said, dismayed.

"I wasn't aware Lord Spenford recently married your sister," he said. "You didn't request leave to attend the wedding."

Serena had rather hoped Mr. Granville wouldn't discover this development just yet. In theory, the financial repercussions of her sister's marriage would be to Serena's advantage—Lord Spenford would feel some obligation to support his wife's sisters—but she refused to benefit from this until she was convinced Constance was happy. At this point, she was by no means certain.

"The wedding occurred rather suddenly, due to the Dowager Countess of Spenford's illness," Serena explained. "There wasn't time for me to journey home."

"I see." Her employer folded the letter and set it on the desk. "I don't recall my sister mentioning your connection to the Spenfords. Are your families old acquaintances?"

In other words, how did a mere governess end up so well connected?

"My father is the Reverend Adrian Somerton, rector of Piper's Mead in Hampshire," she said. "Papa was given his parish living by the Dowager Countess of Spenford, his patroness." She hoped that would be enough.

"There must be more to it, for Spenford to have married a parson's daughter. Somerton…" Mr. Granville drummed his fingers on the desk as he contemplated her. "I'm acquainted with Sir Horace Somerton, brother of the Duke of Medway."

"Sir Horace is my grandfather," she admitted reluctantly.

Her father disapproved of any boasting of their high connections. "We're all equal in God's eyes," he often said.

Mr. Granville blinked. "So your father is the nephew of the Duke of Medway? Does my sister know? Why on earth are you working as a governess?"

She clasped her hands demurely, in the dwindling hope it might make her look more governess-like. Her prospects here at Woodbridge Hall appeared increasingly dim. "Miss Granville is aware… It came out in conversation one day. But, sir, my father became estranged from most of his family the moment he took his holy calling more seriously than they would have liked. Before I was born, my parents spurned London society in favor of a simpler existence."

"You will forgive my intrusion into your affairs—" that was an order, not a request, Serena noted "—but even if your father is estranged from the Medways, your family is surely not destitute."

"Our circumstances are comfortable," she admitted, embarrassed.

"So why do you need to work? Surely the life of a governess is not *comfortable*."

"I love my work," she said in surprise. "The children are wonderful and Miss Granville is kindness itself."

At the mention of his sister, he gave her a sharp look. Some people considered Miss Granville a little odd; Serena wasn't one of them.

She carried on. "But in answer to your question, my father has recently been in disagreement with his bishop. Papa favors preaching the Word to people wherever they may be— in the fields, if necessary. The bishop sees his approach as Methodism, and is afraid Papa will create disunity in the church. Which he never would—" aware of rising indignation in her voice, Serena took a moment to calm herself "—but he worries the bishop might remove him from the parish."

If that happened, her parents would lose their home and livelihood.

"And that's why you sought this position?" Mr. Granville asked.

"I don't want to be a burden on my parents if their circumstances change," she said, which was true, but not the entire truth. That had been the impetus for applying to be a governess, but not the reason she'd accepted this post over the two others she'd been offered. "I should explain, I'm the oldest of five sisters."

Many fathers would consider five daughters a burden. Serena's parents made it clear their girls were their joy. They'd never exhorted them to marry, though as Papa had said when she was home at Christmas, "If God should provide wonderful husbands for any or all of you, my dears, I will not quarrel." Serena hadn't been able to discern from her parents' letters what they thought of Constance's marriage. Whether Lord Spenford was "wonderful."

Mr. Granville leaned forward, pressed his fingertips together. "Miss Somerton, you must see it's impossible for you to remain a governess now that you have an earl as brother by marriage."

She lowered her eyes. He was right. But this wasn't just about what society, or even Lord Spenford, considered proper. She grasped the edge of the desk and said, "Mr. Granville, please don't say I must leave."

He eyed her encroaching fingers warily. "Of course you must."

"Sir, the children need me. It's been such a joy to teach them, to see Thomas develop his interest in nature, and Hetty learn to form her own opinions."

Mr. Granville appeared doubtful about the joys of both of those. She considered telling him the truth: that when Marianne Granville had explained how the children had lost their mother, and implied that their father had grown distant and cold, Serena had seen the possibility for a second chance for this family. A chance for the widowed Mr. Granville to put behind him the mistakes he'd made out of grief. To start afresh with his children. Serena, who knew about making mistakes, would help him. And just maybe, she would earn her own fresh chance.

But it was difficult to explain all that without causing offense. Better just to talk about the children. "Then there's Charlotte's wonderful—"

"Compassion," he interjected. "Yes, so you said."

She beamed at him. "And William. He was so shy when I arrived, but just the other day he took the starring role in a drama we created."

"Really?" Mr. Granville might well be surprised; his second son was notoriously bashful. "That drama lesson wasn't, by any chance, at the expense of something more useful?" he asked. "Arithmetic, for example?"

"Of course we do arithmetic," she assured him. "But I'm thrilled to say William positively relished the limelight in our drama." One only need look at the crippling shyness of Marianne Granville, Mr. Granville's sister, to see that helping William become more sociable was of far more use than practicing his already excellent arithmetic. "The fact that he got to brandish a carving knife for much of the last scene was a useful incentive," Serena recalled fondly.

Alarm flashed across her employer's face, reminding her of that day he'd scolded her for letting the children slide down the banister. What child wouldn't eventually take advantage of such smooth, tempting wood? Far better they do it under her supervision. She moved swiftly on. "And Louisa." She felt her face soften at the mention of the youngest Granville. "As long as she has someone to hold on to, she's the happiest girl in the world."

"She sounds clinging," Mr. Granville said.

"She's five years old," Serena pointed out. "Sir, it would be a very bad idea for me to leave now."

"Bad for them or for you?" he asked. "Frankly, Miss

Somerton, it sounds as if you're having the time of your life, while my children's education could be suffering."

Just in time, she refrained from leaping to her feet in self-defense. The kind of reaction Mr. Granville wouldn't appreciate. Instead, she pressed her slippers firmly into the carpet, anchoring herself. "I report regularly to Miss Granville on my curriculum and the children's progress. She has always expressed her satisfaction."

It was both true and, Serena hoped, a tactical masterstroke. Mr. Granville was inclined to let his sister have her way. "But I see my role as more than that of a teacher of reading and arithmetic," she continued.

"I would hope," he said, "the curriculum of which you boast also includes French for the older children. And sketching and the like for all of them."

Maybe she could just *hint* at her deeper purpose.

"When Miss Granville appointed me," Serena said, "she told me the children were worried they might forget their mother. Yet they were afraid to talk about her."

Mr. Granville's jaw—strong, with a tendency to square when he disapproved—showed definite signs of squaring. "That's absurd. My sister shouldn't have said such a thing to you."

"The reason they were afraid to talk about your late wife was a sense that *you* discourage such conversations," Serena persisted. Oh, this confrontation was long overdue! And now, under pressure, she was making a hash of it. She should have asked to see him months ago, and approached him with a carefully reasoned argument as to how he could improve his children's happiness.

"I see no reason to wallow in things we cannot change," he said. Both tone and glare were designed to intimidate.

So it was a blessing that she'd been raised to disregard intimidation in the pursuit of right.

"Naturally, Louisa doesn't remember her mother at all," she said, "since she was just a babe when... And William also has no recollection. I've made a point of asking the older children to share their memories with them." As a concession, she added, "Without *wallowing,* of course."

Mr. Granville opened his mouth, but seemed oddly stunned and didn't speak.

Serena pressed on. "While the children still miss their mama, they're happier for being able to talk about her. French and arithmetic are certainly important, and I believe I do an excellent job in academic matters. But I count influencing your children's happiness as the greatest achievement of my tenure here." She'd noticed, even in her brief observations of him, that he deflected anything that hinted at emotion. His children deserved better.

"That's enough," he growled. "Miss Somerton, I don't doubt that in your own woolly-headed, parson's daughter-ish way, your intentions are good...."

She gasped. *"Woolly-headed?"* She could not, of course, take offense at being called "parson's daughter-ish." She was proud to be that.

He ignored her. "But regardless of your calling, you cannot stay on as governess. I will inform Lord Spenford by return mail that your employment has been terminated. You will leave by the end of the week." He pressed his palms to the desk and stood.

She was forced to look up at him. "Is that your last word on the matter?" To her annoyance, her voice held a tiny quaver.

"It is."

"Because I should point out—"

"That was my last word," he reminded her.

She sagged. Twice she opened her mouth to raise a fresh objection, but Mr. Granville kept his gaze on her until, under that dark intensity, she subsided completely.

He observed her capitulation. "That will be all, Miss Somerton," he said, sounding satisfied for the first time today.

Serena remained in her seat, not moving, considering what to do for the best. *Father, guide me, please.*

"You may go, Miss Somerton," Mr. Granville reminded her. He cleared his throat. "Thank you for your service. I do appreciate your fondness for my children." He smiled, a little grimly perhaps, but it appeared he intended encouragement.

Inspiration struck, though she suspected it had more to do with her prayer than his smile.

She smiled back as she rose from her chair. His gaze dropped, and it seemed to Serena that he scanned her from top to toe.

"Mr. Granville," she said. Her voice was clear and composed. *Much better.*

He brought his gaze back to her face as he moved around the desk. "Yes, Miss Somerton?"

"Would you consider marrying again?"

Chapter Two

Serena watched as her employer—her *former* employer—turned a remarkable shade of red.

Her question had been unutterably forward. If her father had heard her, even his famed tolerance would be taxed. But she'd spent eight months biting her tongue, save for one or two lapses in diplomacy. Maybe three or four. The point was, her "parson's daughter-ish" good manners meant she'd failed to make any lasting difference here. Now that she'd been dismissed, she no longer needed to exercise restraint.

"Miss Somerton," Mr. Granville said with rigid control, "while I am very conscious of the honor you accord me, I feel your offer springs from a certain desperation."

What was he talking about?

He took two steps backward, away from her, as if she were a victim of the Great Plague she'd been teaching the children about in their history lessons. Yes, she did actually teach them history.

"Therefore-I-must-decline-your-proposal," he said in a rush.

Serena stared…then broke into a peal of laughter. "You think I was proposing marriage!"

He remained red, but was suddenly less rigid. "Er, weren't you?"

"Certainly not!" Goodness, how embarrassing. She could only hope she could pass the days before she left Woodbridge Hall without encountering him again. "Even if I hoped to marry in the near future—which, believe me, I have no expectation of doing—it would be somewhat presumptuous of a governess to set her sights on the master of the house, would it not?"

A reluctant smile widened his mouth, much more natural than the forced version with which he'd tried to reassure her a moment ago. It made him extremely handsome.

"You *are* the sister of an earl now," he pointed out. "And have always been, it seems, the great-niece of a duke. I rather fear, Miss Somerton, you're my social equal."

"I'm an *estranged* great-niece," she reminded him, suddenly distracted. How peculiar that she should notice how handsome he was twice in half an hour. The first time, he'd been inches away from her, trying to detach that dashed lizard. And this time he'd just accused her of proposing marriage—so no wonder her observations were so inappropriate. This was hardly a regular day at Woodbridge Hall.

In which case, the irregularity might as well continue.

"Perhaps I *will* presume on the new status, such as it is, that comes courtesy of my sister's husband," she said. "Sir, your children need a mother."

He was squaring his jaw again. Serena chose to ignore it. "Which means you need a wife," she said. "I'm sorry to bring this up so abruptly—if I'd known I was about to be dismissed, I would have mentioned it sooner—"

"I'm overjoyed that you didn't know," he interrupted.

"The children love their aunt, of course, but they need someone whose constant presence they can depend on. If Miss Granville should marry…"

"No one can promise a constant presence," he said harshly. He closed his eyes a moment. When he opened them, he spoke with excessive calm. "We both know my sister is unlikely to wed, so you may consider her quite dependable." Measured strides took him to the library door, which he opened wide in a clear message that Serena should depart.

He was right about no one knowing the future. His wife, Mrs. Emily Granville, had doubtless never expected to be carried away by measles when Louisa was just six months old.

But Serena was right, too. She drew a restoring breath, gripped the back of her chair and carried on. "Sir, Thomas and Hetty are about to enter a critical period in their adolescence. They need the guidance and nurturing of a parent who loves them, not a governess who's paid to care." And since Mr. Granville showed no inclination to nurture his children, there should be a new *Mrs.* Granville.

"Is that why *you* care?" he asked.

"You dismissed me," she pointed out. "In that process, you made some slurs about my ability as a governess that I consider—"

She stopped. She was getting distracted. What really mattered here?

The children.

In which case…Serena sat down again.

Mr. Granville glanced from her to the open door. "Miss Somerton, you are dismissed. In every sense of the word."

"I will leave, but I'd like to say something first."

He remained by the door, only a slight air of resigned expectancy acknowledging her request.

They could hardly hold a conversation like this.

"Such discourtesy to a sister of the Earl of Spenford," she said lightly.

Granville's eyes narrowed. But he returned to his seat behind the desk. Serena sent up a brief prayer that she could articulate her thoughts in a way that would convince him. She'd never thought she would have the chance to speak her mind, but hadn't he just told her she was now his social equal?

Even better, a social equal who after this week would never see him again.

"Mr. Granville," she said, "your sister has mentioned your faithfulness to the memory of your late wife, and I strongly admire that. But it may be that God has someone else in mind for you. Remarriage wouldn't necessarily be disloyal."

"That's enough," he said sharply.

Serena estimated she had maybe half a minute to persuade him, before he picked her up and bodily threw her out, social equality or not. "Even if you're certain you don't wish to, er, fall in love with some young lady, we could look at this from a purely practical perspective."

"By all means, Miss Somerton, why don't *we* do that?"

The silky menace in his invitation made her pause.

Best to hurry on, before courage deserted her altogether.

"There are many ladies—I can think of several wellborn spinsters in an instant—who would welcome an alliance with a wealthy, handsome man like yourself, without requiring declarations of love."

"Hmm." For a moment, he appeared to be considering her eminently useful suggestion. Then he said, "So, you consider me handsome?"

Heat flooded her face. "I—did I say that?" *Yes, I did.* "I— I'm sorry, I was merely making a point, I shouldn't have…"

Satisfaction with her discomfort gleamed in his eyes.

Now that he'd questioned her opinion of his looks, Serena couldn't help appraising what she could see of him: dark hair, eyes an intriguing hazel, a strong face, a mouth that… She dropped her gaze quickly. Broad shoulders, impeccable dress sense. And he was tall. Any woman would find him handsome, as he was doubtless well aware. And now, confound it, she'd lost her train of thought.

"So," he said, with an affability that was just as disconcerting as his earlier menace, "your expert opinion is that I should marry a spinster who's after my fortune?"

As so often happened, a laugh gurgled out of Serena at quite the wrong moment. "Perhaps I didn't make the prospect sound honorable. Or tempting, for that matter. And I cannot approve such motives for an alliance." A stance she was being forced to rethink, given that her sister's marriage was one of convenience.

"Oh, well, if *you* don't approve, I'd better not." He leaned back in his chair, hands clasped behind his head, emphasizing the breadth of those shoulders.

"But, er…" What had she been saying? Oh, yes. "I believe—" she kept her eyes fixed firmly on his "—such convenient marriages can offer mutual benefits, and there's every chance that over time, love would blossom." She hurried on. "Besides, you really shouldn't make spinsters sound like such a last resort. My aunt, Miss Jane Somerton, is both a spinster and very attractive. In fact, I could introduce you…."

"I'm acquainted with Miss Jane Somerton," he said. "I have no wish to marry her."

"Maybe you should stop thinking about what you *wish,* and think about what your children *need,*" Serena snapped. *Drat.* She braced herself for that forcible removal.

"Miss Somerton," he growled. "If you don't cease your impertinence this instant…"

"You'll dismiss me?" she suggested. "Might I remind you, Mr. Granville, my sister's marriage has put me in the position—rare for a governess—of having nothing to lose. While your children have everything to gain."

Silence. Should she take that as victory?

He pinched the bridge of his nose. "Miss Somerton…"

Merely regrouping, then. Serena braced herself.

"I don't understand why you feel compelled to comment on my domestic arrangements, when you're no longer employed here," he said. "Nor why these outrageous views have come upon you so suddenly."

He sounded so confused, she felt almost sorry for him. "I've felt this way since the day I arrived," she admitted. "But until now, I've been more subtle in my approach."

"You've been subtle?" he said incredulously.

"You possibly haven't noticed that I've been extending the time you spend in your daily greetings and good-nights to the children." She was rather proud of having stretched that stiff, formal five minutes to a whole seven minutes. Still stiff and formal, but one step at a time.

"How Machiavellian of you." He appeared to be laughing at her.

"There are many fathers who spend a great deal of time with their children and find it very rewarding," Serena said coolly. Her own papa was a perfect example, but she knew other families of Quality where the father enjoyed the company of his offspring.

"Again," Granville said, "I wonder why you've taken it upon yourself to try to introduce me to their ranks."

Maybe she should tell him at least part of the truth.

"Do you believe in second chances, Mr. Granville?"

"In theory," he said guardedly. "Is there something else you need to confess?"

"I'm talking about you," she said. "Your family has suffered loss, but you have a chance to build a loving home for your children. If only you'll take it."

"And you intend to force me to take this chance you've conjured up in your imagination?" He scowled. "If you must indulge your penchant for good works, Miss Somerton, I suggest you go home and feed the poor. Surely they're in greater need of second, third and even fourth chances than I am."

"The poor are well provided-for in Piper's Mead," she said. "My sister Isabel practically runs the orphanage, and Charity, my youngest sister, knits for the babies. Mama grows vegetables for the elderly—"

He held up a hand. "Your family can't have such a monopoly on good works that there was nothing left for you but to travel all the way to Leicestershire to inflict a second chance on *my* family."

"Of course not," Serena said levelly. "I chose this position—" he blinked, as if he hadn't realized she'd had a choice "—because I believe this is where I'm meant to be." She knew in her head that she'd been forgiven the foolish mistake she'd made years ago. A mistake entirely unworthy of her upbringing, which would grieve her parents sorely if they knew of it. But in her heart, she despaired of receiving a second chance. If she could help the Granville family grasp *their* chance, then maybe God would send one her way.

"Grateful though I am for your efforts," Dominic Granville said, "your assistance isn't required. Let me remind you, to put your mind at rest before you depart, my children have an aunt right here in this house, who loves them very much and who, as I've said, will likely always be here with us."

Serena hesitated. To speak bluntly about Marianne Granville seemed harsh, but... "If you're suggesting Miss Granville will play a more active role in the children's upbringing than she does now, you're quite wrong."

His mouth tightened. "I'm not suggesting anything to you at all. It's none of your business."

"Are you saying that when Hetty makes her come-out into society," Serena persisted, "she will be chaperoned by your sister?"

He eyed her with hearty dislike. "Not necessarily. Hetty's come-out is six or seven years away."

"Will your loyalty to your wife vanish in that time?" she asked.

"Of course not."

"Even if you could force your sister into the role of chaperone, I doubt you'd have the stomach for it," Serena said. Not that Mr. Granville was in any way *soft,* but his attitude toward his sister was rightly protective. "I understand you have no other suitable female relatives. It's possible you have a female friend who might help—" a flicker of doubt crossed his face "—but a girl's come-out is such a…a complicated time that you'll want someone very close to your daughters involved."

Serena drew a breath. "Which means you'll at some stage need to marry, if only to help your daughters find their place in society. I say, do it now and give them all the benefits of a loving stepmother." She spread her hands as if nothing could be simpler. It didn't take a mathematical genius to add two and two, did it?

She could see from his distracted expression that he was performing the calculation himself and coming up with the same, unpalatable answer.

Then he blinked, as if to dismiss his conclusion. When he spoke, the set of his shoulders, the jut of his jaw, told Serena he had no intention of discussing this further. And every intention of ignoring her advice. "Prepare to leave this house on Monday, Miss Somerton. My own carriage will convey you to your parents' home." His offer of transportation likely spoke as much of his desire to be sure he was rid of her as it did of his determination to acknowledge her social standing.

Serena bowed her head, defeated.

She had failed.

* * *

Dominic found his sister in the greenhouse. She'd commandeered its southwest corner for her botanical project, a move that Gladding, the head gardener, tolerated with an air of long-suffering. Dominic called a greeting from the doorway, to give Marianne a moment to adjust to his presence. By the time he reached her, her face was rosy. But not bright red, as it would have been if he'd startled her.

"So this is the new arrival." He scrutinized the gray-green leaves, if one could call the sharp-tipped spikes that, of the plant she was digging in. "It survived the journey, then." Just as well, since it had cost a small fortune.

"If it survived the trip from India to England, I daresay London to Leicestershire was nothing." Marianne patted the soil around the base of the plant with her trowel, then stepped back to admire it. "Aloe vera. Pretty, don't you think? Even if it doesn't work, it'll at least look nice." Her careless tone didn't fool Dominic.

"Very nice," he said.

She picked up on his sympathy, and her cheeks turned a deeper pink; she fanned her face. "This place is so warm."

"We could step outside if you're finished," he suggested.

She shook her head. "The others need water. I've forbidden Gladding to do it—he tends to drown them."

The gardener didn't hold with newfangled tropical plants. Dominic preferred the more restrained beauty of English plants himself, but he wouldn't deny Marianne her search for a cure for her condition.

She bent to pick up the watering can at her feet; Dominic intervened. "Let me do that. I promise I'll obey your instructions to the letter."

She smiled in gratitude as she dabbed at her cheeks with a damp handkerchief. The slightest exertion, even lifting a watering can, would make her face redden further. Even though there was no one but Dominic to see her, she preferred to avoid exacerbating her complaint.

"While you do that, I promised Cook I'd snip some chives for dinner." She pulled a small pair of scissors from her pocket. "I ordered the honey-glazed duck for tonight."

Dominic's stomach growled at the mention of his favorite dish. "Have I told you you're the best sister in the world?" he teased, as he sprinkled water over the threadlike leaves of the nigella she'd planted last year, having heard the seeds could be ground into a paste for the skin. Like every other remedy, it hadn't worked.

"You've told me many times, but there's no such thing as too often." Marianne signaled that he'd dampened the nigella enough. "What brings you here, Dom? Shouldn't you be out inspecting fences, or the like?"

He moved on to the next plant, a tropical flax whose leaves could reputedly be laid over the skin for a healing effect. "Miss Somerton's sister has married the Earl of Spenford."

Surprise flashed across Marianne's face. "I didn't know." Like him, she never read the London society news. He abstained because he was too busy. For Marianne, reading about a world she had every right to be a part of, but never would be, disheartened her. "So Serena will be leaving us. What a pity, for her and for us."

"I don't see that it's a bad thing for her," Dominic countered. Nor for them, either. The governess had overstepped every conceivable boundary during their conversation; he couldn't remember feeling so provoked. But at the same time, he'd admired her determination to fight on his children's behalf. Even if she was quite wrong.

"She can return to her parents in Hampshire, or no doubt the Spenfords would be happy to have her in London," he said. Serena might be helter-skelter, but she was pretty enough. With some self-discipline and the backing of the

Earl and Countess of Spenford, she'd find herself a husband by the time she'd been in town a month. Maybe less than a month. Dominic had noticed she had a fine figure, the kind to attract male attention.

"Well, it's awful for us," Marianne insisted.

"Will Miss Somerton be such a sad loss?" Dominic asked lightly. Images of the governess's blue eyes and graceful neck rose in his mind as he wielded the watering can over a glossy-leafed something-or-other. "I have the impression that under her care, the children are somewhat rambunctious."

"They adore Serena," her sister said. "And not only does she love them, she can keep up with them." Marianne's excessive, uncontrollable blushing meant she couldn't exert herself with the children—not unless she wanted to spend the next several hours hot and crimson-faced. "But more importantly, although I love them with all my heart and they love me back, Serena seems to know better what they need." She peeled off her garden gloves. "That's enough watering for now. We'll stop at the herb garden for those chives on our way back to the house."

What his children needed… The governess had tried to lecture him on that subject.

"I know you found appointing a governess a tedious experience last time," he said, as he held the greenhouse door open for his sister. An understatement. "But could I trouble you to do it again?" He'd do it himself, but Marianne needed to select someone with whom she'd feel comfortable.

"I can try," she said gloomily. "But don't expect it to be a quick process."

"I offer a generous wage as compensation for looking after five children," he reminded her.

Marianne held his gaze. "The trouble is, Dominic, you want—and the children deserve—a respectable young lady of good breeding. But ladies of that ilk have their choice of position, and some things cannot be compensated for."

"Don't talk like that," he ordered.

"We both know it's true. Younger ladies are so embarrassed by my condition, they don't know where to look. Older ladies are blatant in their pity." Both reactions only caused her skin to flare up more violently. "It's hard to say if I or they are the more miserable," she said.

"It's been a while since we consulted a physician…" Dominic said.

Marianne grimaced. "You know I would be only too happy to try a new treatment. But I haven't heard of one, and to subject myself to those same examinations to no purpose…"

"I suppose you're right," he said. "But if your condition didn't deter Miss Somerton, perhaps others won't be deterred, either."

"Serena is a parson's daughter," Marianne said. "I think she saw this position, this family, as an opportunity to exercise her Christian compassion."

"Has she condescended to you?" Dominic said sharply. It was all very well Miss Somerton spouting her nonsense to him, but if she'd hurt Marianne's feelings he would go upstairs right now and throw her out of the nursery on her pretty ear. He'd been close to that ear, thanks to that blasted lizard, and it was indeed attractive.

"Of course she hasn't," Marianne said. "She asked me about my condition the first day we met—a directness I appreciated—and accepted it with equanimity. She would never presume to condescend."

She presumed to tell me I should marry again. Outrageous. And yet, when he remembered his mistake in imagining she was proposing marriage, amusement blended with his outrage.

"Dominic," his sister said, "we were lucky to have had

Miss Potter—" the governess from their own childhood "—for so long, but you must remember the string of substandard governesses we had before Serena. The few who considered your money worth putting up with my *oddness*. I got so sick of feeling as if I didn't belong in my own home."

"You should never have to feel like that," he said gruffly.

"In a perfect world…" Marianne spread her hands. "But we live in *this* world, and there's no point complaining about something neither you nor I can fix. I will advertise for a governess, and we will pray for a smooth path."

Miss Somerton's outrageous suggestion floated through Dominic's mind.

"Would it be easier—" he studied the glossy toe of his right boot as they walked "—if I were married?"

Marianne turned her head to eye him as if he were a simpleton. "Dominic, of course it would! If you were married, your wife would take charge of these things." She broke away as they reached the herb garden, saying over her shoulder, "My presence would seem a trifling thing to a governess, since I'd no longer be mistress of the house. There's every chance I could avoid her altogether." She snipped some chives from a bushy clump. "And, of course, looking ahead to when Hetty and then the other girls must make their debut in the *ton*." She blinked rapidly. "Dom, just the thought of having to chaperone them makes me want to die." Her flush deepened as she spoke.

Again, Serena Somerton came to his mind. She had already considered these issues, ones that ought to have occurred to him.

"You think I should find a wife." He tugged at his cravat, loosening it.

"Not at all," Marianne said, as they started back toward the house. "I know Emily was the only woman for you. I would never suggest… It's just—" she smiled faintly "—if you were the more fickle sort, it might be more convenient for us all."

Convenient. A convenient marriage.

People do that kind of thing. It's perfectly acceptable. Perhaps it wasn't the biblical ideal of marriage...but wasn't the Bible full of people in arranged marriages that prospered? The instruction for a husband to love his wife didn't specify a romantic love. Presumably it could as easily refer to more of a responsible kind of love, a sacrificial kind of love. He could do that.

And yet...he had a sudden urge to make a run for the stables, and ride his horse up into the hills for a very long time. Decades.

"Dom, I didn't mean it." Marianne shook his arm, jerking him back to the present. "We'll find a solution. Perhaps by the time Hetty comes out there'll be a new treatment. Maybe my aloe vera will do the trick."

He would love to believe that. But the doctors said her condition was incurable. Indeed, it seemed to have worsened in the past couple of years.

If he married again, his new wife would need to understand that Marianne would likely always live with them. As he'd told Serena, his sister was unlikely to marry.

He shuddered. He wouldn't think about the possibility of remarriage now. Besides, he had another unpleasant revelation for Marianne, one that the day's events had driven temporarily from his mind.

"I have more bad news, my dear," he said.

"More?" Marianne said, aghast. "Beyond Serena's departure?"

"My groom met the groom from Farley Hall when he was out exercising the bay mare this morning."

"It's been far too long since I called on Sir Charles." Their neighbor at Farley Hall, Sir Charles Ramsay, had lost his son in a carriage accident nearly a year ago. Marianne's brow wrinkled. "Is he unwell?"

"Not at all. In fact, it's good news for Ramsay, though not so pleasant for you," Dominic said. "His new heir, a Mr. Geoffrey Beaumont, has arrived to stay for a month or two, to acquaint himself with the property. I'll have to call on him next week."

Marianne groaned. "If he has any manners at all, he'll return the call." Meeting strangers was torment for her.

Dominic nodded.

"And we, as owners of the largest home in the district—"

"Farley Hall is as large." But she was right, the Granvilles were the incumbent gentry.

"—we'll have to host a dinner to welcome him to the area," she said miserably.

"I'm afraid so."

"And I, as always, will be your hostess." She swallowed. "It won't be so bad. If we invite enough of our friends from around here, Mr. Beaumont will barely notice me, let alone feel compelled to stare at me as if I'm a freak."

"I'm sorry, but it's our duty," Dominic said. "It may be scant comfort, but I always think you look lovely, Marianne, you know that."

"I know, and I thank God daily for your delusion." She squeezed his arm, then walked ahead of him through a side door into the house. "I wish I had a friend nearby, someone my own age, that I could invite to dinner. Someone I could laugh with, in whose company I wouldn't care about others' opinions. Or at least, would care less."

Marianne's secluded life meant she corresponded energetically by letter with a few girls from the seminary for female education she'd attended. But she didn't like to travel, or to invite guests to stay. Her local friends were older women.

Not close confidantes. Dominic could understand her need for a friend nearer her own age.

If he remarried, his children would gain a stepmother. Might his sister gain a friend?

Even if that were so, he could hardly marry in time for dinner with Mr. Beaumont.

Serena had asked a footman to set up quoits on the lawn for the children. Although it was only late April, the sun shone warm and the fresh air would do them good.

Thomas had brought Captain Emerald out from the stable, still in his jar, and had replenished the lizard's stock of leaves, grasses and a few unfortunate insects. He and Hetty had given the younger children a fighting chance at quoits by setting the juniors' throwing mark some ten paces in front of theirs. Dominic's two dogs were wreaking havoc by chasing the rings as they sailed through the air.

Louisa wasn't playing; she was content to cling to Serena's skirts. Serena was referee…and though the children were good sports, there were sufficient squabbles to require regular intervention.

She was mediating a dispute between William and Charlotte when a shadow fell across her. She turned to see Dominic Granville.

He smiled.

How unexpected.

"Good afternoon, Mr. Granville," Serena said. She hadn't seen him since she'd left the library two days ago, but she imagined he was still railing against her impertinent interference—yes, she could acknowledge she'd taken unfair advantage of her change in status, had breached courtesy even among equals.

And yet he was smiling. Though, on closer inspection,

his smile was not one of unadulterated joy. It was, in fact, rather tense.

Charlotte and William ceased their dispute immediately and straightened up in front of their father. "Hello, Papa," they chorused. Louisa echoed them. The two older children were picking up the quoits at the other end of their pitch. They waved to their father, but knew to finish the job before they stopped to talk.

"Have you come to play quoits?" Serena asked. He'd never yet accepted one of her invitations to play with the children, but she lived in hope.

"No, thank you." Today was obviously not to be the exception. "Miss Somerton, I wish to talk. Would you care to walk around the lawn with me?"

William and Charlotte had taken a few stealthy steps backward; as soon as they were out of their father's line of sight, they trotted toward the twins.

"If this is about William tearing a page of *Robinson Crusoe*—" Serena decided to anticipate the problem rather than appear to be concealing it "—you can be sure I was very cross, and William has undertaken to repair it. On the bright side, his reading improved enormously...." She trailed off; Mr. Granville had closed his eyes in a pained sort of way.

"That's not what I want to talk about," he said. "Shall we walk?"

She inclined her head toward Louisa, who was unfortunately sucking her thumb through the muslin of Serena's dress. He shook his head.

"Stay here, dearest, and watch the big children play," Serena told the little girl. "Your papa and I must talk privately."

As she brushed grass off her skirt—once again he'd found her covered in undergrowth—and made an attempt to rub dry the damp patch where Louisa had been sucking, she wondered what he wanted to discuss. Since he'd already dismissed her from her position, whatever he had to say now couldn't be that bad. She realized he was watching her cleanup with disapproval.

"All done," she said brightly, if not entirely truthfully. "Let us go."

His arm moved involuntarily, as if he might offer it for her to take. But that would suggest a level of acquaintance they didn't have. Instead, they walked side by side, a respectable two or three feet of lawn between them. Mr. Granville's hands were clasped behind his back; he appeared lost in thought.

He didn't speak for some time. But as they neared the sundial at the far end of the lawn, he said, "I've been considering our conversation from Thursday."

"The one in which you dismissed me from my post," Serena said.

He cleared his throat. "Yes, that one." He paused, squinting up at the sun, then down at the shadow on the sundial. "It pains me to say, I believe you're right. It's time I married again."

Serena halted, forcing him to do the same. "Really?"

"Why the surprise? You seemed convinced of the excellence of your idea."

"I was— I am. But, Mr. Granville, if I may be frank—"

"Are you ever anything else?" he asked. "If so, I suspect I might prefer it."

"I'm afraid not," she admitted. "My father always encouraged me and my sisters to speak boldly and to speak the truth, as the Bible advises."

"That must have made for some rather alarming conversations around the dinner table."

She snickered. "I should remind you, the complete biblical instruction is to speak the truth with love."

"That's even worse. There's nothing more irritating than people who tell one things for one's own good."

Serena laughed out loud. "So true!" At his sidelong look, she said, "Don't think I don't know I'm guilty of it myself. As temptations go, it's one of the most insidious."

"Hmm." He pushed aside the branch of a shrub that threatened to dislodge her bonnet. "Is your sister, the one married to Lord Spenford, as bold as you?"

Serena considered. "Not on first acquaintance, but Constance has hidden depths. I'm the oldest daughter, so perhaps I'm more..."

"Impertinent?" he suggested.

"Forthright," she corrected.

"And what is your advanced age, Miss Somerton?"

"I'm twenty-one. Constance—Lady Spenford—is twenty." She followed him through the arbor into the rose garden. The roses, the pride and joy of Gladding the gardener, were in varying stages of bloom, from tight buds to full blossoms on some of the China varieties. None were yet overblown. Serena sniffed the air appreciatively. "Mmm, you can just catch the scent, if you try."

"Very nice," he said, making no attempt to sniff. "I assume your younger sisters are not yet married?"

"No," she agreed.

He shook his head. "Your poor father."

"Mr. Granville!" she exclaimed, outraged. Then she caught a gleam of humor in his eyes. "You'll be relieved to know Papa doesn't consider himself *poor*. He's been known to say he'd love all five of us to live with him and Mama forever."

"Diplomacy is an important skill for a parson," Mr. Granville said.

Serena found herself laughing again.

His gaze drifted down to her mouth, then jerked back up. "I daresay your sisters will be easy enough for your father to marry off," he said abruptly. "Assuming they don't make a habit of wearing lizards in their hair."

"That habit is uniquely mine," she assured him. "Though I'm devastated to learn it might cost me a husband."

His eyes narrowed. "It's a matter of decorum, Miss Somerton."

"A man who loves me will not care about decorum."

"Is that so?" he said dryly. "Will he also appreciate your excessively free speech?"

"Might I remind you, Mr. Granville, you started this unusual conversation, for reasons you have yet to reveal. The only reason I'm participating so *freely* is because I'm about to leave."

He rubbed his chin. "Ah."

He looked…awkward.

"If you're feeling guilty about dismissing me, you needn't," she said. "I was aware that once you learned of Constance's marriage my position would be untenable."

"I'm not feeling guilty," he said, as if he'd never heard anything so absurd.

She almost managed not to roll her eyes. "So what *is* the reason for this conversation?"

"Ah, that," he said. He cleared his throat. "Given that I've now decided you were right about a convenient marriage being a good idea…"

"I said I couldn't wholeheartedly approve of such pragmatic motives," she corrected. "But that I understand the necessity."

He ignored her. "I personally have no faith in this *second chance* of yours, nor do I desire to marry again, but I see no option. The kind of alliance you mentioned will do nicely." His frown deepened. "It will do," he amended, dispensing with any niceness attached to the concept of marriage.

"Oh," Serena said.

"Have I shocked you, Miss Somerton? I expected a more vocal response."

"I…" She stopped. Thought. "I can't deny it'll be wonderful for the children, but it does seem a shame you won't even consider finding a *real* wife."

"My wife will be as real as you are," he said. "Miss Somerton, in the light of my new intention, there's something I must ask you."

Realization burst over Serena like a lightning flash.

Mr. Granville's unexpected friendliness. His questions about her family. *My wife will be as real as you are….*

He was going to ask her to marry him!

"No!" Serena squawked.

"No?" He plucked a leaf from a rosebush and rolled it between his fingers as he looked down at her, more confused than distressed.

But then, why would a man be distressed if a convenient bride turned down his proposal? The thought made it easier to say what she had to. "Mr. Granville, you are a most estimable gentleman, and I can't deny I love your children, but to marry for convenience would be truly repugnant to me, and therefore…"

She stopped.

He was laughing.

"You…weren't asking me to marry you?" she guessed. Suddenly, she was perspiring all over. How hideous!

"I'm afraid not," he apologized. "It seems you and I share an unusual conviction of our own desirability as spouses."

Relief at his acknowledgment that she wasn't the only one who'd made an idiot of herself recently made her chuckle rather more loudly than was ladylike. Which wouldn't surprise him.

"Shall we agree we're equally deluded when it comes to nonexistent marriage proposals," he said, "and move on?"

"Yes, please."

"So…I gather from your refusal of my, er, proposal, that you cherish notions of a romantic love?"

Is this what he considers moving on? "Yes," she said. Though she doubted such a love would come her way.

His dark brows drew together. "I suppose that's not unusual in a young lady of your age."

Serena merely nodded.

"My sister speaks highly of you," he said.

The change in topic disconcerted her. "Thank you—I mean, Miss Granville is one of the nicest people I've met."

"For some people, character is not the only consideration," he said. "As I'm sure you know. You must also know that Marianne is uncomfortable meeting new people."

"I'm aware," Serena admitted. "And I can't blame her."

"I would go so far—" he seemed bemused "—as to say Marianne likes you a lot."

"How odd," she replied.

He smiled.

"I'd say I return the sentiment toward your sister," she said, "but you'd probably consider me impertinent."

"Miss Somerton," he said calmly, "may we call a truce?"

Serena realized she was enjoying the cut and thrust of their conversational duel. It made her feel at home. "The Bible does say we should live peaceably with one another," she admitted.

He chuckled at her marked lack of enthusiasm. "A truce, then. Good. For I would like to offer you a new position, Miss Somerton. That of companion to Marianne."

"You want me to stay?" This was the last thing she'd expected.

"Let's not get into personal preferences. I'm *asking* you to stay."

She choked on a mix of shock and laughter. "Completely different," she agreed.

He folded his arms across his chest and stood, watching her, a gleam in his eye. "Well, what do you say?"

"Mr. Granville, I— How can you even ask such a thing!"

Flustered at her own outburst, Serena turned away. She leaned over to smell the bouquet of a Maiden's Blush bud. She could just see the furled petals, white barely tinged with pink, vivid against the dark green foliage. It was known to be one of the most fragrant rose varieties, so she drew in several breaths deep enough to dizzy herself, in the hope he would have the tact to walk away.

When she straightened, he was still there.

"You gave the impression on Thursday that you were reluctant to leave," he said coolly. "Are you now reluctant to stay?"

"No, I— Yes!" She clasped her hands in front of her. "Mr. Granville, in the last few minutes—and let us not forget Thursday!—I have spoken to you far more boldly than a governess should, on the understanding that I was no longer employed."

"*Far* more boldly," he agreed.

Infuriating man! If she'd hoped for courteous reassurance, she was looking in the wrong place. But her father preached the need to "confess your faults to one another." Not that she'd done that with her parents, as far as her past indiscretion was concerned. Still, she persevered now. "And now, having stated views that, to be quite honest, are none of my business—"

"At last," he murmured.

"—and speaking in such plain terms about matters of the heart—"

"My heart in particular," he reminded her. Unnecessarily.

"—you're asking me to stay. If I'd had any idea this would happen, I would never have presumed…"

"I suspect you would have," he assured her. "Though perhaps with more subtlety."

She made a sound of exasperation. "Mr. Granville, this is most embarrassing." She paced, agitated, to a bush heavy with pink roses, and began fidgeting with a just-opened bloom.

"That variety is a China rose called Parson's Pink," he told her. She released it quickly. "If I promise to expunge this entire conversation from my memory, and Thursday's, too," he said, "will you stay?"

She shook her head, but couldn't help smiling. "I doubt your ability to expunge so much. Tell me, why does Miss Granville need a companion now, when apparently she didn't before?"

"I intend to begin my search for a wife immediately," he said.

If that was meant to answer her question, she'd missed it. "Are you saying you'll be traveling to London? And that your sister will need company in your absence?"

He strolled over to join her by the Parson's Pink roses. "We spoke a moment ago about Marianne's dislike of meeting new people," he said. "Woodbridge Hall has a new neighbor whom I'll be required to entertain in the near future. If I'm inviting guests, I might as well commence my hunt for a bride at the same time. With so much going on, Marianne will need support. For you to assist her as a companion, paid an allowance—which I assure you will be generous—is very different from a governess paid a wage. It's entirely acceptable in the eyes of society."

"True," she murmured.

"There's another benefit," he said. "The more people in

the house, the less 'on display' my prospective bride will feel when she visits."

"Hmm." Serena was unsure of his logic. Wouldn't a lady feel *more* on display, the more people there were to inspect her? Then she registered his use of the singular noun. "Just *one* prospective bride, Mr. Granville?"

"I only need one wife."

Which was quite the silliest thing she'd heard. "What if the first lady you invite here proves unsuitable?"

"There will not be a *parade* of single ladies," he said ominously.

Oh, dear. Serena changed the subject. "So you will invite them—*her*—here for the children to meet her. An excellent idea." Perhaps if she praised the concept first, she could then suggest improvements.

"It's for my prospective bride to meet my children, not the other way around," he said. "The children will have no say in my decision."

Serena tried not to look alarmed. After all, few men would ask their children's opinions. But Dominic Granville didn't know much about his children's needs....

"If I left it to Thomas, he would choose the lady most courageous in the handling of lizards." His annoyance suggested she hadn't succeeded in disguising her concern. "You may rest assured of my good judgment, Miss Somerton. Now, will you stay? As well as pleasing my sister, the continuity of your presence would benefit the children."

"And I'd be delighted not to leave them just yet," she admitted. "I assume I could still spend time with them, though I'd be Marianne's companion?"

"Certainly, though you wouldn't be teaching them," he said. "It's only just over a month until summer—the children can take an early break from their studies." His tone was ironic, as if he didn't believe they studied too seriously under Serena's supervision.

Well, they didn't. Not *too* seriously. She believed in a balance of work and play. If she stayed, she could continue to encourage Mr. Granville to get closer to his children. With a great deal of tact, of course.

"Nurse is quite capable of managing their daily activities," he stated, then paused. "So, you will stay?"

A chill gust of wind blew a sprinkling of rose petals off the bush, to land at Serena's feet. Poor petals, so easily parted from the security of the plant, then left to wither and die.

"Miss Somerton, everything is proceeding according to your wishes," he said, his patience wearing thin. "You'll have longer with the children, and I've undertaken to provide the stepmother you insist upon. Yet—"

He put a finger to her chin, lifting it.

Serena gasped and took a step back.

"I—I apologize." His face had reddened, whether from the wind or embarrassment, she wasn't sure. "I was merely observing you appear to be sunk in gloom."

She laced her fingers tightly, so she wouldn't be tempted to explore the place where the memory of his touch lingered. She struggled to marshal her thoughts. "I'm not gloomy," she said. That was the wrong word for her doubts about his approach to remarriage. And certainly the wrong word for her reaction to his touch. *Don't think about that.*

"You will stay," he said.

It wasn't a question, but Serena answered it, anyway.

"I will stay."

Chapter Three

"You must call me Marianne." Marianne Granville served herself some stuffed lettuce from the platter in front of her. "I call you Serena in my head, anyway, so your name comes naturally to me."

"Certainly, if you wish." Serena smiled at Marianne, then listened with half an ear as brother and sister chatted about some matter related to the estate's tenants. Her elevation to the role of companion required her to dine with Miss Granville—Marianne—and her brother. Prompted by her embarrassment at her free speech with Dominic Granville, Serena had given excuses for why she should eat at the table in her own little sitting room the past two evenings, but today Marianne had insisted. The other woman had embraced the idea of having her as a companion with such alacrity, Serena felt Mr. Granville was right that she was needed by more than just the children. Not that he'd admitted the children needed her.

"You're very quiet tonight, Miss Somerton." Dominic's comment jerked her out of her reverie.

"Not at all, Mr. Granville," she murmured. She'd decided life would be simpler if she didn't engage in conversation with him, beyond grasping opportunities to subtly encourage him to spend more time with his children.

"Maybe you should call Dominic by his Christian name, too," Marianne said.

A frown from her brother. Serena was relieved, and unsurprised. Though she had thought of him as Dominic several times over the past few days—it was hard not to, with Marianne saying his name all the time—they weren't related, and were certainly not friends.

He made no response to her sister's suggestion, nor did Serena.

"Dom, I've made a list of whom I think we should invite to dinner next week," Marianne said. "As soon as you approve it, I'll send the invitations."

No one listening to her would know how much she dreaded the occasion. Looking at her was another matter; her face was crimson at just the thought of entertaining so many people, even though most of them were familiar.

If Marianne hadn't been afflicted with this excessive, uncontrollable blushing, she would have been one of the most beautiful women Serena had met. Not surprising, given how handsome her brother was. Her blue eyes were large and well spaced, her cheekbones beautifully defined, her mouth a perfect bow. Her dark hair was lustrous and thick; Serena had seen it down and admired its natural, loose curls.

But then…there was her Condition. Serena had never seen Marianne in an unblushing state. Even in the company of family, her cheeks were lightly flushed. And it took no more than a question from one of Woodbridge Hall's longtime servants to make her color flare. In wider society, her skin ranged from rose-pink with friends to a vivid puce with strangers. Serena wasn't sure what had come first, Marianne's blushing or her shyness. Whatever the answer, the two were now inextricably linked, feeding each other.

"Excellent," Dominic said of the plan for dinner invitations. He started on one of the second course dishes, poached turbot with lobster sauce. "When I called on Mr. Beaumont, he said he'd be pleased to attend."

"What kind of man is he?" Marianne asked. She'd told Serena yesterday that she liked to know as much as possible about people before she met them, in the hope that minimizing the surprise would also minimize blushing.

Dominic poured more sauce over his fish. "Very friendly."

He spoke as if that was a bad thing. Serena could imagine him pulling back from an excess of neighborly warmth.

"He sounds the type to want to converse a lot," Marianne said dubiously. She set down her knife and fork. "Serena, we might go into Melton Mowbray on Thursday to see what Mrs. Fletcher has on offer."

Mrs. Fletcher was a dressmaker, the best in the village.

"Thank you, I'd love to," Serena said. Her wardrobe wasn't sufficient for her elevated status of companion, and certainly not for a dinner party. With her new allowance, she could easily afford a new dress. Perhaps even two. And if she took her gray silk with her, Mrs. Fletcher might suggest alterations that would bring it into the current fashion.

Despite her concern for Marianne, Serena found herself looking forward to the upcoming dinner. As rector of Piper's Mead, her father was invited, along with his family, to all the social events of the local gentry. Serena had always enjoyed the occasions.

"Shall I tell you who else is on the guest list, Dom?" Marianne said, with a smile that was painfully forced. "One name will be of particular interest to you, I think."

Her arch tone suggested she was referring to a lady.

Dominic's glance flickered in Serena's direction; she sensed his reluctance to open the subject in her presence.

"Mrs. Gordon," Marianne announced, before he could refuse. To Serena, she said, "Colonel Gordon was killed in the

Peninsula three years ago. She's a very capable lady, and her children have excellent manners."

"She has children of her own?" Serena asked, dismayed. It had never occurred to her that the new Mrs. Granville might bring her own offspring to the marriage. "I'm not sure that's a good idea."

"Your opinion is not required, Miss Somerton," Dominic said. "Indeed, it is unwelcome."

Belatedly, Serena recalled her intention not to engage in discussion with him. But she could hardly ignore such thoughtlessness! Besides, as Marianne's companion, she was no longer a servant to be instructed as to what she could and couldn't talk about. She wouldn't force her views on him as bluntly as she had when she'd thought she was leaving. But a less personal, more reasoned discussion should be perfectly acceptable.

"It's natural for a mother to favor her own children over someone else's," she observed. She addressed the remark to Marianne.

"Serena may have a point, Dominic," Marianne said. "I don't think Mrs. Gordon would willfully do such a thing, but perhaps unintentionally... Maybe I shouldn't invite her."

"Invite her," he ordered. "She's a very pleasant woman, and she already calls this district home. She will do very well."

Just like that, he'd decided this Mrs. Gordon was The One? Serena bristled. Convenience was one thing, expediency to the point of carelessness quite another. His eyes met hers, daring her to challenge him. She held his gaze for several long seconds. Then his focus shifted infinitesimally, lowered, and she was reminded of his touch on her chin. A quiver ran through her.

Serena picked up her cutlery and turned her attention to her fish. For the next few minutes, the only sound was the clink of silver on china. Judging by her high color, Marianne was lost in fretful contemplation of the upcoming dinner party. Dominic doubtless thought he'd solved his marriage dilemma in one easy step; the measured pace of his eating radiated smugness.

Serena reined in her impulse to argue further. She was the one who'd suggested Dominic should marry. To object to how he went about it was unreasonable…at this stage.

Dominic couldn't sleep. A few days ago he'd thought he would never remarry. Now he'd not only decided to walk down the aisle again, but Marianne had identified a candidate who seemed exactly what he needed.

Everything in him rebelled.

He stared at the elaborate ceiling cornice above his bed, only just able to discern the acorn-and-leaf pattern in the light of the half-moon. *Lord, there must be another way.*

He'd loved Emily from childhood, and at their wedding he'd promised to love her until death parted them. A promise all too easily kept. The truth was, he would love her forever. Was it fair to propose marriage to another woman, even one who accepted—perhaps welcomed—the convenient nature of the alliance?

The alternative was worse. Even if it were possible to feel again the way he'd felt about Emily, why would he want to? The agony of losing his wife was no longer rapier-sharp, but he remembered it well. When Serena had talked of a second chance, all he'd been able to imagine was a second chance to suffer. A man would be insane to expose himself to that again.

Which brought him back to a convenient marriage. Deep down, despite his prayer, Dominic knew there *was* no other way. Not if his daughters were to be successfully presented to society, if his sister was to be spared the agony of a chaperone role.

He thumped his pillow into a more amenable shape and turned over.

From a distance—upstairs?—he heard a cry. Then another. In the next moment, it became full-on wailing.

One of the children. Likely a bad dream; Nurse would attend to it. Dominic pulled his pillow over his head.

A minute later, the noise hadn't abated.

Dominic lay there another minute. Was it possible Nurse had gone suddenly deaf? Maybe Marianne would... No, she was a famously sound sleeper. Suppressing a curse, he pushed the covers aside and got out of bed, pulled on his breeches and shirt. And since he could hardly go wandering around the house in his shirtsleeves, a dressing gown on top.

The noise was louder outside his room, deafening by the time he reached the nursery. He pushed open the door.

"Nurse, what is this infernal—"

He stopped. The woman standing at Louisa's bed wasn't the comforting figure of his sixty-year-old nurse. It was Serena—Miss Somerton.

She scooped Louisa up into her arms, staggering a little as she straightened.

His daughter's cheeks were brilliant red, her eyes glassy.

Dominic charged forward. "What's wrong with her? Where's Nurse?"

"Her granddaughter was due to be delivered of a baby tonight." Miss Somerton blushed at the intimate topic. "Marianne gave Nurse permission to attend her."

He touched the back of his hand to Louisa's forehead. "She has a fever. Have you summoned a doctor?" He made for the bellpull.

"The doctor can't do anything." Serena raised her voice so he could hear over his daughter's cries. "It's an ear infection."

"How do you know?" Even as he asked, Dominic noticed that Louisa's left earlobe was red. "It might *look* like an ear infection, but what if it's something more serious?"

Like measles.

"Louisa suffers these infections quite frequently, though more often in winter." Serena's tone said he should know that. "Experience suggests there's nothing much to do beyond comforting her." Rocking his daughter in her arms, she murmured, "Hush, dearest, I'm here now."

Louisa continued to scream.

"There must be something we can do," Dominic said, aghast. "She's obviously in pain."

"I've sent the nursery maid for some laudanum. A few drops won't harm her, and it'll help her sleep."

"What about Nurse's special tonic?" he said desperately. "That seems to fix anything."

Serena smiled, and her face took on that impish look he was beginning to associate with her. Highly inappropriate in a governess.

She's not a governess anymore.

Still, to be smiling like that, she couldn't be too worried about Louisa; Dominic felt his own panic ease.

"Nurse's special tonic is just lemon barley, I'm afraid," she said. "I've discovered that unless Nurse herself administers it, it doesn't work."

"Lemon barley?" He struck a hand to his chest. "That tonic has cured me miraculously numerous times."

Serena's smiled widened as she stroked Louisa's hair. "I apologize for disillusioning you."

"Let me take her," Dominic said. "She's heavy."

He half expected her to protest, convinced as she was that she knew better what his children needed, but she willingly offered Louisa over.

The transfer proved awkward, as Louisa burrowed into

Serena's neck. Dominic's suddenly clumsy fingers brushed Serena's shoulders and upper arms through her clothing. She stiffened.

By the time he held his daughter, he felt as if he'd been wrestling quicksand. Serena's cheeks were pink, her gaze downcast.

It occurred to him that the high-necked garment she wore might be a dressing gown. It certainly wasn't the dress she'd worn to dinner, which had been white, with a pink ribbon and a ruffled hem. Simple, but pretty. Whatever this peach-colored garment was, it boasted the shabbiness of long wear.

To allow them both time to collect themselves, Dominic paced the room, trying to keep his steps rhythmic. With no better plan of his own—indeed, he didn't have a clue—he followed Serena's example, stroking Louisa's hair, hushing her. Inept though he felt—should he be stroking or patting?—it seemed to soothe the child.

Serena yawned and sank down onto the edge of Louisa's bed. Dominic walked past the chest filled with toys, many from his own youth, and over to a table where pencils and paper and paints were laid out. One of the chairs had a cushion tied to it, presumably for Louisa. On the table was a painting—if you could call the mess of colors that—anchored with two stones from the garden. Dominic eyed the "masterpiece" with misgiving. Was Serena a poor tutor, or was his daughter entirely lacking artistic talent?

"Louisa uses color to great effect." Serena had followed the direction of his gaze.

"It's a mess," he said.

"It's the work of a five-year-old, Mr. Granville."

The sudden frost in her voice was a defense of his daughter, he realized. About which he could hardly complain.

"Actually," she continued, "it's a portrait of you."

Dominic leaned over to get a better look at the painting.

Louisa's head flopped forward; quickly, he cupped it, hugging her securely. "I appear to have three eyes."

"It's perhaps not a good likeness," Serena admitted. "Maybe," she continued, still frosty, "that's because the children don't see enough of you to remember what you look like."

Dominic had heard the phrase *midnight madness*... This must be it, the casting aside of daytime's social inhibitions. Mind you, Serena seemed to indulge the urge to speak her mind at any time, thanks to her father's unusual liberality.

Dominic would not be indulging in madness. No matter what the provocation.

"I see my children morning and evening," he reminded her calmly.

"For all of seven minutes each time."

"I have an estate to run, Miss Somerton. It ensures my family's daily provision and future security, and it occupies a great deal of my time."

"You have five children. You're their only parent."

"A situation I intend to rectify."

"Your sons in particular need more of your time," she said.

It was growing more difficult to maintain his polite demeanor. "I know you mean well, Miss Somerton, so even though I have explained to you that well-meaning people are among my least favorite, I will overlook your interference."

"William's fear of the dark—"

"He'll outgrow that." Actually, Dominic had assumed his son had long ago outgrown the fear that beset him after his mother died.

"—is getting worse," she said. "Perhaps if you talked to him..."

Before she could give him the benefit of any more of her advice, the maid appeared, carrying the laudanum. She gave a little gasp of surprise to see Dominic.

"Mr. Granville, could you set Louisa on the bed?" Serena asked.

Laying Louisa down wasn't easy. Her little fingers clutched at his lapel. Detaching them seemed to hurt her, and she squalled.

Dominic took a hasty step away from the bed, the back of his neck hot, as if he were the one with the fever.

"Hold her hand, please," Serena said crisply.

Out of his depths, unsure if there was some medical reason to obey, he reluctantly approached the bed again and took his daughter's hand. Serena administered the laudanum. Louisa settled almost instantly, whether from the effects of the medicine or from a belief that it would do her good. Dominic let go of her hand, feeling as if he'd just run a mile.

Serena dismissed the maid. "You may go, too, Mr. Granville," she said.

Eager though he was to get back to bed, he didn't like being dismissed in his own house by an uppity governess. *Companion,* he corrected mentally.

"What about you, Miss Somerton? You need your sleep."

"I'll wait a few minutes, to be sure she's asleep."

As if to prove the wisdom of her strategy, Louisa writhed suddenly. "Mama," she moaned.

Dominic drew in a sharp breath. Louisa didn't remember Emily; she'd been only six months old when her mother died. Of course, she'd heard the other children talking of their mother over the years. More so recently, going by what Serena had told him the other day.

Could another woman possibly fill the gap in his children's lives, if she couldn't fill the gap in his?

Serena's gaze met Dominic's. "If you're questioning the wisdom of your plan to marry, believe me, the children will appreciate it."

Had she read his mind? Discerned his doubts? "Stepmothers are often vilified in literature," he said lightly.

Her lips curved. "Naturally, you should avoid those who plan to feed the children poisoned apples, who possess magic mirrors or who will force the girls to live among the cinders."

"Useful advice," he murmured. "Thank you."

He noticed again the graceful length of Serena's neck—she was so well covered that was all there was to notice. Other than her eyes, the blue of cornflowers. And her lips, rather full and rosy for a governess. From his own childhood, he recalled governesses with pursed lips and tight mouths.

"It seems strange you're such a firm proponent of my remarrying," he said, his eyes still on her lips, "yet you're in no hurry to enter the matrimonial state yourself." That's what she'd said, when he'd accused her of proposing to him. He grimaced at his own conceit, and dragged his gaze back up. "Most women of your age and connections would be eager to launch themselves into London's marriage mart, rather than rusticate with my children and my sister."

Serena shrugged, a delicate lift of her shoulders. "I can't speak for most women, only for myself. And your situation and mine are not at all alike—I don't have children who need a father. I shall marry when I find a man who loves me with all his heart."

A silence fell, during which they both stared at Louisa, now sleeping, her breathing loud.

"You don't have a suitor back home?" he asked.

She looked away. "No."

Another silence.

"About Mrs. Gordon…" she began.

"Serena, could you set aside your objections to Mrs. Gordon for now?" he asked. He realized he'd used her Christian name. She blinked, whether at his familiarity or his plea, he wasn't sure. "After all, we have no reason to believe the lady will have the slightest interest in marrying me."

Serena looked him over, so quickly he could have missed it.

"If you say so," she said.

Something hung in the air between them. Something that to Dominic felt like *She thinks I'm handsome.*

"I mean, how does one even introduce the thought of marriage?" he asked quickly, distracting her from any possibility of reading his mind, which had taken a turn for the absurd. His conceit was still alive and well, it seemed! "I've spent years making it clear to the world that I don't intend to marry."

The first few years after Emily died, women had made their interest plain, some of them while he was still in mourning.

"There's a simple way to convey your change of heart to everyone who needs to know," she said. "Tell your valet your intentions."

"Trimble would never—" Dominic broke off, seeing her readiness to disagree. No point encouraging her to argue. Even if those arguments were as exhilarating as they were irritating. "I'm prepared to try your suggestion," he said generously. "But I have more faith in my valet's discretion than you do." In a way, he hoped Trimble would say nothing. Though the world needed to know, Dominic quailed at the thought of reversing the impression of confirmed bachelorhood he'd worked so hard to create.

Of course, if he wanted a wife of good birth, conveniently located and who liked his children, Miss Somerton herself was eminently qualified.

"I commend your reluctance to wed," she said surprisingly. Surprising given that the whole thing had been her idea. "Your loyalty to your late wife is admirable."

It struck him that her admiration was a thing some men might covet. Before they realized how argumentative she was. No one would want a wife so provoking.

"Emily and I loved each other from childhood," he said. What an odd conversation to be having with a near stranger. Something about the lateness of the hour, the flickering shadow of the candle on the wall, invited confidence. It seemed he wasn't immune to midnight madness, after all.

Madness or no, she needed to understand this one thing about him. He fixed his gaze on the wavering shadow. "When I was thirteen, and Emily was twelve, I told her we would marry one day. Neither of us faltered in our determination. We were married a week after she turned eighteen, and the twins were born a year later. We were happy every day we were together." He ran a hand around the back of his neck, suddenly tired. "I don't believe a person finds a love like that more than once in their life."

"I hope and pray you're wrong," Serena said.

Something in her tone put him on the alert. It sounded personal. As if she, too, had loved and lost. He would have said twenty-one was too young to be seriously brokenhearted, but of course, he and Emily had been married three years by the time Emily was of age. He wondered who Serena…

He dismissed the thought. Likely she was moved by his own tale, not referring to a doomed romance of her own.

The silence grew awkward. Serena broke it.

"How will you determine if Mrs. Gordon is fit to be your children's stepmother?" she asked.

"She's a woman of good sense and few expectations," he said. "I consider that an excellent start."

Those cornflower eyes widened. "Oh, dear, she sounds rather uninspiring."

He couldn't help it; he groaned. "If by uninspiring you mean calm and reasonable…"

"That must be what I mean," she said with that now-familiar mischievous twinkle.

"Her lineage is impeccable," he said. "If not as elevated as your own."

"I can't help feeling Mrs. Gordon has attained the position of front-runner merely by coming from a good family and living close by," Serena said. "Is your aim to make the nearest choice or the best choice?"

He refused to rise to that bait. "Since this will be a marriage of convenience, proximity seems a logical criterion."

"What about whether she adores your children?"

Adores. What a word to use.

He straightened the storybook sitting on the chest of drawers next to the bed. "She will need to care about the children, of course. And to know how to nurse them and employ a governess and, when they're older, introduce them to the world. She's a mother already, so I'm sure she knows these things."

"Hmm," Serena said. It wasn't a sound that expressed confidence in Dominic's judgment. "What other qualities should the future Mrs. Granville possess?"

Like most of her questions, this one fell into the none-of-her-business category. But it was, he supposed, something he should be considering.

"Intelligence," he said, "of course."

"There's no *of course* about that," she said. "I hear many men don't want an intelligent wife."

"I'm not afraid of a woman with a brain, Miss Somerton."

"Excellent," she said warmly.

He shook off the pleasant feeling her approval induced. "For my wife to be attractive would be nice, but not essential."

"A Christian woman," Serena suggested.

"Naturally," he said. "I believe most ladies of my acquaintance are Christians."

"Someone…playful?" she proposed.

He frowned.

"You don't object to play, do you?"

"Of course not," he said. "It's good for children to play. When it's appropriate."

Her quick grin said she considered him stuffy. To a twenty-one-year-old girl, he probably was. "I expect my wife to be mature," he said. "Close to my own age."

She nodded as if that made complete sense, which, perversely, left him feeling insulted. Who was to say he couldn't find himself a younger wife if he wished?

Though a more mature woman was less likely to have romantic notions.

"The main thing is," he said, putting an abrupt end to a conversation that had already become too personal, "the children should have someone to take the maternal role in their lives."

"You mean, to love them." Why did she have to twist everything, yet at the same time make it sound so uncomplicated?

"You really are very young, Serena." Blast, he'd used her Christian name again.

"I suspect you mean I'm naive," she said. "If believing in the power of love to transform lives is naive, then, yes, I am."

"No doubt you're right." But Dominic would settle for a successful come-out for his daughters, and for a more comfortable existence for his sister.

Serena's tsk suggested she knew he was fobbing her off. But she didn't argue. "I think Louisa will sleep through now," she said.

"Excellent." He looked down at his sleeping daughter. Louisa had always been a small child, but huddled as she was, she seemed tiny. He had the urge to caress her in some way…but he didn't know how. Awkward, he rubbed the bump in the blanket made by her foot. "I will do my best for my children in this matter of my remarriage, Miss Somerton, you may rely on that. I am more than conscious that they depend on me. Indeed, I would give my life for any of them."

What on earth had possessed him to say something so dramatic? *Blame it on the midnight madness.*

Serena made a smothered sound. Dominic raised his eyebrows at her, daring her to comment.

She shook her head. "It's time I returned to my chamber." She bent over and kissed Louisa's forehead. That was what he should have done, he realized, castigating himself. It seemed obvious now. The way Serena smoothed a lock of his daughter's hair reminded him of Emily. For one moment, he found himself wanting that touch on his own hair, that tenderness directed at him. *No.*

Yet instinctively, he drew closer, and as Serena straightened, she bumped into him. Dominic grasped her arms to steady her. Immediately, he released her.

They stood staring at each other.

"Good night," she blurted. And almost ran from the room.

Chapter Four

The next morning, Marianne's complexion was redder than usual—one of those inexplicable days when her face started off the color of the crimson walls in the breakfast room and stayed that way. Small wonder that, having swallowed the last of her baked egg, she took to her room to lie down with damp cloths on her cheeks, with a plan to play some solitary chess later. A devotee of the game, she had a board set up in her private sitting room.

Outside, a spring storm had blown up, lashing the windows and bending trees at dangerous angles.

Serena visited the nursery and found the children fidgety, snapping at each other. Louisa was feeling much better, but her mood was subdued.

"What we need is a nice game," Serena announced.

"Can we slide down the banister again?" William begged.

"No, dearest." Even though it was exactly that kind of day, and Serena felt so peculiarly unsettled that she'd have relished the chance to climb onto the banister herself. Not that she ever would, of course. "We'll play dominoes."

The children pounced on the suggestion, and the twins soon had the game set up. Luckily, it didn't require much concentration, because Serena's mind was busy elsewhere.

Wondering at Dominic's unguarded, late-night declaration of love for his children.

Not that he'd said anything as simple as "I love them." Instead, he'd said, "I would give my life for any of them."

She doubted he'd been thinking of the verse from John's gospel: "Greater love hath no man than this, that a man lay down his life for his friends." But *she* had thought of it, and had recognized a declaration of ardent love.

He would probably be horrified by her interpretation. What a pity that he should feel so much for his children, yet not show it in his words or deeds! During her eight months at Woodbridge Hall Serena had observed him as a cool, distant father. A provider and protector, but not a loving papa. When he embraced his children, she saw only duty on both sides.

Until last night, she'd assumed his behavior was a reflection of his thoughts.

She'd been wrong.

Yet she doubted even Dominic knew how much he loved his children. Given his attitude to love in a new marriage, he might not even *want* to know.

For his own sake, and that of his children, he needed to admit to his deeper feelings. And if this was another example of Serena deciding what was best for others...she didn't care.

The game of dominoes came to an end, with William the winner.

"What shall we play now?" Charlotte asked, as the older children packed away the dominoes.

"Time for spillikins, I think," Serena said. "Louisa, perhaps you could ask your father to join us?"

Louisa was hard to resist on any day. Today, when she was still pale from her sleepless night, even the hardest-hearted brute would succumb. Dominic was certainly not that.

"Ask Papa to play a game?" Thomas said, astounded. "In the middle of the day?" It wasn't clear which idea he found more outrageous: that Dominic might play or that they might see their father outside the prescribed times.

"Why not?" Serena said. "He's probably as bored as we are."

Thomas's expression said she had lost her mind, but of course, he didn't contradict her. The Granville children were all, with the occasional exception of Charlotte, well-behaved, as they should be.

Serena escorted Louisa downstairs to the library, where Dominic usually spent the morning on his correspondence and accounts. She knocked on the paneled oak door.

"Come in," said a mildly irritated voice.

He'd been deprived of sleep, Serena reminded herself. She opened the door and gave Louisa a little push.

"Hello there." Dominic's voice softened immediately. Serena could hear him smiling. "How are your ears this morning?"

Still holding the door handle, Serena pressed her own ear to the opening in an attempt to hear the conversation—only to stumble a moment later when the door was wrenched open.

She gave a little squawk of dismay, and straightened up.

"Eavesdropping, Miss Somerton?" Dominic asked.

So, in the cold light of day they were back to "Miss Somerton." If not for the flicker in his hazel eyes of a recognition that went more than skin-deep, she'd have said their midnight conversation had never happened. And perhaps his eyes were just a little too fixed on her own, as if he wouldn't allow them to stray. Last night, she was almost certain he'd been looking at her mouth.

"I apologize," she said, slightly breathless. "I wanted to hear how well Louisa framed her request."

"You could have come in with her."

"True," she agreed. "But then I couldn't have observed you without your knowing."

He gave a startled laugh. "That honesty of yours."

"There's no point pretending otherwise, when you caught me red-handed," Serena said.

"A fair point," he conceded. "And at least this time your ruthless honesty isn't directed at my private life." He propped one shoulder against the doorjamb. The casual power of the pose suggested he had the world at his feet, his to command or ignore. When he looked like this, the task of reforming a man so distant into a loving, playful father seemed an impossible fantasy. Then he surprised her by saying in a tone that wasn't distant, "So…spillikins, hmm?"

Serena nodded. She tried not to sound too eager. "Marianne is resting in her room, so I thought I'd spend some time with the children. With such beastly weather outdoors, we're looking for entertainments."

"Please play with us, Papa," Louisa asked, with plaintive sweetness.

Dominic swung her into his arms, a tenderness in his eyes that made Serena's heart jump. *This* was more like it.

"If you insist." His agreement told Serena just how worried he'd been last night. "But I warn you—" he set Louisa back on the floor and ruffled her hair "—I shall win."

"Not with those big hands you won't," Serena said. Gracious! What was she thinking of, commenting on his hands? Besides, strong though they looked, the tapering of his fingers suggested he might not be entirely graceless.

Not at all.

"Miss Somerton, are you too warm?" he quizzed her.

Serena pressed her palms to her cheeks. Heat. *Pull yourself together, my girl.* "I'm quite comfortable," she said.

The children were surprised but delighted when their father entered the nursery.

Only Charlotte didn't show her pleasure—like her papa, her natural state was one of wary distance. Serena had learned that Charlotte would never risk a display of affection unless she was certain it would be returned. When the others ran to greet Dominic, she carried the spillikins over to Serena.

Dominic frowned in her direction, but didn't comment. Nor did he greet her. "Where are we playing?" he asked. He looked as if he already regretted the impulse to indulge Louisa.

"On the floor, of course," William said.

"I feared as much." Dominic eased himself down onto the pale pink-patterned carpet.

"Charlotte, could you do the drop?" Serena asked.

Charlotte held the sharpened sticks in her fist an inch or two off the floor, then dropped them. Immediately, all the children focused intently on the lay of the sticks, trying to identify the easy pickings. Dominic traded an amused glance with Serena.

"Who starts?" he asked.

"Me!" William said. Then, at his father's querying look, he said in a more subdued tone, "I mean, I do, Papa, since I won our last game of dominoes."

He picked up an easy first stick, one that had rolled away from the others. He used the tip to separate two more from the pile before disturbing one of the neighboring sticks.

"My turn," Charlotte whooped.

"Ladies don't shout, Charlotte," her father reminded her.

The girl's face reddened. During her turn, she failed to retrieve any sticks before knocking one out of place. Her father grimaced—in sympathy, but she took it as criticism.

"It wasn't my fault," she said. "William bumped me."

Serena gave her a sharp look, a reminder that sulks were not permitted. Charlotte's chin jutted—again, so like her father—but she said no more.

Though Dominic proved to have a surprising aptitude for

the game, despite his large fingers, he was no match for the practiced nimbleness of the children. Thomas won quickly.

They played another game, this time won by Hetty, then Thomas won again. Charlotte was looking crosser and crosser, and Dominic didn't look too happy, either. Somehow, Serena wasn't quite sure why, the mood in the nursery turned cool. When Dominic declared he needed to get back to work, no one but Louisa begged him to stay. This time, he had no difficulty refusing her request.

Serena got to her feet. "I will check on your aunt. Children, I suggest you read quietly. Nurse will be up with your luncheon soon."

She hurried out of the nursery in Dominic's wake. "Mr. Granville?"

"What is it?" He seemed intent on rushing downstairs; he slowed to let her catch up, but didn't pause in his stride.

"Please." Serena was forced to stay him with a hand on his arm. As soon as he stopped, she let go. "Thank you for joining the children in their game. They love to spend time with you."

He nodded with scant patience. Then he said, "Charlotte clearly didn't love it. Is she always so sullen?"

Shouldn't he know the answer to that?

"She takes offense too easily," Serena said. "She's the sweetest thing when people show kindness to her first." She hesitated. "Is that why you seemed to be vexed?"

He bristled. "I wasn't vexed."

"Your mood cooled," she said. "It dampened the children's spirits."

His expression grew stony. "Then perhaps it's a good thing I don't play spillikins more often."

She burst out laughing. "Really, Dominic, you sound just like Charlotte in one of her sulks."

The flare of his eyes made her aware she'd called him by

his Christian name. Should she apologize? No, better not to concede a weakness right now.

To her surprise, he smiled ruefully. "Perhaps that's where she gets her moods."

"So if not Charlotte, did something else cause your misgivings?" she asked.

"You're not going to let me just walk away, are you?" he said, exasperated. "I don't like to criticize my children—" no, he preferred to stay away from them "—but if you must know, I was disappointed in Thomas and Hetty. Winning the games so fast and not letting the younger ones enjoy some triumph."

Serena beamed. "Is that all?"

"That's no cause for good cheer," he said. "I consider sportsmanship very important."

"So do your children," she promised. "Usually Tom and Hetty would deliberately fluff a few rounds to let the younger ones win. Today, they were both too anxious to impress you."

He looked doubtful.

"Truly," she assured him. "Your children are generous in spirit, all of them. Their stepmother will be a fortunate woman—you *will* marry someone kind, won't you?" she added impulsively.

He stared at her.

"Of course you will," she muttered. "I apologize."

"Miss Somerton," he said, "your interest in whom I intend to marry has gone beyond the curious and into the nosy."

"I just want—"

"I don't doubt you mean well." Which they'd both agreed was a thoroughly obnoxious habit, so she couldn't derive any comfort from that, and he knew it. "But I will choose my wife without further comment from you. Is that understood?"

"I was just— The children—"

"If you continue to interfere, you will be removed from this household. My sister will have to find a new companion."

He was bluffing, surely! But he appeared entirely serious.

"Is that understood?" he asked again.

Though he stood close to her, his coldness put distance between them. Serena swallowed. He'd told her at dinner to keep her opinions to herself. But then, late last night, he'd talked so openly, she'd thought...

Obviously not.

It would serve him right if he ended up married to a shrew who nagged him from dawn to dusk—except that wouldn't be fair on the children.

"I understand," she said, with an attempt to match his iciness.

Evidently, she failed; his eyes lit with a flash of humor that was far from cold. But he merely said, "Good."

She watched as Dominic walked down the stairs and into the library.

Yes, she understood, but she would not obey.

Dominic Granville might not look for happiness for himself, but she would do everything in her power to make sure his children had their share.

The more she thought about Dominic's criteria for choosing a wife, those qualities he'd mentioned as they nursed Louisa last night, the more she found them disturbingly vague. Mrs. Gordon didn't sound objectionable, but neither had Dominic considered how she would fare with his children. Though to see them as an amorphous clump of "five children" was to do them a disservice. Each was different from the other. Did he even know that?

Charlotte could easily be deemed surly; he'd said so himself. He needed a wife who understood that Charlotte's prickly nature was an invitation to show kindness, a sort of test as to whether people liked her, without comparing her to her whip-smart older sister, Hetty, or the adorable little Louisa. Then there was William, who'd started off so shy, but was gradually finding confidence. Embarrassed about his fear of the dark, but fearless beyond his years when it came to horses. The twins were both so strong-minded, they needed to believe in something before they would do it— would Dominic respect that?

A man who considered the things he didn't know to be irrelevant was doomed to make mistakes.

Dominic's choice of wife was too important for mistakes. This was a second chance, whether he saw it that way or not, and Serena wouldn't let him squander it.

I will assess this Mrs. Gordon, and if I don't think she's right, I'll make sure Dominic doesn't propose to her.

She had no idea *how* she could stop Dominic proposing marriage to an unsuitable bride. She only knew that she would do it.

Chapter Five

The Granville carriage slowed as it entered Melton Mowbray. In this busy village, it seemed everyone crossed the road without looking. At least, that had been the dire warning from Carver, the coachman, as he'd helped Marianne and then Serena into the carriage at Woodbridge Hall.

Which explained why he proceeded at not much more than walking pace until they pulled up outside Mrs. Fletcher's establishment. Carver opened the door and let down the steps. Serena disembarked first.

"Could you make sure there's no one coming?" Marianne begged. "I don't want to be any redder than necessary when I talk to Mrs. Fletcher." The more people she was forced to speak with, the deeper her color.

Serena stepped down, careful to avoid a puddle left by yesterday's storm, and scanned the street. No one coming, from either the left or the right. "You're safe," she reported.

But just as Marianne emerged, a gentleman appeared around the back of the carriage. He must have just crossed the road—without looking, judging by the disapproval on Carver's face. Since the gentleman was unlikely to be visiting Mrs. Fletcher, his destination must be the stationer's shop next door.

Marianne hadn't seen him. "I've warned Dominic to be prepared for a large bill," she said chattily. "It's so long since I've bought any new dresses, I need at least—" She broke off the moment she registered the presence of a stranger. Ducking her head, she froze, as if that might render her invisible.

But the gentleman had stopped, arrested, it seemed, by their conversation. He bowed in their direction.

Go away, Serena thought.

"Good afternoon, ladies," he said. "Forgive my intrusion, but I couldn't help overhearing…are you, by any chance, Miss Granville?"

He addressed the question to Serena. She must indeed look more like the lady of the house, with Marianne huddled behind her like the most downtrodden companion.

"I'm Serena Somerton," she said. "Companion to Miss Granville." She indicated Marianne.

Marianne raised her face, as scarlet as Serena could ever remember seeing her.

The gentleman blinked, but his face didn't betray any awkwardness. "Forgive me, Miss Granville," he said, "you must think me terribly rude, accosting you in the street. I'm Geoffrey Beaumont, a guest at Farley Hall."

Marianne licked her lips. "Sir—Sir Charles's nephew." She shook the hand he offered. "Good afternoon."

"I heard the mention of your brother's name and couldn't resist the opportunity to introduce myself," he said, still apologizing. He had blue eyes that smiled, Serena noticed, and his well-cut coat and impeccable boots enhanced what was already a pleasing appearance. "I'm very much looking forward to dining at Woodbridge Hall next week."

"As are we," Marianne murmured. "I mean, looking forward to you joining us…not looking forward to dining there ourselves, since we do that every night…." She trailed off into inarticulateness.

Serena stared at her. She'd never heard Marianne volunteer so much conversation.

Mr. Beaumont laughed in appreciation of her wit. "Now that I've met you, I'm looking forward to it even more."

Marianne's color deepened, if that was possible. "Our cook does have a wonderful reputation in the neighborhood."

Her modest reply inspired a warm smile from the gentleman. "Good news, indeed. Ladies, I won't detain you any longer."

He shook Serena's hand again, then Marianne's.

"Good day, Miss Granville." He half bowed over her hand.

"Good day," Marianne said faintly.

He seemed to become aware that he still held her hand. Looking slightly sheepish, he relinquished it. As a gentleman should, he waited until Serena had pushed open Mrs. Fletcher's door, causing the bell to ring, before resuming his walk.

Serena and Marianne didn't have a chance to talk during their appointment with the dressmaker. Poor Marianne stayed an unfortunate shade of red throughout Mrs. Fletcher's measuring and pinning, and was correspondingly quiet.

When at last they were back in the carriage, Marianne having ordered four dresses, and Serena two plus an alteration to her gray dress, Marianne tipped her head back against the seat. She pulled her fan from her reticule and began fanning herself.

"Your new neighbor seems very charming." Serena uttered the comment she'd been holding in since they arrived.

"He was *wonderful,*" Marianne agreed.

Which was a more effusive word than Serena would have used.

"And quite the most handsome man I've ever seen," Marianne added.

Serena blinked. Gracious! Still, she supposed Marianne could hardly be expected to consider her own brother the handsomest man she'd seen. "He *was* nice looking," she agreed. "He seemed rather taken by your wit, Marianne."

Her friend's color had been fading slowly as they drove; now, it flared again. "Don't be absurd." But Serena heard the longing in her voice.

She thought carefully about Mr. Beaumont's behavior before saying more, since the last thing she wanted was to raise false hopes. "I really do think he liked you," she said. "Not everyone is preoccupied with appearances." Besides, if one ignored her condition, Marianne had a classic beauty few could match.

"*You* are not," Marianne agreed. "But Mr. Beaumont came down from London, and I can tell you from my one season there, everyone in the ton is obsessed with looks." The carriage rounded a bend in the road, causing Marianne to reach for the strap next to her.

"I didn't know you had a London season," Serena said.

Marianne shuddered. "I try not to think about it. I was eighteen, Mama was still alive." Her father had died some ten years ago, Serena knew, and her mother had been carried off four years later. "She insisted I be presented at Court and go through one season. It was mortifying, from start to finish."

"Did anyone offer for you?" Serena asked.

Marianne delivered another surprise. "Two gentlemen. They were both fortune hunters. That's the kind of man who wants to marry a woman like me." She attempted a joke. "I've realized the only knight in shining armor in my life will be the one on my chessboard."

Serena squeezed her hand. "Are you certain the men were fortune hunters?"

"Dominic investigated their circumstances, then chased them off by threatening to withhold my dowry." She tipped her head back against the seat again. "I suppose I'm glad."

"You wouldn't have wanted to marry a fortune hunter, surely?" Serena asked.

"I suppose not…but I would like to have children one day. For that to happen, I would probably have to marry for something other than love."

"You sound as bad as Dominic," Serena said.

"Unlike my brother, I would prefer to marry for love. But I don't meet many men—by choice, I know—and Dominic tends to be overprotective when I do. He forgets I'm twenty-five, no longer an eighteen-year-old romantic."

"If Mr. Beaumont is Sir Charles's heir, he will have a fortune of his own," Serena said. "He's under no obligation to find a wealthy bride."

Marianne looked briefly intrigued. Then she sighed. "The fact is, Serena, he's a man of beautiful manners, and I will be hostess at dinner next week. Naturally he was charming. There's nothing more to it than that."

"You can't be sure. If you were better acquainted with him… I know!" An idea struck Serena. "You could host a house party at Woodbridge Hall. It's usual to invite neighbors in most days to boost the numbers for your activities—I attended several parties in Piper's Mead that way. You'd see Mr. Beaumont nearly every day for at least a week."

"I can't think of anything worse than a house party," Marianne said. "I'm so relieved Dominic has chosen Mrs. Gordon without the need for anything so deplorable." She smiled ruefully. "Serena, trust me when I tell you Mr. Beaumont has no interest in me. I have more experience than you in matters of the heart."

It was on the tip of Serena's tongue to confide her own history to Marianne, so that her friend would understand that she knew a genuine attraction when she saw it. Only the thought that Marianne might mention it to Dominic prevented her.

"I believe one day you will meet a man who loves you

for yourself," she said obstinately. "Just as I hope I will, too. Even if it takes a miracle for both of us."

The dinner guests were invited for six o'clock on Wednesday. This was Leicestershire, not London, so they kept "unfashionable" country hours.

Dominic checked his cuffs—still pristine—then looked at his watch. Ten to six. The drawing room seemed bare without a fire at night, but the evening was warmish and the heat would have played havoc with Marianne's complexion, so he'd instructed Molson not to light one. He strolled to the window to inspect the skies. The moon was at its fullest tonight; there should be no carriage accidents on the way home.

Despite the uncomfortable reality that the dinner party was a bride interview, Dominic was looking forward to the evening. For Marianne's sake, they almost never entertained. And he seldom went to London; since Marianne had no desire to act as his hostess, opening up Granville House for the Season seemed too much effort. These were practical decisions, but they made for a life that was sometimes too quiet.

Perhaps that was why Serena's intrusions into his ordered existence hadn't been altogether annoying. Woodbridge Hall felt more…alive.

That's because of this dinner, not because of Serena. All day, the house had been in a pleasantly purposeful bustle. Trimble, Dominic's valet, had relished the challenge of dressing his master to a higher standard than usual tonight.

At a sound from the doorway, Dominic turned to greet his sister. And Serena.

A fraction of a second was sufficient to register Marianne's overly detailed deep blue dress and her predictably elaborate coiffure, as her maid had standing orders to do anything and everything to draw attention away from Marianne's face. Dominic didn't intend to pass quite so quickly over her to Serena, but somehow...

Governesses—companions—weren't supposed to look like this! Their function was to blend into the scenery as they smoothed the path of the lady of the house. Not to draw the eye of every man in the room, as Serena would do tonight.

Her dress was the palest of pinks, cut lower than a day dress, its scooped neckline showing the creamy skin of her shoulders. Her hair was more complicated than her usual simple knot, with artistically arranged curls spilling over her shoulders.

A constriction in his chest informed Dominic that he'd forgotten to breathe. He rectified that omission with a noisy exhalation that he turned into a throat-clearing. "You look lovely. Both of you."

"I had Grimes do Serena's hair," Marianne said. "It becomes her, doesn't it?"

Before he could comment, Serena said, "It was very kind of you to lend me your maid, Marianne." She gazed with pleasure around the room, at the silver candlesticks on the mantelpiece, the faded Aubusson carpet that was brought out only on special occasions. She was looking forward to tonight, too, Dominic realized. Unlike his sister, who would be dreading it, no matter that she'd pinned on a bright smile.

Serena would be accustomed to society events, he assumed. In any parish, a wellborn rector's family was an asset when it came to making up numbers at parties, with the added benefit to the host of a sense of being on good terms with the church. Indeed, Marianne had invited the rector from Melton Mowbray tonight. Dominic wondered if the gentlefolk of—where was Serena from?—that's right, Piper's Mead received the same bracing dose of truth she had subjected him to. He suspected not. For reasons he couldn't fathom, he hoped not.

"Sir Bertram Shelton and Lady Shelton," Molson announced from the doorway.

Dominic stepped forward to greet the Sheltons, neighbors on his western boundary and a most pleasant couple.

"Granville, good of you to invite us." Shelton's manner was hearty, with no archness in his demeanor, or his wife's, to suggest they'd heard he was in the market for a wife. Dominic had mentioned the matter to Trimble, his valet, as Serena suggested. But obviously Trimble was as discreet as he believed. While it was a relief not to be the subject of gossip, at the same time it raised the question of how he was supposed to convey his *availability* to Mrs. Gordon, and gauge her interest in return. He was dashed if he would flirt with her.

Marianne greeted their guests. She knew the Sheltons well, but that didn't stop her cheeks from firing. At least their color would fade sooner than in the company of strangers.

Molson announced the Reverend Horace Goodham and his wife.

"May I introduce Miss Serena Somerton," Dominic said, after he'd greeted the clergyman. "Her father is Reverend Adrian Somerton, of Piper's Mead in Hampshire." That took care of the need to converse with the rector; he and Serena immediately launched into the kind of talk designed to find the closest link between him and her father.

To keep the numbers even, Marianne had invited Baron Spence, a bachelor of middle age who never entertained at home but liked to be invited out. He arrived soon after the clergyman, and as he made his bow, Marianne fanned herself discreetly. She'd taken a new herbal concoction this morning, but despite making her gag on her breakfast, it didn't seem to have helped.

Then came Mr. Beaumont.

Dominic had met the man just the once, when he'd called at the Ramsay home last week. He was a likable enough chap, with easy address. His clothing was expensively tailored—coat by Weston, boots by Hoby, Dominic guessed, as he watched the man bow to his sister.

Dominic winced when he realized Marianne was the color of a radish.

"A pleasure to see you again, Miss Granville," Beaumont said.

Ah, yes, they'd met in the village, Dominic remembered. Marianne murmured something indistinguishable, but made a visible effort to hold the man's gaze. Dominic felt a rush of affectionate pride for her. She was courage itself. He wished there was something he could do to make her life easier.

There is. Get married.

Beaumont greeted Serena without the stunned admiration that seemed the logical response to her appearance tonight, then turned back to Marianne. Which was only proper, since she was the hostess, and Serena a mere companion. But still…Dominic himself was having trouble tearing his eyes from Serena; it hardly seemed possible that Beaumont hadn't been captivated.

It was another fifteen minutes before Molson announced Mrs. Gordon, just as Dominic could see Marianne starting to fret about the timing of their meal.

When the lady walked in, he knew immediately that Serena had been right about his valet's propensity to gossip.

Dominic might ordinarily have described Mrs. Gordon as a woman of low expectations, but that didn't appear to be the case tonight. She was definitely staging an entrance. Her dress bordered on too much for a country dinner, but showed her trim figure to perfection. Her coiffure was at least as elaborate as Marianne's. Most telling of all was the way she studiedly avoided Dominic's eyes, as she went to greet his sister…in tones that were loud enough to carry to Dominic as she complimented Marianne on her appearance.

Dominic tamped down a surge of annoyance. He was being unfair to the lady. He had set up this occasion with a view to considering her suitability as a wife; he could hardly complain if she sought to present herself in the best light. When one wasn't looking for romantic love, marriage became about practicalities. He should be pleased that Mrs. Gordon was a willing player in this kind of courting game.

When he greeted her, her manner was perfectly comfortable, and Dominic felt himself relax.

Molson summoned them to the dining room almost immediately. Marianne had seated Mrs. Gordon at Dominic's right hand, with Lady Shelton to his left. The other guests could choose their own places. Beaumont sat next to Marianne, while Serena ended up with Reverend Goodham and Baron Spence on either side of her.

Dominic invited the rector to say grace. After that, the serving of the food obviated the need for conversation for several minutes, beyond offers by the gentlemen to serve the lady next to them with buttered crabs or beef tremblant.

Dominic exchanged pleasantries with Mrs. Gordon, who was an attractive woman, no doubt about that, and who knew just what level of depth a dinner table conversation should reach. Talk turned to the wars that had finally ended last year, to the recent insinuations in the *Times* that the British government was trying to hasten Napoleon's death by providing poor living conditions on Saint Helena, the island of his exile. They were such a small group, only ten of them, most of whom knew each other well, that conversations could be conducted with more than just one's neighbor.

"I fear you will think me unchristian," Mrs. Gordon said, after Baron Spence expressed a concern that it simply wasn't British to treat even a deposed enemy emperor harshly. "But my fervent hope is for that man to die of some plaguey condition. He robbed me of a husband, robbed countless English families of sons, brothers, nephews."

It *was* an unchristian sentiment, Dominic supposed, but he couldn't condemn a widow for her resentment of the man whose lust for power had been responsible for her husband's death.

Reverend Goodham quoted some verse about vengeance belonging to the Lord. Dominic expected to see Serena nodding wholehearted agreement, given her expressed belief in compassion. He'd been avoiding looking at her, but now he did so…and found her lips clamped together in a way that suggested she was biting back an opinion at odds with that of the reverend.

Intrigued—shouldn't a parson's daughter agree with a clergyman?—Dominic asked, "What do you think, Miss Somerton? What's your preferred fate for Bonaparte?"

After all, she was apparently encouraged by her parents to express her opinions at the table. Though he'd noted tonight that she didn't put herself forward in company—she reserved that dubious behavior for him.

Some of his other guests seemed surprised that he should consult a young woman rather than the wiser matrons.

She hesitated. "I have no wish to see anyone suffer," she said. "But I confess, news of the death of that particular warmonger would be a relief."

Reverend Goodham looked disapproving, but Mrs. Gordon said warmly, "You are a lady of sense, Miss Somerton."

Why did Serena feel so strongly about Bonaparte? She'd mentioned four sisters…had she had a brother who'd died in the wars? Dominic could tell she'd had to quell the urge to speak more strongly. The fire in her eyes accentuated her prettiness; Baron Spence looked at her with fresh interest.

Marianne, who found that listening to arguments exacerbated her condition, changed the subject. "Mrs. Gordon,

I hope your family wasn't affected by the recent influenza outbreak."

"Thank you, Miss Granville, but no." Mrs. Gordon served herself a ladylike portion of damson jelly. "My children have inherited my own strong constitution."

A strong constitution was an excellent qualification for a bride, Dominic decided. If Emily hadn't been prone to infections all her life, would she have been able to resist the measles? He would not want to lose a second wife, even one of convenience....

"And you, Miss Granville?" Mrs. Gordon asked. "Are your nephews and nieces well?"

"The children are thriving." Marianne blushed deeply, as she always did when asked a question. "Are they not, Dominic?" He wasn't sure if she was deflecting attention, or trying to provide an opening for him to impress Mrs. Gordon.

"They are," he said, somewhat lamely. Doubtless he was meant to present his children in the most positive light at this stage of a courtship. Rather than mentioning Thomas's predilection for bringing wildlife into the house, Charlotte's sulks and thieving, William's fear of the dark and Louisa's repeated ear infections.

Put like that, he was amazed Marianne had managed to recruit a governess at all.

"The children are all very intelligent," Serena interjected. "Even little Louisa possesses such an inquiring mind."

"Thank you, Miss Somerton," Dominic said quellingly. She didn't need to blow the trumpet for his children. Just because he hadn't quite got around to it yet didn't mean he wasn't going to. It was simply…he had a lot on his mind, and right now couldn't think of specific attributes to which he could refer.

"Inquiry is not always necessary in a little girl, of course," Mrs. Gordon said.

Dominic saw indignation kindle in Serena's eyes. Her views regarding his children were strong, and it seemed she would defend them whenever and wherever she deemed necessary.

In the interest of his future domestic harmony with Mrs. Gordon, Dominic intervened. "Louisa is an enthusiastic artist. She particularly enjoys painting."

He was rather pleased with the way he'd phrased that. He hadn't had to lie and say his daughter was actually *good* at painting.

Serena spotted the distinction—she squinted at him. Dominic found himself smiling.

Mrs. Gordon nodded her approval of that more feminine pursuit. "My Elizabeth is a most talented artist. I'm sure she'd be delighted to show Louisa her work." She seemed to realize she had perhaps anticipated too much, for she added, "Should they ever meet."

"How old are your children, Mrs. Gordon?" Serena asked.

Dominic remembered her concern about the woman favoring her own offspring over his.

"Elizabeth is ten and James is eight," the widow said. "They've been such a comfort to me since Colonel Gordon died. So sunny-natured...I do like a sunny-natured child, don't you?"

Who knew what she would make of Charlotte, then. Dominic suspected the overloud scrape of Serena's knife against her plate was an attempt to catch his eye in order to communicate that very thought.

He smiled encouragement at Mrs. Gordon. "A sunny nature is very attractive," he agreed.

His erstwhile governess, one of the sunniest people he'd met, looked thunderous.

"And my James is fearless," Mrs. Gordon continued. "Quite fearless."

Dominic was beginning to wish she would quiet down on the subject of her incomparable offspring…but then, it was right for a mama to be proud of her children, wasn't it?

"How admirable," Serena said, to his surprise. He'd expected her to counter with Thomas's intrepidness with animals. "So often children that age have unexplained fears. Of the dark, for example."

Ah. He should have guessed.

"If courage isn't naturally present, one must *teach* it, Miss Somerton." Mrs. Gordon's tone held a touch of condescension. Dominic winced. It wouldn't be the first time Serena had encountered that attitude, whether as a parson's daughter, a governess or a companion, but he'd rather his future wife hadn't been the one to deliver it.

"We must face our fears in order to vanquish them," Mrs. Gordon pronounced.

Perfect love casteth out fear. The Bible verse flitted through Dominic's head.

"That sounds easier than perhaps it is," Serena said. Dominic wondered if anyone else noticed her emphasis on *sounds*. As if reality might differ. Her attention was fixed on Mrs. Gordon with an intensity that reminded him of a painting he'd seen of a lioness with its cubs.

"It works," Mrs. Gordon insisted. "I myself was frightened of horses as a child. My father had the servants put me on a horse every day, until I stopped screaming."

Marianne gasped, Lady Shelton tutted. Dominic winced. Only Serena appeared unmoved at the plight of a young Mrs. Gordon—or whatever her name had been—terrified on the back of a pony.

"It didn't do me any harm," Mrs. Gordon assured them. "Indeed, Colonel Gordon used to say I grew up into a very good whip."

"Most interesting," Serena said, all thoughtful innocence.

Dominic groaned inwardly.

"Do you think," she asked, "that kind of experience could be used to cure a fear of the dark?"

"I'm sure of it," the other woman said. "Any fearful child would benefit from a minute or two each day confined in a dark space…a cupboard of some sort…supervised from the outside, of course."

"Of course." Serena beamed.

Dominic sighed.

So much for Mrs. Gordon as the future stepmother of his children.

Serena sat back in her chair and willed herself to be satisfied with this moment of triumph. Dragging Mrs. Gordon to the nearest cupboard, then locking her in and throwing away the key might be a tempting prospect, but it would hardly be good manners. Plus, she wouldn't have the strength—Mrs. Gordon was a good three inches taller—and Serena doubted an attempt to enlist Dominic's help would succeed.

"Is one of your children prey to such a fear, Mr. Granville?" Mrs. Gordon asked.

"Not as much as *I* am prey to a fear of harsh cures," Dominic said.

The chill in his voice made Serena rethink her decision. Maybe he *would* help her drag Mrs. Gordon to that cupboard. She hadn't seen him like this before: his voice cold, his eyes warm. Hot, even, with anger. And, she chose to believe, with love for his children.

How silly that a man so capable of love should plan to marry without it. Yes, Serena was anxious for him to marry, and if it had to be for convenience, then so be it. But if he was capable of tender feelings, why rush into union with a woman who didn't engage those feelings?

Serena paused, struggling to reconcile Dominic Granville

and "tender feelings" in her mind. If he met the right woman, surely those sentiments would burst into life.

Everyone deserved to love and be loved. Including Marianne who, though her behavior was perfectly decorous, was clearly infatuated with Mr. Beaumont. If their neighbor got to know her better, could he come to love her? They would probably never find out, since Marianne's seclusion made it unlikely she would see much of him. Unless…

Serena pulled her thoughts up short, as she realized an awkward silence had developed in the wake of Mrs. Gordon's comment and Dominic's unmistakable rebuke. She made an instant decision to restore social harmony and at the same time lend Marianne a helping hand.

"Miss Granville and I have had the most wonderful idea," she announced.

Everyone—except Marianne, who looked baffled, but trusting—clamored to hear it. Anything to break the silence.

Serena knew a moment's misgiving. This was certainly one of her bolder schemes. But tonight had proved that the Granvilles—both Marianne and Dominic, were in desperate need of assistance.

"We were talking about the possibility of a house party here at Woodbridge Hall," she said. She neglected to mention that Marianne hadn't liked the idea at all. "If it's sufficiently informal, it could take place early next month."

"A house party," Lady Shelton echoed. "What a lovely idea."

As others around the table voiced their approval, Marianne's mouth opened and closed; she was too horrified to utter a word.

Serena caught her eye and tipped a discreet but meaningful glance toward Mr. Beaumont, who had paid attention to no one but Marianne tonight. She couldn't possibly doubt his interest now.

Marianne's eyes widened. Serena could almost see her thought processes, torn as she was between her abhorrence of large gatherings and this perfect excuse to see Mr. Beaumont day after day.

Dominic cleared this throat, the intention to deny all possibility of a house party etched on every feature.

Then Marianne stuttered, "Y-yes, indeed. I should enjoy a house party above all things. May we do it, Dominic?" She looked appalled and delighted at her own nerve.

"It sounds very jolly," Mr. Beaumont chimed in, his eyes on Marianne.

Dominic stared at his sister. "Marianne, are you well?"

"I'm fine." To their guests, she said, "When we have the party, you must all join us for the activities and excursions."

"Delighted," Mr. Beaumont murmured.

"We expect to have my niece staying with us next month," Lady Shelton said quickly. "I know she'll enjoy any excursions."

Her husband's exclamation of surprise collapsed into a muffled grunt. Serena suspected his wife had trodden on his toes to keep him quiet. From Dominic's grim expression, it was clear he'd realized the niece's visit was a hastily concocted plan to enter the girl in his hunt for a bride. His valet had clearly spread the news of his intentions far and wide.

"May we, Dominic?" Marianne asked again.

With nine pairs of eyes on him, he had no other option. "Certainly," he said, his voice tight.

Serena pressed her lips together to avoid any hint of a smirk. He hadn't wanted a parade of women through his house, but he would get one. Dominic would have every chance not just to choose a new wife, but to fall in love again.

Chapter Six

Two days later, Serena stood behind Marianne at the writing desk in the blue salon, reading the list of house party guests penned in Marianne's elegant hand. Dominic would likely join them soon. Right now, he was doing whatever it was men did after dinner, while the ladies withdrew.

"It's amazing how many locals, like Lady Shelton, happen to have unmarried relatives coming to stay at the very time of our house party." Marianne smiled wryly. "Serena, you have no idea how thrilled I am that Dominic plans to wed. The thought of having to accompany the girls into society as they grow older..." Her face turned scarlet at the mere idea.

Serena squeezed her shoulder. "It's just a shame you have to endure a house party in order for Dominic to find a bride. Which is all my fault, and I appreciate that you haven't complained."

"You know very well why I haven't," Marianne said.

"The delightful Mr. Beaumont." Serena had hoped he would call after Wednesday's dinner, but he hadn't. He was doubtless busy getting to know the estate that would one day be his.

"I don't suppose I have a chance with him." Marianne twisted to face Serena. "This house party is a wonderful idea for increasing our acquaintance, but knowing me, I shall spend the entire two weeks looking like a—what's the name of that fruit that Cook insists only foreigners should eat?"

"The tomato. Though in your case, maybe we should give it its English name—the love apple."

Marianne rolled her eyes. "Yes, one of those. I've never heard of a man marrying a tomato, have you?" She didn't wait for a reply. "But, do you know, Serena, I really want to try. If there's any hope at all, I could never forgive myself for squandering it."

"Exactly," Serena said.

"And even if nothing comes of this house party for me—" Marianne set the pen back in the inkwell "—there's a strong chance Dominic will meet a nice woman. If he marries, I can abandon my lady-of-the-manor duties and become a nun." She sounded as if she was only half joking.

"Marianne, you know you enjoy your food too much for a nunnery's plain fare."

"Very true." She sighed. "Besides, my blushes make me look so *guilty,* they'd never admit me."

Serena laughed. When Marianne joked like this, when she wasn't fussing about her herbal remedies or her damp cloths, she was so attractive, it was hard to believe she couldn't catch Mr. Beaumont, or indeed any other man. A gentleman just needed to spend enough time with her to get to know her. The house party would be perfect.

"Tell me about the ladies on your list," she said. "Are there any your brother might fall in love with?"

Marianne turned back to her paper. "He didn't mention love. He said to invite women I thought might be good for the children."

An improvement, at least, on "women who live within five miles of Woodbridge Hall." Serena considered Dominic's progress a personal victory.

"Don't you agree it'd be nice for him to fall in love?" she said. If he opened his heart to a woman, it would be so much easier to open it to his children.

"I don't think he could," his sister said. "Not after Emily."

"Was Emily very wonderful?"

Marianne leaned back in her chair. "She was…perfect for Dominic, I suppose. Calm and well-ordered, with never a hair out of place, always thoughtful of others. She was a most loving mother."

"She sounds like a saint." Serena was conscious of a metallic taste in her mouth.

"Emily had her flaws," Marianne assured her. "She could be indecisive at times. But Dominic's so decisive, that scarcely mattered."

If indecisiveness was her worst fault, then Emily Granville sounded depressingly perfect. She and Dominic couldn't have disagreed much.

Peace in the home was a good thing, of course. Even if it meant sacrificing robust discussion.

"Is there anyone on your list who's like Emily?" Serena asked.

Marianne read the list aloud. "Lady Mary Carruthers, Sarah Seton, Annabelle Peckham, Penelope Carr. And their parents, of course." A single lady of marriageable age couldn't attend a house party without a chaperone. "Mrs. Anne Evans—another widow." She grimaced at the memory of Mrs. Gordon.

"What qualities would you say Dominic might fall in love with?" Serena asked casually. "I mean, we should be sure to point those things out to him when these women arrive."

"Oh…the usual, I suppose," Marianne said.

"Marianne, you must be able to do better than that!"

"One doesn't think about one's brother in that way," she

said sheepishly. "Oh, I know, a gentle voice. That was one of the things he loved about Emily."

Serena sighed and moved to examine the tapestry hanging on the wall between the two windows. It depicted Jesus healing a leper; some earlier Granville had reportedly acquired it during his travels in France.

"You know, Marianne, five children might seem rather a lot to a lady who has none. We need to show the children to advantage during the house party."

"They'll be confined to the nursery," Marianne pointed out.

"Surely Dominic intends for them to at least meet his prospective wife. When they do, it would be too awful if Thomas chose that moment to release a lizard."

"I can just see it," Marianne agreed, laughing.

The more she thought about it, the more it occurred to Serena that something might go wrong. "Any encounter between the children and the guests will need to be well managed," she reflected. Which went against her view that Dominic's wife should love his children just as they were. But first impressions did count for a lot. "Maybe we should stage a musical performance."

"Are the children very musical?" Marianne asked.

Serena wandered away from Jesus and the leper, and over to the window. Woodbridge land stretched as far as her eye could see. "I admit I've neglected that aspect of their education, since the older ones have a music tutor and my own skills on the pianoforte are mediocre," she said. "But all children are adorable when they sing. They barely have to hold a tune."

"And my nephews and nieces are especially adorable," Marianne said.

"So true." Serena grinned. "I'll start training them in a small performance."

"You'd make a wonderful mother yourself, Serena." Marianne sanded her page to dry the ink. "I plan to invite two or three bachelor friends of Dom's to the house party, so that it's not quite so blatant a marriage mart. Perhaps one of them will fall in love with you."

Serena fiddled with the tieback of a bronze damask curtain. "I'll be very much in the background, with so many eligible ladies present."

"You have a case of the fidgets tonight, my dear," Marianne observed. "Ah, Dominic, you're just in time to approve my guest list."

Serena turned quickly, to see him standing in the doorway. He was watching her.

Or maybe looking past her, out the window.

Marianne pushed her chair back. "I'll ring for tea."

"I'll do it." Serena crossed to the fireplace and pulled the bell rope.

"Dom, take a look." His sister held out her sheet of paper.

He muttered something under his breath, but took the list and scanned it. "I don't know most of these women."

"They're all delightful," she assured him.

Dominic stared down at the page for a long time. "Are you certain we need to do this?"

"Think of the children," Serena said, chivying him. "If it will help persuade you, William had another incident last night."

Dominic tsked. "I remember noticing there was no moon at all."

"His sheets were soaked with sweat—and before you ask, my room is nearest his and I run much faster than Nurse." Serena wrapped her arms around her middle at the memory of William's distress. "He let me comfort him, but I feel so sorry for him. Every time the moon is obscured with cloud…"

Marianne sighed. "It's too dangerous to leave a candle burning. Maybe Serena's right, that if you marry…"

"There's no guarantee a stepmother will cure his phobia," Dominic said.

"The problem started after his mother died," Serena said. "I believe that if he has a permanent mother figure, his subconscious worries might subside."

"So I'm supposed to marry one of these women—" he dropped the paper on the desk "—on the basis of your *intuition*."

"Inviting a few ladies to attend a house party with the thought there may be a match isn't the same as walking down the aisle." What Serena really wanted to say was *Stop feeling sorry for yourself, and start thinking about your children.* "You can step down off the gallows any time before you put your head in the noose."

He laughed reluctantly, and his whole face lightened, making him devastatingly attractive. "What a delightful analogy."

"It's one of my father's favorites," she said. At Dominic's raised eyebrow, she said, "Admittedly, Papa uses it about sin, rather than marriage."

"Interesting," Dominic observed. "So Reverend Somerton advocates waiting until the last second to resist temptation?"

She rolled her eyes. "Papa says we might feel we've as good as sinned merely by deciding to do so, but we still have a choice. We can pull back from it at any time."

"Are you saying I can pull back from this madcap idea right up until my wedding day?"

"Certainly not," she said. "Obviously a gentleman can never jilt a lady. But just because you have several prospective brides visiting, you're not obligated to propose marriage to one of them."

"A great relief," he said dryly. He glanced at the list again. "Marianne, did you consider… What about Hester Lacey?"

"Hester!" Marianne said. "Of course. Is she still unwed? She must close to thirty by now."

"We exchanged letters last Christmas and she didn't mention she'd married."

"I daresay she'd welcome the chance to change her old maid status," Marianne said. "And she's so nice."

"She has the same name as Hetty," Serena observed. *Whoever she is*.

"Hetty was named for Hester Lacey," Marianne explained. "She was Emily's best friend."

A little shock ran through Serena, one she couldn't explain. "I didn't know."

"How could you?" Dominic asked, frowning.

"So…Miss Lacey knows the children?" Was she as perfect as Emily?

"Of course," Dominic said. "I haven't seen her since she and her mother stayed a night on their way to Yorkshire, maybe two years after Emily died."

"Hester Lacey," Marianne said slowly. "I can't believe I didn't think of her. I'm certain you'll approve, Serena." She picked up her pen again and added Miss Lacey to the list.

Dominic's snort said Serena's approval was irrelevant.

"Wonderful," Serena said brightly.

The next morning, Serena and Marianne walked the bridle path along Woodbridge's eastern boundary. Serena dangling her bonnet from her fingers by its ribbons. The spring sunshine was so tempting, it was worth the prospect of attracting a dreaded freckle to feel the sun's warmth on her face. The risk of freckling was low, she hoped, given the rays were mostly filtered through the trees.

"I'm certain I saw some lemon balm along here." Marianne carried a basket for gathering wild herbs for the concoctions with which she treated her complexion. "In the glade next to the pond."

"Will you apply it to your face?" Serena asked.

"Apparently one makes a tea. Which can be served cold." Marianne avoided hot drinks outside of the compulsory evening teatime. "I don't suppose it'll work, though." She made a sound of impatience. "I'm sorry to seem so gloomy. But, Serena, I've had enough. I have done everything that's possible and reasonable, and plenty that's unreasonable. I have prayed the prayer of Saint Paul, 'Lord, take this thorn in my flesh away from me,' every day since I was nine years old. But nothing changes."

"He hears you," Serena said.

"But why doesn't He act? He can't *want* one of His children to be so hideous, can He?"

"My dear, you know perfectly well you're not hideous. You do a disservice to those with serious disfigurements."

Marianne kicked a pinecone from the path, and didn't respond. At last she said, "You're always so *right*."

Serena laughed. "What a thing to say! I detest people who are always right. With the exception of my papa, of course."

Marianne's mouth tugged into a smile. "I apologize. I should have— Oh, my."

A horse and rider had rounded the bend in front of them. The black horse was magnificent. So was the rider—at least, Serena guessed, in Marianne's opinion.

Mr. Beaumont lifted his hat. "Good morning, ladies."

A sidelong glance at Marianne revealed a flush so deep as to be almost purple. Serena returned his greeting. "Are you visiting Woodbridge, Mr. Beaumont?" she asked. "I'm afraid it'll be some minutes before we reach the house, and Mr. Granville is out with his steward."

Beaumont smiled. He certainly was a nice-looking man.

And yet Serena's pulse failed to quicken the way it did when Dominic did something as unremarkable as raise an eyebrow.

"This path traverses the boundary between Woodbridge and Farley Hall," he said. "I believe at this point I'm on Farley land." He dismounted from his horse.

"You are indeed." Marianne found her voice at last. "We are the intruders. I'm sorry."

His answering smile held a gentleness that made Serena catch her breath. If this wasn't genuine regard for Marianne, she would eat her bonnet!

"Are you helping me by clearing my land of weeds?" He indicated her basket. "That's above and beyond the call of neighborly duty, Miss Granville."

"I—I gather herbs in these woods," Marianne stammered. "I hope I haven't inconvenienced you."

"Of course not," he assured her. He investigated her basket more closely. "Is that ragwort?"

"Yes, do you know it?"

"My nurse used to make a poultice of it when I had a bee sting. Here, let me hold that for you while we talk." He took the basket from her, a chivalrous gesture that left Marianne more flustered than ever. "What do you use it for?"

Marianne hesitated. "According to Nurse, it's very good for inflammation."

A neat evasion, Serena thought.

Mr. Beaumont eyed Marianne consideringly, but didn't comment.

"We're also looking for lemon balm," Marianne said in a rush. "You wouldn't know…?"

He shook his head. "I'm afraid you've gone beyond my knowledge of herbs in a few short seconds." With his free hand, he steadied his horse, which was beginning to show signs of impatience. "My uncle knows a great deal more— he fancied himself something of an apothecary in his days at Oxford, and has quite a collection of volumes dedicated to herbal remedies."

"How fascinating," Marianne said.

For a moment, Mr. Beaumont's mouth twisted, as if he heard such words too often from simpering misses. But Marianne couldn't be further from a simpering miss, and the basket he carried was testimony to her genuine interest. Mr. Beaumont's mouth softened. "I fear the books are sadly out of date, but perhaps you'll have occasion to visit my uncle, and see for yourself."

"Sir Charles isn't known for entertaining," she murmured.

Mr. Beaumont chuckled. "Believe me, I've noticed! The evenings are dashed quiet in this part of the world." He spoke a calming word to the horse, which settled. "Do you go up to London often, Miss Granville?"

Poor Marianne turned puce with horror at the thought. "I do not," she said. "I find it doesn't suit my—my constitution."

A flicker of Mr. Beaumont's eyes said he understood. "May I walk with you on your quest?"

But a search of the glade next to the pond failed to turn up any lemon balm. "Thank you for your company," Marianne said to him when they'd abandoned the hunt. "We must be getting home now."

"If you've no objection, I'll walk with you, at least as far as the Woodbridge lawns," he said. "I saw signs of a poacher earlier this week, and I worry for your safety."

Serena and Marianne walked in these woods often, and had seen no such signs. Serena wondered if Beaumont was conjuring an excuse to spend time with Marianne. A strategy she heartily applauded, since she was here to chaperone.

Marianne accepted his offer with fetching demureness and only minimal additional staining of her cheeks.

Mr. Beaumont was courteous enough to ensure Serena wasn't left out of the conversation, but she chose not to speak unless directly addressed. *Dominic would be amazed at my tact.*

A discussion of the pastimes that might liven a country existence revealed that Mr. Beaumont enjoyed the game of chess as much as Marianne did.

"I almost never play with Dominic," she confided to him, her manner more relaxed than Serena had seen her with anyone outside of Woodbridge Hall. "He's too easy to beat—he looks for the most direct route to victory and assumes he'll be able to storm through." Marianne shook her head.

"No sense of strategy, of the long game," Mr. Beaumont suggested.

"That's it exactly. Of course, that means I end up playing myself, mostly." She would play both sides, black and white, Serena knew, in games that could last days, if not weeks.

"I like a long game, too," Mr. Beaumont said, as they approached the east lawn. "Tell me your preferred opening move."

"If I was playing against you…" Marianne wrinkled her brow, presumably consulting the chessboard in her head. "Pawn to D4."

Mr. Beaumont narrowed his eyes, envisaging. "Hmm. A rather conventional start."

"What would your move be in response?"

"Pawn to D5, of course—I'm as conventional as you at this point. But now, I must leave you. My uncle's physician said he wished for a word with me this morning." He bowed, then mounted his horse. "Remember, Miss Granville, the next move is yours."

That afternoon, Serena gathered the children in the drawing room. The space was generally used only in the evenings, unless the Granvilles were entertaining, so she and the children had it to themselves.

"We need to start planning for when your papa's guests are here," she told them. "Some will want to meet you—" namely, any lady angling for the role of Mrs. Granville "—and when they do, you'll need to behave as wonderfully as always…and maybe a tiny bit better. Thomas, Captain Emerald will be confined to quarters for the duration of the house party."

"Yes, Miss Somerton," he said.

"I know you all have enough common sense to conduct yourselves in the proper fashion, but just to remind you, we should probably not shriek as we play." Serena hugged Louisa, the most talented shrieker in the family, to her. "That goes for me, as well as you."

Louisa giggled.

"Lastly," Serena said, "your father is likely to want to show you off to his friends. I've decided we'll prepare a musical item for their entertainment. We'll sing the song 'Scarborough Fair.'"

She'd chosen the tune for its simple melody. The children knew it already, and she'd found the sheet music in the folio kept near the pianoforte.

"We'll need all of you singing, apart from Thomas, who will be playing his flute," Serena said. "Hetty, you'll play the pianoforte, and, Charlotte, we'll have you on the harp." The three older children took lessons once a week with a tutor from the village. "William and Louisa, you needn't do anything other than sing."

The advantage of employing the two youngest as vocalists was that any missed notes would be overlooked by an indulgent audience. The way Serena saw it, not only would the hearts of the female guests melt, but their sighing approval would soften Dominic's heart, too.

It was an excellent strategy, if she said so herself. Combined with her other strategy of pointing out to Dominic the ladies' most lovable qualities, she had every hope of breaking through that armor of his.

"I'll play the tune the first time, and you can all sing the words with me." She skimmed the sheet music before she started. She was an adequate pianoforte player, but by no means a brilliant sight reader; Charity was the musically talented Somerton sister.

Satisfied there was nothing too taxing in the music, Serena began to play. She sang, too, to encourage the children. "'Are you going to Scarborough Fair…'"

The children joined in. Unfortunately, the younger ones lagged a beat or two behind her and the older ones. Thomas's singing bordered on a monotone; it was just as well he'd be playing the flute.

After one verse, Serena stopped. "That was a good beginning, my dears, but perhaps you're not as familiar with the song as I assumed."

"We know it," Hetty assured her. "Mama used to sing it."

Serena bit her lip. "Maybe we should choose another one." She didn't want to upset the children with a painful reminder of their mother. Nor Dominic.

"Please, Miss Somerton," Charlotte said suddenly. "I like this song. Please may we sing it?"

The others backed her up, and it was so unlike Charlotte to be in agreement with her siblings that Serena acquiesced. "But let's try to sing a little more in tune. Hetty, you take over on the pianoforte, so I can concentrate on listening."

The children sang the first verse again, on their own. Louisa still lagged behind, listening for the words from her siblings. William was all over the place. Hetty was shrill, Thomas hesitant and wheezy on the flute. If Mrs. Emily Granville had possessed a musical ear, her offspring hadn't inherited it. Only Charlotte could sing, but her volume was low. Her harp playing was very good, but again, quiet. She resisted Serena's urging to play louder.

"Perhaps, Hetty, you could play the piano a little louder, then," Serena said.

"But then they won't hear us sing," the girl objected.

"They'll hear enough," she assured her. "I think, my dears, we'd better practice every day." Her vision of an audience enraptured by her melodic young charges had dimmed somewhat.

"Excuse me, Miss Somerton," Charlotte said, with unusual timidity.

"Yes, my dear?"

"Is it true that Papa is getting married? And that our new mama will attend the house party?"

Hetty said authoritatively, "Of course it's not true—Papa would tell us if we were to have a new mother. Wouldn't he, Miss Somerton?"

"He wouldn't," Thomas said. "He didn't even tell us when Mama died. Nurse told us."

Really? Serena wanted to grab Dominic by those broad shoulders and shake him. That was too bad of him. And foolish of him not to have mentioned to the children that he was thinking of marrying. Although many fathers likely wouldn't share that intention with their children, she couldn't see the point of allowing such momentous news to come as a shock. Especially when "enhanced" by the gossip of servants.

"He would so tell us that," loyal little William chipped in.

Only Louisa seemed to have no opinion. She wrapped her left arm around Serena's knee and sucked her right thumb, a habit Serena was trying to break.

"Charlotte, who told you your papa might marry?" Serena asked.

"Mr. Trimble was talking about it to Miss Grimes," the girl said. "I heard them in the servants' dining room." She preempted Serena's next question, about why she was anywhere near the servants' dining room, by saying, "I was in the kitchen, helping Cook make a cake."

Dominic would be sadly disillusioned to know how much his valet liked to blab. Serena put an arm around Charlotte. "I don't know if your father will marry again." The intention and the doing were two very different things, after all. "But it's common practice for a widowed man to do so. Adults can be lonely if they don't have a husband or wife."

Louisa looked stricken at the thought of her dear father pining away. Which wasn't truly accurate.

"I'd *like* a new mother," William said, somewhat defiantly.

"I shouldn't like one at all," Hetty said. "Well, maybe if she's very kind, like Mama." Serena suspected the girl was torn between loyalty to her mother and her desire to have a maternal presence.

"I don't need a mother," Thomas said. "I'm going to Eton in September."

"Miss Somerton?" Louisa tugged at her skirt. "Why don't *you* marry Papa?"

Serena felt her cheeks heat in a blush worthy of Marianne. "Louisa, dear, that's not possible."

"That'd be lovely," Hetty said. "Wouldn't it, Thomas?"

"If Papa must marry someone, Miss Somerton would do," he admitted.

Serena couldn't help chuckling. "Such high praise. Thank you."

"You should tell Papa to marry you," Hetty said. "Or we can tell him, can't we, Thomas?"

Serena's chuckle turned to a choke, as she imagined Dominic's reaction to that advice. "You mustn't," she ordered. Best to make that unambiguously clear. "It would be quite improper for your papa to marry a governess."

"But you're not our governess anymore. And Aunt Marianne has a novel called *The Prince and the Governess,*" Hetty said knowledgeably.

That didn't sound like Marianne's usual edifying reading, Serena thought, intrigued. It sounded more like that of her own sister Amanda, who devoured romance novels. "You must understand, children, it wouldn't be right for me to marry your father. Not least because I don't love him."

"Not least because he hasn't asked you," Dominic said from the doorway. "Despite your assumption to the contrary."

She spun around, her hand pressed to her chest. "I'm not the only one to have made such an assumption." She was trying to get past that urge to argue with him, but sometimes a woman needed to stand up for herself. If she wasn't to look like a complete idiot.

He advanced into the room. "Is there a reason you're discussing my matrimonial prospects with my children, Miss Somerton?"

"The children overheard the servants—including your valet," she couldn't resist saying, "discussing the subject, and brought it up with me."

"I see." He frowned toward the children, who'd sat down in a circle to play a game that involved passing whispers between them, but it was more distracted than disapproving. "Don't you have better things to do than indulge in such fruitless speculation?" he asked Serena. "Such as spend time with Marianne?"

"Your sister wanted to write some letters in her room," Serena said. "She was tired after our long walk with Mr. Beaumont this morning."

"Beaumont?" Dominic glanced toward the window. "Why was he here?"

She realized she didn't know where Mr. Beaumont had been going. "I assume he was exercising his horse. He walked the bridle path with us for a while."

Dominic wedged his hands in the pockets of his pantaloons. "Hmm."

"I assure you it was all aboveboard." Serena checked that the children were still engrossed in their game. "He acted the gentleman with Marianne the entire time."

"With Marianne?" he said sharply.

Too late, it occurred to Serena that Dominic hadn't noticed the mutual interest between Marianne and Beaumont. Not that he could possibly object, but it would have been better for him to hear it from his sister. "We were talking," she clarified. "All three of us."

"About what?" he demanded.

"Er…herbs. And chess."

"You're a keen chess player are you, Miss Somerton?"

"I've never played," she admitted.

"Which rather suggests you didn't participate in that conversation."

"It was entirely innocent," she said. "I don't understand your— Oh!"

The butler had somehow materialized right next to her.

"Molson, where on earth did you come from?" she asked. "Is there a secret passage into this room?"

He allowed himself a half smile. "I came from the hallway, miss. Mr. Granville, sir, you asked me to remind you to pen a letter to your lawyer before the post is collected."

Dominic checked his watch. "Thank you, I will. And now there's another letter I must write."

The butler glided from the room.

"How does he do that?" Serena watched him leave. "Just *appear?*"

"Dashed if I know. I fully expect to collapse in a fit of fright one day." Dominic rubbed his chin. "Serena, I didn't intend to interrogate you about Mr. Beaumont. Marianne will tell you I'm overprotective."

"She has mentioned it once or twice." Serena gave him a tentative smile, and was relieved when he responded in kind. "I'm aware your sister is my first responsibility," she promised. "As soon as I'm finished here with the children, I'll go up to see her."

"Are you afraid I'm an ogre who'll have you flogged if you're not working every minute of the day, Miss Somerton?"

Aware of the children's sudden attention, caught by the wood *flogged,* and their uncertainty as to whether their father was being serious, she said, "Only since I saw you munching on that small child yesterday."

William giggled at the thought of his father as an ogre in one of his favorite fairy tales.

"Papa, we think you should marry Miss Somerton," Hetty said. "She's pretty, she's kind and Aunt Marianne likes her...."

"And she knows about lizards." Thomas inadvertently confirmed what his father had warned would be his assessment criteria.

"I've told them the notion of you marrying me is absurd," Serena assured Dominic. "I believe it's quite common for children to suggest such a thing with regard to their governess. You shouldn't take it seriously."

"I have no intention of taking it seriously," he said. Of course he didn't.

"Papa, *are* you going to marry a new lady?" Charlotte demanded.

"Possibly," he said. "But rest assured, I will certainly not marry Miss Somerton."

So adamant was his tone, he might as well have added, *not if she were the last woman on earth.*

Chapter Seven

Dominic's home had metamorphosed from a gracious English country estate to some kind of Oriental bazaar, where merchants—matchmaking mamas and proud papas—did their utmost to convince Dominic that their product—a dutiful daughter—was superior to all others.

Unfortunately, the "product" he'd been most interested in, Miss Hester Lacey, wouldn't be attending, thanks to a bout of influenza. Which left him a mere five women of looks, breeding and intelligence to choose from.

When Dominic led the gentlemen into the drawing room after their postdinner drinks on the first evening, the room teemed with women clad in every imaginable hue. The mamas whispered instructions to their daughters to be charming, judging by the number of feminine shoulders that straightened and mouths that curved in demure but welcoming smiles.

This was the first night of the house party, so he'd barely done more than greet most of them. Dinner had been formal, with conversation confined to those on his immediate right and left.

"Ah, there's Sarah," said Phillip Seton, father of Miss Sarah Seton. "Shall we go and talk to her, Granville?"

Dominic allowed the man to lead him toward his daughter. Seton had had the grace to be subtle as they lolled around the dinner table, far more relaxed without the ladies. The mention of his daughter's substantial dowry had been couched in the context of some other matter. But Dominic had got the message.

Sarah Seton was engaged in conversation with Serena, which was useful, since Dominic needed to talk to his sister's companion. He hadn't seen much of her the past few days—she'd been busy with house party preparations—but she needed to know about the letter he'd received yesterday. She looked delightful tonight, in that same pink dress he'd admired a few weeks ago, but she also, when her eyes met his, seemed decidedly cool. He wondered why.

The ladies were talking about painting.

"Miss Seton is an accomplished artist," Serena informed him, with an enthusiasm at odds with her coolness. "She specializes in watercolors of the landmarks around her home in Gloucestershire." Serena tilted her head expectantly.

"Excellent," Dominic said. "Er, what do you find the most difficult aspect of painting, Miss Seton?"

The young lady began to talk of light and shadow and other artistic challenges.

When she wound down, Serena said, "Could you excuse us, Miss Seton? I particularly wish Mr. Granville to speak with Miss Peckham."

He had no great desire to talk to the woman himself, but he went with Serena.

"Miss Peckham works with some of the poor in London's East End, under the auspices of her church," Serena said, as she introduced them.

"Admirable," Dominic said. "Your efforts must be very rewarding, Miss Peckham."

"I don't do it for me, Mr. Granville, I do it for them," she said earnestly.

Ten minutes later, even the tiny desire he'd had to hear about her charitable impulses had evaporated. Miss Peckham's do-good spiel droned on, without discernible pauses for breath. When Serena claimed an urgent need to talk to Lady Mary Carruthers, and they escaped, he could have kissed her. On the hand, of course.

"Save me from do-gooders," Dominic muttered as they crossed the room. "Is your family like Miss Peckham?"

"Not at all." Serena didn't take advantage of the opportunity to talk about her family, as she usually did. Had Dominic offended her?

"Serena, I need to talk to you about Marianne...."

"What about her?" She glanced across the room to where his sister was conversing with a group of the mamas. Tacit acknowledgment she wasn't in the market for a husband.

Dominic's friend Benedict Trent approached. "Miss Somerton, I believe there's an excellent Reynolds portrait in the gallery. Would you be able to show me?" he asked. He'd sat next to Serena at dinner.

"Certainly." She bestowed a warm smile on him, of the kind she hadn't offered to Dominic.

"No, she cannot," Dominic snapped.

Trent raised an eyebrow.

"I'd be delighted, Mr. Trent, but at some other time." Serena scowled at Dominic, then swapped the scowl for another smile at Trent. "We were just about to beg Lady Mary to play the pianoforte for us. You won't want to miss that."

Even Trent, whom Dominic knew to be ramshackle and devoid of interest in the pianoforte, was too good-mannered to disagree. Indeed, his manners toward Serena were quite charming, Dominic noted. As they arranged themselves into an attentive audience for Lady Mary's musical performance,

Trent sat down on Serena's left. Dominic made sure he took the place to her right. She was, after all, a member of his household and therefore under his protection. She was also an inexperienced girl who might have her head turned by a London gentleman intent on flirtation.

Lady Mary launched into an enthusiastic rendition of "Greensleeves," singing the ballad in a very pleasant alto. She would be quite relaxing company of an evening, Dominic decided. When the song finished, he leaned in to Serena. "May we talk now?"

"Lady Mary is talented, isn't she?" Serena said. "And she has a delightfully *gentle voice.*" She said that as if it was of some significance.

"You won't fob me off again," he said. "I want to speak to you on the terrace, now."

Her jaw set, as if she might refuse.

"Serena," he said, in a "gentle" voice of his own, intended to convey dire consequences if she didn't cooperate.

Two minutes later, they were at the terrace rail, staring out into the darkness. Naturally, they stood apart, in full view of the drawing room.

"Have you spoken to Miss Penelope Carr yet?" Serena asked brightly. "She's a notable wit and, I hear, a woman of strong faith."

"Serena, what's going on? One moment you're glaring at me, and the next you're a ray of sunshine. I wish you'd stop listing these women's good qualities as if they were *horseflesh.* Next thing, you'll have me inspect their teeth. I find this most uncomfortable."

"I don't exist to make your life comfortable," she snapped. "Your sister and I have been forced to parade these women in front of you in the hope of finding some kind of connection. And believe me, if watercolor skills and gentleness of voice won't do it, I haven't ruled out inspecting their teeth—

purely because you're too much of a coward to choose for yourself a woman you might actually *love*."

"*What* did you call me?" he demanded.

She hesitated, as if realizing she'd gone beyond the bounds of what was acceptable. That if she were a man, he'd be obliged to call her out, no matter that the authorities these days took a dim view of dueling.

Then she said, "I named you for a coward, sir, and I stand by it."

"How dare you!" His heart was thumping so hard it was setting his blood to boil in his veins. "The moment I became aware of the need to marry, of my sister's concerns for my children's future, I undertook to find a wife. I will do it, just as I'll do whatever is necessary for the care and protection of those within my charge. That, madam, is not cowardice. It's the very opposite."

"If you were acting from ignorance, I could understand it," she said. "But you know the joy of a loving marriage, and you deem it a risk not worth taking."

"That's my prerogative," he growled.

"Not when a fear of intimacy means you refuse even to engage in discussion with your children." She snorted. "Beyond telling them *I* am the last woman in the world you would marry."

"I don't have a fear—" He broke off. "What are you talking about? I said no such thing." He would never be so rude. Unlike *her*.

Her skin was alabaster-pale in the moonlight, her eyes glittering. "Perhaps not those exact words," she said. "But the children were worried and confused. They wanted to talk to you about the prospect of a stepmother—I don't think for one moment they seriously intended me for the role—and you fobbed them off, as you do at the first sign of threat to the aloofness you so carefully maintain."

"I did *not* say you were the last woman I would marry." Hang it, he couldn't remember exactly what he *had* said, only that he'd been anxious to close down the line of conversation.

To avoid hearing concerns from his children that might upset his plans.

To fob them off.

She was right.

He'd said something about not marrying Serena—though nothing about "last woman in the world"!—and charged out of the drawing room.

And his thoughtless words of self-preservation had hurt her. That was why she'd been so cool.

"I'm sorry," he said, feeling like the biggest wretch in history. "I shouldn't have said I would never marry you."

"That—that's not what I'm objecting to." A blush rushed into her cheeks.

"It should be," he said. "I was appallingly rude. How could I have been so mean-spirited, when you have never been anything but generous of heart?"

Where had that come from?

She was staring at him.

"Despite also being too forthright," he reminded himself and her.

Suddenly, she smiled. It was like seeing the rainbow after the rain, and he only now realized how much the lack of her smile, seeing it shining on others but not himself, had dampened his evening.

My enjoyment is dependent on the smiles of Serena Somerton?

Not possible.

Not acceptable.

Dominic became aware that his breathing was rather labored, his chest constricted.

"Dominic, thank you." She sounded slightly breathless herself. "That was a *generous* thing to say."

He had to get out of here. No matter that he hadn't yet spoken to her about that blasted letter burning a hole in his pocket.

Very stiffly, very correctly, he bowed. "I spoke unwisely, Miss Somerton, and I apologized. That's all. Do not, in your usual unguarded manner, read any more into it."

He had the relief of seeing that captivating smile vanish.

The house party kept Serena busy day and night, arranging activities and seeing to the comfort of the guests. She bore the brunt of the load for Marianne—that was her job— and she was enjoying it. She was far too busy to have much to do with Dominic, who was fully occupied in getting to know his female guests.

By the third day of the party, there was still the distance between them that he'd been careful to create at the end of the first night. *Heaven forbid he should say something heartfelt and not feel obliged to retract it,* she thought with irritation, as she instructed the servants on the setting up of today's picnic lunch. Several folding tables had been brought outside, and there were blankets for the younger members of the party to sit on.

Nearby, several of the ladies were sketching, while the men were mostly engaged in comparing hunting stories from last winter. Archery targets had been set up on the south lawn. Crawley, the gamekeeper, was a proficient archer whose instruction skills, Marianne said, would be in great demand, since the sport had recently become so fashionable again.

Serena had already witnessed Dominic, from the corner of her eye, landing three arrows right on target. She enjoyed archery herself, and knew just how difficult that feat was.

"Look there," Miss Peckham, one of the sketchers, said. "Just what I needed to liven up my picture."

An approaching horseman trotted down the middle of the lawn.

Lady Mary giggled. "A definite improvement on the view."

Serena tried not to consider that too forward from a lady she scarcely knew. If one of her sisters had made the comment, she'd have thought nothing of it. Indeed, she would have agreed; the visitor had an excellent seat on his horse, which was itself no hack.

A moment later, she realized the horseman was Mr. Beaumont. She glanced at Marianne and found her already fanning herself.

Dominic left the archery range and sauntered toward them. Except it wasn't really a saunter; Serena observed the stiff set of his shoulders.

"Dominic, it's Mr. Beaumont," Marianne said.

"So I see." Her brother's voice was cool.

Mr. Beaumont dismounted a few yards away. A stable boy came running to take the reins of his horse. One of the dogs came out, too; a sharp word from Dominic stopped its growling.

"Good afternoon, Mr. Granville, Miss Granville," Beaumont said. "I must apologize for intruding on your party. I had hoped to call in before you grew busy with today's activities."

"Alas," Dominic said, with clearly feigned sympathy.

Mr. Beaumont looked momentarily awkward. "It's you I came to see, Miss Granville. I found this in my uncle's library, and prevailed upon him to lend it to you." "This" was a leatherbound volume. The title, stamped in gold, read *A Cornucopia of Herbs and Their Remedies*.

Marianne's face lit up as she accepted the book. "This is exactly the kind of volume I like to pore over. That's very thoughtful of you, Mr. Beaumont. Isn't it, Dominic?"

"Very," he agreed.

"I have something for you, too, Mr. Beaumont," she said. Dominic tensed.

"Pawn to C4," Marianne said.

Another chess move, presumably a follow-on to the opening moves they'd mentioned on the bridle path, Serena guessed.

"Risky," Mr. Beaumont murmured. "I wonder what's in your mind, Miss Granville?"

Dominic twitched, as if about to object to a perfectly innocuous conversation about chess.

Serena remembered what Marianne had said about her previous suitors. How Dominic had taken it upon himself to chase them away. Had become overprotective—he'd admitted it himself. It would be too bad if Marianne lost her chance to get to know their new neighbor because of Dominic's lack of courage in matters of the heart.

Beaumont observed the sketching ladies, the archery targets. "What a splendid scene on this beautiful day."

It seemed clear to Serena he was angling for an invitation. It was equally clear that courtesy dictated that Dominic must extend that invitation.

Dominic said nothing. Funny how he could lecture Serena about proper behavior, then entirely disregard good manners when it suited him.

"Did you find your lemon balm, Miss Granville?" Beaumont asked. A transparent attempt to prolong the conversation.

"Not yet," Marianne said. "I read that it grows in more exposed areas, so maybe Miss Somerton and I will climb a hill one day."

A silence fell. Stretched into awkwardness.

"I don't suppose…" Marianne began, then trailed off. She wouldn't ask him outright to stay, for fear of provoking gossip among their guests—nothing could be more humiliating than to be accused of "setting one's cap" at a man. Perhaps she worried, too, that Beaumont would refuse the invitation. Though it was plain to Serena that he wouldn't.

Mr. Beaumont didn't pester Marianne to finish her sentence, displaying a discretion Serena knew she would appreciate. Finally, he bowed and said, "Well, I suppose I should—"

"Would you like to join us, Mr. Beaumont?" Serena asked. "We're about to sit down to a picnic luncheon." She sensed, rather than saw, Marianne's sag of relief.

As for Dominic's disapproval...no sensing required. It was fully evident in the slash of his dark brows drawn together.

Marianne said breathlessly, "Please do, Mr. Beaumont."

Which meant Dominic could do nothing but agree. "By all means, join us."

His endorsement was offered with a total lack of enthusiasm that Mr. Beaumont proved able to ignore as he accepted with grace. Serena rather admired that.

Marianne introduced Beaumont to Lady Mary and Miss Peckham. Mr. Trent came over to join them. Serena deemed Marianne well enough chaperoned that she could walk away from Dominic's glare.

She murmured her intention to try her hand at archery, and left.

Crawley soon had her equipped with a longbow and a quiver of arrows. Serena pointed the bow toward the ground to load her first arrow, nocking it to the bowstring. She positioned herself with her forefinger above the arrow, the next two fingers below, then raised the bow. It had been a while since she'd done this, so she drew back carefully, testing the curve of the yew wood. Unfortunately, she released too soon, and the arrow flew embarrassingly wide of the mark.

"Drat," she muttered, and reloaded.

"You didn't find your anchor point, Miss Somerton," Dominic said behind her.

Her second arrow, which she'd been in the process of pulling back, veered wildly toward the rose garden.

"You should know better, Mr. Granville, than to speak when an archer has her bow almost at full draw," she said.

He bent to the quiver and handed her another arrow. "I suspect you were anchoring at the ear. Try the corner of your mouth."

He was right that she preferred to use her ear as the anchor point that would stay consistent from shot to shot, allowing her to reassess her aim.

"Thank you, but I know what I'm doing." She nocked the third arrow.

"I've frequently observed, Miss Somerton, that you assume more knowledge than you have. This bow is likely heavier than you're used to."

She raised the bow.

"The corner of your mouth," he instructed again.

He'd hit the target with three consecutive shots, she remembered. And he was right, this bow was heavier than the one she used at home. In one fluid movement, she drew the arrow back to the corner of her mouth, then relaxed the fingers of her drawing hand.

The arrow sailed straight, and struck the outer rings of the target.

"Good work." Dominic handed her another arrow. "You could try moving your back foot a little closer to the front one."

She did as he suggested.

"Now your shoulders are misaligned." His hands came down on her errant shoulders and adjusted her position slightly. For one moment, his fingers rested there. Then he stepped back.

She took her shot; the arrow landed just outside the bull's-eye.

"Thank you," she said to Dominic. "That was good instruction."

"Will you trust my instruction on another matter?" He sounded serious.

Serena searched his face. "If it makes sense to me."

He huffed what might have been a laugh, if his expression hadn't been so grave. "Will you ever just agree to what I ask, without arguing?"

"It's unlikely," she admitted.

He relaxed, and his face assumed less austere lines. "That cursed upbringing of yours." He pulled an arrow from the quiver, presumably to preserve the appearance of an archery lesson, then took her bow. "Mr. Beaumont's intentions toward my sister are dishonorable."

Despite his coolness to the other man, this was the last thing she'd expected.

"Are you sure?" she asked. "You say yourself you can be too protective of Marianne."

Dominic pulled a folded sheet of paper from his pocket. "I received this letter a few days ago. This is what I wanted to speak to you about."

The night she'd accused him of cowardice, and he'd accused her of generosity of heart.

"I shouldn't have called you a coward," she said quickly. The burden of her unguarded tongue had been on her conscience.

One corner of his mouth twitched. "No, you shouldn't. Read this, and I'll forgive you."

"I can't read your private correspondence," she demurred.

"Are you saying, Serena, that you're reluctant to involve yourself in my affairs?" His eyes gleamed, and suddenly she was very, very glad she'd apologized.

"I don't suppose I could say that with any credibility," she admitted.

He laughed. "Then read it."

She took the letter. Dominic lined up perpendicular to the archery target and shot his arrow. The trajectory was straight and true: another bull's-eye.

"How smug of you." Serena unfolded the page he'd given her—two pages, as it turned out. "What is this?"

"After you mentioned encountering Mr. Beaumont on the bridle path, I wrote to a friend in London requesting a report on our new neighbor," he said.

Serena's heart sank. She grasped the pages with both hands—gracious, the crest at the top was that of the Marquess of Severn—and began to read. Which proved easy, as the letter was written in one direction only. The marquess was clearly an extravagant man. Serena didn't know anyone who would send two sheets of paper, rather than crossing and if necessary recrossing the lines on a single sheet.

Once she passed the greeting "My dear Granville" and ensuing platitudes, Beaumont's name and various phrases began to jump out at her. They started off fairly innocuous— "always in the pink of fashion...to be seen at any and all ton parties"—and grew progressively worse. "Expensive habits. Given to gaming. Excessive drinking—his father was the same."

"I suppose any young man might commit youthful follies," Serena said hesitantly. "These sound bad, but possibly Mr. Beaumont has reformed."

"Read on," Dominic ordered.

She obeyed.

"Short of funds." Serena drew in a breath. *"Beaumont has acquired a reputation as a fortune hunter,"* Severn wrote, *"his charming manners having made inroads into the hearts of several heiresses. I believe most fathers are aware of his*

conniving nature and odious intentions, and have taken steps to protect their daughters...."

Serena let the paper fall to her side, the fingers of her left hand pressed to her lips. "Oh, no."

"Indeed." Dominic sounded sympathetic. He set the bow on the ground. "Serena, I know that as a parson's daughter it's in your nature to see the best in everyone, even, occasionally, including me." At her querying look, he explained, "You seem convinced there are tender feelings lurking deep within me. But I can't let Beaumont prey on Marianne. I can see she likes him."

Serena nodded. "*I* liked him, too."

Dominic's smile was grim. "The young ladies Beaumont pursued in London needed their parents' permission to marry, and had the purse strings controlled by their fathers. Marianne is twenty-five and in complete control of her fortune. She needs no one's permission to wed, at which point her funds become her husband's."

"So you'll tell her what you've learned." Serena winced at the thought of his sister's disappointment. "The sooner the better."

He shook his head. "Twice before she was chased by fortune hunters, as you may know. Although I believe I did right persuading those men to drop their suit, I suspect Marianne resented my interference, in one case in particular. The man was the lesser of the two evils, to be sure, but still a fortune hunter."

"She feels you deprived her of a chance to marry and have children," Serena admitted.

"She told you that?" He looked shocked, and hurt to have his suspicion confirmed.

"I know you only wanted to look after her," Serena said impulsively.

He smiled. "You mean, I decided what was best for her."

Serena smiled back. "Which can be a very good habit. Dominic, I understand you not wanting to incur her resentment again, but surely this is too important…"

"I would rather attempt to separate them more subtly," Dominic said. "If Severn's report of his London lifestyle is accurate, Beaumont must already be chafing at the quietness of the country."

"He has mentioned the dullness of the evenings," Serena said.

"He'll be torn between Marianne's fortune and a desire to return to London. Once this house party is over, there'll be nothing to look forward to. I'm hopeful London will seem even more attractive."

"There's nothing to stop him corresponding with Marianne after he leaves," Serena said.

Dominic hesitated. "When he gets back to town, he'll see the contrast between the fresh-faced debutantes and my sister. He might have to work harder for his money, but he'll end up with a wife he can parade proudly in society. Severn suggests his image is important to him."

Serena's heart broke for Marianne.

"She will recover," Dominic said roughly, reading her face. "Absence is a powerful anesthetic, and Marianne has met Beaumont only a handful of times. If we let this attachment run its natural course, rather than forcing it to end, then when Beaumont leaves, Marianne won't have been humiliated in front of me and you."

"And she won't have the story spread around the district through servants' gossip," Serena said, feeling guilty that she was discussing her friend, plotting against her, this way.

"The main thing is to protect her from any actions that might have ruinous consequences," Dominic said. "Which is why I wanted you to know the truth. I suspect that by the time we rejoin our guests, Marianne will have insisted Beaumont join tomorrow's expedition to Oakham Castle and attend our supper dance on Saturday, along with goodness knows what else."

Serena groaned.

"You're the person best placed to make sure she doesn't spend time alone with Beaumont, or behave indiscreetly," Dominic said. "Can I rely on you?"

"Of course." Instinctively, Serena stretched out a hand.

He took her fingers in his and smiled down at her, his eyes warm. "Thank you, Serena."

Ridiculously, her heart leaped at the sound of her name on his lips.

For a long moment, their gazes meshed.

"You're looking at me in a…an unusual way," he said.

His bluntness startled her. "Whoever marries you will be a fortunate woman," she blurted.

His eyebrows shot up.

"I meant that you're thoughtful…and loyal," she said.

She seemed to have silenced him.

"I don't hesitate to tell you when I think you have things wrong," she reminded him, embarrassed. "It's only fair I should point out what you do well."

Still, it took him a while to find a response.

"Let's hope," he said at last, "that these other ladies—" his gaze swept the lawnful of prospective brides "—agree with you."

It was as if a sudden shadow had been cast across the garden.

"Let's hope," Serena echoed.

Chapter Eight

"**W**here is Charlotte?" Serena asked. "We can't practice without her." Not without the most musical member of the Granville family. The children's performance had improved enormously, but it was Charlotte's talent on the harp that would make it audience worthy.

If she ever turned up.

"She's helping Cook," William said.

Serena sighed. Charlotte had developed a passion for baking, it seemed. Which wasn't a problem just now, but Serena hoped she grew out of it before she reached an age where it was considered unladylike to spend time in the kitchen. Knowing Charlotte, there would inevitably be strife. Of course, dealing with that would be her father's problem. And her stepmother's.

"Hetty, can you fetch her, please?" At least that would stop the ker-plunk, ker-plunk of the pianoforte keys that was giving Serena a headache. She'd barely slept last night for worrying about Marianne and ruing her own part in inviting Geoffrey Beaumont into their midst. As Dominic had predicted, the bounder had already been invited to this afternoon's castle expedition and to the supper dance by the time she and Dominic rejoined the party.

Serena yawned, which prompted William to do the same. "Are you tired, dearest?" she asked.

"No," he said, and yawned again. He'd worked himself into a terror in the night again, Nurse had told Serena. Typically, it took him a long time to settle after those episodes.

Hetty returned to the drawing room. "Charlotte's not there. Cook said she went outside."

Serena groaned. "We shall have to start without her. Thomas, isn't that flute tuned yet?"

He blinked at the sharpness in her voice, and set down the instument, which he'd been tinkering with for the last ten minutes. Serena shook her head. "I'm sorry, I'm in a crotchet today. Come on, my loves, this is our very last rehearsal— we're performing tomorrow, so we need to get it right."

Louisa tugged at Serena's skirts. "I know all the words, Miss Somerton."

"Wonderful." She kissed the top of her head. "Places, everybody."

Actually, they weren't too bad, she thought, as she listened to verse after verse of "Scarborough Fair." Rather good, in fact. If Charlotte had been here, covering any lapses from her siblings with her nimble fingers on the harp strings, they'd have been close to excellent.

"Again," she instructed. She moved over to the window to gain a more distant impression of the sound. Outside, it was a beautiful day, which had prompted several of the gentlemen to go fishing. A figure running across the lawn toward the house caught Serena's eye.

Charlotte. Where had she been, the little minx? And what was that, glinting in the sunlight?

Oh, no.

Charlotte was carrying a silver platter.

"Keep going, children," Serena said. "I'll be right back." She hurried from the room and let herself out the front door. She met Charlotte as the girl was about to sneak around the side of the house toward the door that led to the gun room.

Charlotte jumped a mile at the touch on her shoulder. She turned to face Serena, sliding the platter behind her back in an ineffective attempt to conceal it. "Hello," she said brightly, as if nothing was untoward.

"Did you steal food from the kitchen again?" Serena asked.

She turned bright red. "It's not stealing, it's our food."

"Did you tell Cook you were taking it?"

The girl clamped her mouth shut and shook her head.

"Because you knew you shouldn't."

Still no response from the child.

"Then why didn't you ask your father, or even me? We could have discussed it with Cook. Your father might have given the man some money...."

"Albert's afraid to come to the house, in case we summon the magistrate," Charlotte said.

Serena gaped. "Albert?"

"Th-that's his name." Charlotte realized she'd erred, and she took a step backward.

"Charlotte, you cannot go off visiting a vagrant in the woods." Serena took the tray from her. "It's unsafe."

"Albert's nice," she said. "He's much nicer than the first man."

"You mean this isn't the same man as the one you gave the lamb to?" Serena said, horrified.

Charlotte shook her head.

Gracious! Every beggar within a hundred miles had probably heard of the bounty to be had from Miss Charlotte Granville!

"Charlotte, this is very naughty," Serena said. "Your papa will be angry." He would punish his daughter, Serena didn't doubt, and she couldn't argue with that decision. Though it was rare, there had been cases of tramps assaulting or even murdering people. The silver platter Charlotte was carrying was probably worth enough to feed the man for a year. Serena shuddered.

"Please don't tell Papa, Miss Somerton," Charlotte begged.

"Of course I must." Serena hustled her into the house through the side door. Dominic would need to make sure the man left Woodbridge land.

"But—but he'll hate me." The cry sounded as if it was wrung all the way from Charlotte's heart.

Serena stopped. "He won't hate you. Charlotte, he wouldn't."

"He already doesn't like me—he never smiles at me, and he gets cross about tiny little things. And when he gets a new wife it'll be even worse." Charlotte rubbed her eyes with her fists. "He'll love her more than he loves me."

Serena wondered if she realized she'd implicitly acknowledged that Dominic did love her. Which was more than his convenient wife could expect. "That's not true," she said. "Your father isn't the sort of man to spout sappy words of love—"

A giggle broke out from Charlotte.

Serena patted her cheek. "—but I know for a fact that he loves you very much. Will you trust me on that?"

Charlotte nodded, but looked unconvinced. She sniffed. "I'm sorry I took the ham, Miss Somerton."

The ham! Serena winced. There went tomorrow's breakfast.

Charlotte saw her anxiety and turned sullen again. "Please, Miss Somerton, please don't tell Papa. I don't mind if he smacks me, but if he shouts at me, I'll die."

"Nonsense, Charlotte, you'll do no such thing." For the sake of Charlotte's rocky relationship with her father, a part of Serena would prefer to keep this quiet. But she had to tell Dominic....

He'd confided in her about Mr. Beaumont, and trusted her to look after Marianne. Could she repay his trust by concealing Charlotte's theft? Not to mention the presence of a vagrant on his land?

"Don't tell him," Charlotte pleaded again.

But if I do tell him, there's every chance he'll confine Charlotte to her room for a day or more. Which meant Charlotte would miss tomorrow's musical performance. The thought of putting on a show intended to impress the visiting ladies and Dominic without its star...

"I need to think about this," Serena said, aware how weak that sounded.

Charlotte threw her arms around her, almost knocking her off her feet.

"That wasn't a yes," Serena warned. As she escorted Charlotte to the kitchen to return the tray and apologize to Cook—and to beg the woman to find an alternative to ham for breakfast—she felt hopelessly out of her depth.

Father, what should I do?

On Friday afternoon, hiding in the library from the constant onslaught of company, Dominic was counting the days until this infernal house party would be over. He'd made polite conversation, he'd acted the fool in games of charades, he'd shot arrows at targets. Night after night, he'd endured interminable dinners, wreaths of cigar smoke and endless rubbers of whist washed down with cups of tepid tea.

All he wanted was his quiet life back...but the awful truth was, things might never be the same again. Not if he proposed marriage to one of the young ladies currently staying in the house. It would be the end of life as he knew it.

No point consoling himself with the hope that his chosen bride might turn him down—he didn't consider himself irresistible, but he wasn't ugly, he had a large fortune and a beautiful home. He'd done nothing to give his guests a disgust for his manners. They still had to meet the children, of course. Dominic wasn't naturally inclined to gush, so he probably hadn't said enough to make them sound irresistible. But none of these women would have accepted the invitation to the house party if they didn't intend to accept a marriage proposal.

Once he married, Woodbridge Hall would feel different. There would always be someone else at the table. Yes, he had Marianne now, but they were used to ignoring each other when the constant company grew too much. Look how he hadn't been able to ignore Serena....

A wife would likely be less distracting than Serena, he decided. That was a good thing. He would guarantee it by choosing a woman of mature, sober disposition like himself. Someone he could ignore. No, that didn't sound right. Someone undemanding. Someone who knew how a marriage should rub along.

How dull, he could imagine Serena saying.

It would not be dull. It would be...nice. *Yes. Nice.*

There was a knock on the library door, and somehow, he knew it was Serena. Dominic stood, tugged his waistcoat down. "Come in."

Serena stuck her head around the door, her eyes bright. "Dominic, the children are about to entertain your guests. Will you join us?"

"Entertain them? How on earth will they do that?"

"Their act is called Thomas and the Amazing Performing Lizard." She grinned at what Dominic suspected was the horrified sag of his jaw. "Don't worry," she assured him, "there's not a lizard in sight."

"I wasn't the slightest bit worried," he murmured untruthfully.

"The children are to sing and play music," she said.

Dominic pushed himself out of his chair. "Are you telling me the small fortune I've bestowed upon that music master is about to pay off?"

"Exactly so." She beamed. "The young ones are involved in the act, too, and believe me, training them hasn't been easy. But they've practiced every day and have come along beautifully."

She'd just solved his problem: how to ensure his prospective brides saw his children in their best light. "Serena, you're a gem," he declared.

Which he probably oughtn't to have done. But something about her unorthodox manners made him unorthodox, too.

She ducked her head. "I—I do think it's nice for the future Mrs. Granville to see your children looking adorable and talented, don't you?"

The future Mrs. Granville. The room felt suddenly too warm. This spring had been unseasonably humid.

Dominic rounded his desk. "Lead on, Miss Somerton."

The switch between her Christian name and a more formal address seemed suddenly necessary, despite the fact they were alone. Or perhaps *because* they were alone. A situation that could be easily rectified, by joining the others in the drawing room.

"Mr. Granville, could I have a word with you after the children's performance?" Serena asked, as she walked briskly alongside him.

"Certainly." He could have slowed his pace to accommodate her. But right now that didn't seem a good idea. Serena Somerton was the sort of woman who, if you accommodated her on one thing, would have you committed to who knows what the next minute.

The guests were already assembled in the drawing room, where the servants had set out three rows of chairs. Serena left Dominic at the doorway and went to collect the children.

When they trooped in, the ladies, old and young, sighed audibly. Dominic had to admit his offspring looked charming. They lined up in age order, scrubbed, combed, dressed in their best clothing, and bowed to the audience. He found himself smiling proudly.

"Mr. Granville, you have the most delightful children," Mrs. Evans said.

At the front of the room, Serena cleared her throat. "Ladies and gentlemen, Mr. Granville's children will play and sing the old English melody 'Scarborough Fair.' Places, children."

The way they moved directly to where they should be was very impressive.

Please, Father, Serena prayed, *let them do well. Let Dominic see how wonderful they are.*

Her heart swelled as the children assumed their positions. They'd worked so hard the past two weeks, improved so much on their disastrous first attempt at the song.... Now they looked excited, but anxious—Charlotte the most anxious.

Serena hadn't told Dominic about the vagrant yet. She'd decided it would be an acceptable compromise to wait until after today's performance, on the condition that Charlotte promised not to go outside before it. Charlotte never made a promise she didn't keep.

Serena nodded at Hetty, the signal to start. Hetty played the introduction that would cue the others in, and off they went.

Hetty fumbled the fifth chord, but—oh, dear, and that one, too.

Luckily, it was time for the harp and the flute to come in. *Good girl, Charlotte.* The harp joined in right on time. On the flute, Thomas just made it, too, and if the notes were breathy, it wasn't too noticeable. And now the vocalists...

"Are you going..." Hetty and Charlotte sang.

"Are you going…" Unfortunately, the younger children came in half a beat late.

And half an octave off-key.

For the rest of the first verse, Serena listened in horror as William's voice roamed up and down the scale without regard for the actual tune. In verse two, Louisa compensated for sudden amnesia as to the words with a loud "la-la-la."

In the third verse, both younger children finally recognized Serena's frown as a sign to fix their timing; they rushed the next few words out. And ended up half a beat *ahead* of the music.

At least Charlotte had both the words and the tune right, Serena thought wildly, as the song instructed some poor woman to wash her beloved's shirt in a well with no water—what kind of man would demand such a stupid thing? But who could hear Charlotte, now that Hetty had decided to compensate for the youngsters' vocal deficiencies by doubling her own volume? She clearly had no idea she'd always been the furthest from the mark, tunewise.

As the fourth and fifth verses alternately limped and galloped along, Serena braved a glance at the audience. Indulgent smiles had frozen like ancient Greek death masks. One gentleman was not very discreetly blocking his ears. Two ladies held their fans in front of their faces. At the back of the room, Marianne was brilliant red—with stifled laughter, Serena realized, outraged. She would deal with *Aunt Marianne* later.

And Dominic… Dominic sat frozen, his mouth slightly ajar. To describe his expression as that of a proud papa would be, quite simply, a lie.

In verse six, Serena gestured to Hetty to play louder and to sing more quietly, then wondered if she'd made a mistake. Certainly, the piano and harp were the most competent elements of the performance…but now the overall volume bordered on earsplitting.

Thank the Lord, they were past the halfway mark.

"Tell him to plow it with a ram's horn," William caterwauled in verse seven—the woman in the song was every bit as unreasonable as the man. The pair deserved each other, Serena thought bitterly. And as for the person who'd thought it a brilliant idea to write *ten* verses of this song…

"La-la-la-la," Louisa sang through verse nine, though a momentary flash of memory did allow her to produce the words "true lover of mine," which, taken out of context, didn't sound quite *right* coming from the mouth of a five-year-old.

"Parsley, sage, rosemare-e-e-e and—*thyme*." William finished the tenth verse with a flourish, an unplanned break in the lyrics that had him thundering out the last word on his own.

It was over.

The silence was stunned. Complete.

Serena closed her eyes.

Then…a solitary round of clapping.

She opened her eyes and saw it was Dominic, on his feet in the middle row. His smile looked forced, his jaw painfully clenched, but he applauded with enthusiasm.

What could the others do but join in?

The gentleman of the blocked ears got into the spirit of the thing and called, "Bravo!"

The children beamed as they curtsied or bowed.

"Thank you so much," Serena said to the audience. *Thank you for not throwing rotten fruit. Thank you for not walking out.*

"Miss Somerton, can we sing it again?" William begged, his face flushed with triumph.

Someone moaned.

"No, my loves, our guests' tea will be getting cold." Serena raised her voice. "Ladies and gentlemen, refreshments are served in the blue salon."

She'd never seen a room empty so fast.

Dominic stood at the door, ushering people through. He steadfastly refused Serena's attempts to catch his eye. Would he dismiss her as Marianne's companion on the grounds she'd humiliated him and his children? But the children hadn't *felt* humiliated.... She started preparing her defense.

When the adults had left, Serena dismissed the performers with thanks and the promise of a special tea waiting in the nursery. They filed past their father. Dominic congratulated each of them, shaking hands with Thomas, kissing Hetty's cheek. When it was Charlotte's turn, he squatted down a little and planted a kiss on her forehead. "You were superb," he said. "I had no idea we have such a talented musician in the family. Just like your mother."

Serena caught her breath. She'd never heard him mention their mother to the children.

Charlotte turned red with pleasure and appeared to be close to tears. She threw her arms around Dominic's neck, almost knocking him over with the unexpectedness of it, but detached herself before he could hug her back.

God might not have answered Serena's prayer for a polished musical showing—not even the most faithful of His flock would say He'd done that—but He'd used that execrable performance to forge a bond between father and daughter. *Thank you, Lord.*

Last of all, Louisa trailed out of the room, tugged along by Hetty.

Serena sagged into a front-row seat, her legs as wobbly as Cook's damson jelly. The sight of the musical instruments brought the performance back to her, and she groaned.

Then she realized Dominic was still here. He walked past

her to the pianoforte, where he picked up the sheet music. He scrutinized it intently, as if trying to ascertain if the children had in fact performed something completely different. Such as, "The Massacre of the Innocents."

Perhaps, Serena thought hopefully, he had an interest in the song because he thought his children had performed well, and thus his applause had been genuine. It was well-known that some parents were blind and deaf when it came to their offspring's accomplishments....

Then Serena remembered the critical eye he'd cast over Louisa's painting that night in the nursery. No, he would be quite objective about this performance.

Dominic set the music back on the pianoforte. He came over to stand in front of Serena, his dark eyes fixed on hers.

"What were you thinking?" he asked conversationally. "To put my children on display in such a manner that their lack of talent should be evident to all?"

This was dreadful.

"They were wonderful in our rehearsals," she said in her—and the children's—defense. She stopped, examined that statement. "Actually, they were terrible the first time. But they worked so hard, improved so much, I started to think they were good. *Very* good. I—I'm afraid I lost my objectivity."

"Which makes you worse than the most obtuse of mothers," he said.

Serena hung her head. "I'm so sorry. I humiliated you."

"You had no idea Louisa would forget the words?"

"She remembered them perfectly yesterday."

"I've never heard 'la-la-la' sung with such enthusiasm." His voice had a curious quality. "And such complete lack of tune."

"I fear singing is not her gift," Serena said. "I did con-

sider having her play the triangle, but her timekeeping…"
She shuddered at the cacophony that would have ensued.

"And Thomas's flute playing," Dominic said. "I'm aston-
ished that after so many years of tuition he can't play without
so much huffing and puffing."

"He's had a cold the last few days…." Not that that made
any difference. Serena buried her face in her hands. "I'm
sorry," she said, her voice muffled.

Dominic's fingers closed around her wrists.

She froze.

"Come now, Serena." He lowered her hands from her face
and tugged her to her feet. "At least have the courage to look
me in the eye."

She swallowed. Lifted her gaze. And found he didn't appear angry.

Yes, his lips were pressed together, but in his eyes…was
that mirth?

"Dominic?" she said tentatively.

"I blame you for the nightmares I'll undoubtedly suffer
tonight," he said. "I'll be haunted by Hetty, banging louder
and louder on the keys of the pianoforte."

Serena smiled reluctantly. "I signaled to her to play louder,
thinking it might…"

"Drown out everyone else," he completed. "Nice idea,
but I'm afraid it would have taken more than that. William's
screech transcended all."

She chuckled. "If ever we need to sound an alarm, he's
our man."

"Parsley, sage, rosemare-e-e-e and thyme," Dominic
yowled, in a more than passable imitation of his son.

"Hush," Serena said, laughing. "I don't think my ears can
take more."

"But William generously offered a repeat performance,"

he said, laughing now, too. "I was going to suggest another concert after dinner."

"Poor William." Serena dabbed at the corners of her eyes with her fingertips. "He and Louisa tried to fix their timing, but they never managed it. Do you think everyone noticed?"

"Noticed what? First the lag behind, then the gallop ahead? I shouldn't think so."

Serena swatted his arm. "Your guests were very brave."

"I think Lady Mary's mama came close to an apoplexy. You have done me a service, Serena."

"Really?"

"If any young lady tells me my children sing beautifully, I'll know she's a brazen liar, and not someone I should marry."

"If she loves the children, she might be deaf to their faults," Serena suggested.

"As you were during the rehearsals," Dominic said.

She paused. "I suppose so." She did love his children, he knew that. So why did she feel awkward?

"None of those ladies know my children—" was it her imagination, or was his voice a trifle husky? "—so we can assume they don't love them."

"Yet," Serena added quickly. "To know them is to love them."

"I daresay they are, in their own unmusical way, rather wonderful," he said.

A lump in her throat prevented Serena from doing more than nodding.

He stared down at her. With one hand, he tucked a loose curl behind her ear. Not breathing, Serena took a step back. Dominic dropped his hand.

A footman entered the room.

"Shall I remove the chairs now, sir?" he asked.

Dominic's gaze broke away from Serena. "Go ahead, thank you. Shall we join our guests for tea, Miss Somerton?"

"Yes, please," she said. "I'm parched."

Which had the effect of drawing Dominic's gaze to her mouth.

"You wanted to talk to me about something," he said. "Perhaps we should have our tea brought to the library."

Spend time alone with Dominic in the library, with this charged tension between them? She could practically hear her father's favorite sermon on the need to turn away from temptation in all its guises.

But she needed to tell Dominic about Charlotte's transgression.

Serena remembered the girl's ecstatic reaction to her father's approval just now. How sad it would be to reverse that so soon.

"We can talk another time," she said. "Your guests deserve your company in the salon as recompense for their battered ears."

Before he could argue, she left the room. *I'll tell him about Charlotte tomorrow.*

Chapter Nine

"I think," Marianne said, "my complexion has improved, don't you?"

She and Serena were walking through the home wood, the woods nearest the house, in the early Saturday morning cool. Despite the low temperature, Marianne's face was flushed with exertion.

"You may be right," Serena said diplomatically.

"The aloe vera has a beneficial effect, I'm certain," Marianne said. "But I still want to find the lemon balm." The book Mr. Beaumont had lent her had waxed lyrical about the calming effect of the herb. Not so much on the skin as on the nerves. Marianne had expressed a hope that if she felt less anxious, her skin would be less inclined to flare up. "From what I've read we're most likely to find it in an open area with plenty of sun. I'm thinking the south side of McGregor Hill. We could encourage a few of the ladies to walk there this afternoon."

"Mmm-hmm," Serena said. The walk they were enjoying now was a prebreakfast stroll. They'd need to return to the house soon, so Marianne could lie down and let her color recede before the morning meal. As soon as they got back,

Serena would seek out Dominic, an early riser, and talk to him about the vagrant.

Three days had passed since "Scarborough Fair," and Serena hadn't found the right moment. She'd forbidden Charlotte to go near the woods—though in all likelihood "Albert" was as harmless as most tramps were—and had kept a close eye on the girl. Still, she needed to talk to Dominic. But it was hard, when, for the first time, he'd expressed such deep appreciation for his children. When harmony prevailed, and when several times a day she caught him eyeing her with keen appreciation.

The moment never seemed to call for a confession of Charlotte's sin, now compounded by Serena's delay.

The sound of someone whistling drifted through the trees.

"Did you hear that?" Serena took Marianne's arm. "I hope it's not a poacher."

"There are no poachers around, as far as I've heard," Marianne said, with unusual calm. Her color had risen, but not as much as Serena would expect.

The whistling grew closer. Serena tightened her grip on Marianne, in case she had to drag her through the trees as they ran for their lives. Then she realized the tune sounded familiar...it was "Oh, for a Thousand Tongues."

What kind of poacher whistled hymns as he went about his thieving?

Just as she realized her mistake, the man himself appeared in the gap between two ancient oaks.

Mr. Beaumont. On foot this time.

"You!" Serena said, unsure if this was better or worse than a tramp.

"Good morning, Miss Granville, Miss Somerton." He bowed. A slight raise of his eyebrows conveyed surprise at Serena's manner of greeting.

"Serena feared you were a poacher," Marianne explained.

"Ah." He chuckled. "A thoughtful thief I would be, to announce my presence by whistling."

Which seemed so exactly what he was—a thoughtful thief—that Serena was tempted to point an accusing finger at him. Marianne snickered at his little joke. She seemed extraordinarily relaxed at this unexpected encounter.

Serena sucked in a breath.

Maybe this isn't unexpected.

Now that she thought about it, Serena realized the only explanation for Marianne's insouciance was that she'd known the "poacher" was Beaumont. But how? Serena was almost certain no notes or letters had been delivered to Marianne, and she'd been with her practically every minute....

The music practices.

Serena and the children had practiced at the same time each day. The perfect opportunity for messages to be sent between Woodbridge and Farley Hall.

Come to think of it, Marianne had suggested an early walk yesterday, but then some of the other ladies had risen early, and it would have been rude to leave them. *At least she realizes she cannot go off and meet him alone.*

But neither could a lady exchange letters with a single man who wasn't a family member or her betrothed. At least, a lady Serena's age couldn't. Marianne might be considered on the cusp of spinsterhood, where she might get away with some liberties without ruining herself.

Drat! Now Serena had more bad news for Dominic.

"I was hoping to see you," Beaumont said to Marianne. "I have a move for you—knight to C3."

Marianne's eyes lit up. But her comment to Serena was an amused, "Predictable."

She and Mr. Beaumont continued in easy conversation. They had spent most of the expedition to Oakham Castle on Thursday in each other's company. Constantly chaperoned by either Serena or Dominic, or both, but they'd had an opportunity to build a rapport. Serena noted with misgiving that they seemed the best of friends. More than friends, by the heated glances they were exchanging.

Serena eyed their neighbor with disapprobation. He should know better than to arrange a clandestine meeting in the woods. Marianne should know better, too. Maybe this didn't strictly count as clandestine, given Serena had accompanied her friend, but an honorable man would visit the house.

Whereas a dishonorable man might be afraid his suit would be discouraged by the owner of the house.

Mr. Beaumont was now telling Marianne how edifying he'd found the sermon at church last Sunday. What better way to convince a lady you're aboveboard?

Serena glared at him.

"You didn't approve of the rector's message, Miss Somerton?" he asked.

"On the contrary, I enjoyed it very much." She stepped over the tree root he'd just helped Marianne avoid. "The reverend's point about the hypocrisy of those who appear outwardly religious, but whose inner motives are evil, was well made."

"I think he was a little heavy-handed," gentle Marianne said. "Everyone knew he meant the choirmaster." The choirmaster was rumored to be too fond of his sherry.

Mr. Beaumont's narrowed gaze suggested he'd understood Serena's implication. "Hypocrisy comes in many forms," he said. "Is the sinner who considers himself—or *her*self—more righteous than others any better?"

Serena's surge of indignation probably did mean that she'd unwittingly considered herself more righteous than Beaumont. How mean of her…and how irritating of him to have made the observation. "We must all acknowledge ourselves sinners," she admitted. "But true repentance involves turning away from wrongdoing."

"And when we do that," Beaumont said, "God is quick to forgive."

"Of course."

"In fact, He washes us whiter than snow. We are, in effect, starting afresh, our past forgotten."

Serena gritted her teeth. A man who could twist any words to his own purposes was dangerous. "A man is known by his deeds, Mr. Beaumont, not the virtue professed by his mouth."

"I don't know how you two got all that out of Sunday's sermon," Marianne said. "Once I realized it was about the choirmaster, I could barely stay awake."

Beaumont darted her a smile, warm and unmistakably tender. "Perhaps you hadn't slept well the previous night."

Outrageous for him to refer to a young lady's bedtime habits, Serena fumed. Unfortunately, honesty compelled her to acknowledge she was taking an extreme stance. If one of the male house party guests were to inquire as to how she'd slept, she wouldn't object in the least.

"Quite likely," Marianne agreed. "It's been warm these past few nights." She held Beaumont's gaze with a boldness that had Serena worried.

"Marianne, we must get back," she said. "The other ladies will be up soon, if they're not already, and wanting their breakfast."

"My apologies, I didn't mean to detain you," Beaumont said. "I'll walk with you to the edge of the woods, in case another poacher is lurking."

Marianne laughingly accepted his offer. Serena would have turned him down, but remembered how alarmed she'd felt to hear Beaumont whistling earlier, and that there could well be a vagrant nearby. She wasn't at all keen to encounter "Albert."

Try as she might, she couldn't prevent Marianne and Beaumont from walking side by side whenever the path permitted. She was so busy glaring at Mr. Beaumont's back and wishing him ill—yes, one should love one's enemies, but it never came easily—she didn't notice a bramble encroaching on the path until it caught her dress.

Her exclamation of annoyance had the other two turning around.

"Don't move, Miss Somerton." Beaumont assessed the situation immediately. "Or you'll tear that flounce. I'm sure you have better things to do today than mend it."

Not that a gentleman should know the first thing about ladies' dresses and the mending thereof. Still, he was right, so Serena waited in place. The narrow stretch of path where she was caught wouldn't accommodate Marianne as well, so at least she'd succeeded in separating the lovebirds. Though she wasn't particularly keen that it should cost her a dress.

With his gloved hands, Beaumont began carefully to peel the bramble away. "This thing is deucedly entangled," he muttered.

Serena kept her head high, trying to ignore the fact that he was touching her skirts.

"So haughty, Miss Somerton," he observed.

Startled, she dropped her chin. "I'm sorry. Haughtiness isn't nice."

"Nor is judging others," he said. "Not to mention listening to gossip."

She pressed her lips together.

"Will it come free?" Marianne called. "I could fetch some scissors from the house...."

"Another minute should see it through," Beaumont replied. He returned to his work. "I saw Granville's young daughter in these woods the other day," he told Serena. "She was carrying a tray of meat. I wondered if she has a hideout around here."

"Charlotte took some food to a tramp who'd come to the kitchen," Serena admitted. "That was what made me think of a poacher when we heard you coming earlier. It was very foolish of her."

"Very," he agreed, shocked. "I know usually these men mean no harm, but a child with a misplaced sense of adventure could easily get hurt. I did enough wandering at that age to know what mischief she might find."

Wonderful. Now Serena was being made to feel guilty by a hard-drinking, hard-living fortune hunter.

Her father would probably say a bit of being humbled would do her good, she realized ruefully.

Still, she was unable to resist defending Charlotte. And, indirectly, her own failure to tell Dominic. "Charlotte was acting out of compassion, rather than adventure."

Beaumont snorted. "I can't imagine Granville falling for that." One last careful separation of thorn from cloth, and the bramble was detached. "There, you're free."

Serena gathered her skirt close, so it wouldn't snag again on this narrow stretch. "Thank you."

"On the other hand," Beaumont mused, returning to their conversation, "Granville was probably the kind of upright youth who didn't get into scrapes. Does he appreciate the risk his daughter took?"

It sounded almost as if he intended to educate Dominic himself. *Surely not.* But what if he did? A dozen possible courses of action filled Serena's head. But only one was viable.

Honesty.

Never had she felt less like speaking the truth, boldly or otherwise. Let alone with love. "Mr. Beaumont, Mr. Granville doesn't know about Charlotte's escapade." She glanced ahead at her friend. "Nor does Marianne."

Beaumont looked so scandalized, Serena felt herself blushing to her roots, much like Marianne.

"Charlotte has been in some strife with her father lately," she explained, feeling disloyal to both father and daughter. "I believe she's put this behavior behind her, so punishing her will serve no purpose."

"I'm relieved to learn that someone benefits from your Christian compassion," he mocked. "I only hope she's worthy of the second chance you so readily extend to her." And not to him, was the implication.

Serena bit her lip. "Charlotte is a child."

"We are all God's children, Miss Somerton." He sounded so smug, she laughed through her worry.

The smile he gave her had a twist that wasn't entirely pleasant. "Very well, Miss Somerton, I'll keep your secret."

"I do plan to tell Mr. Granville myself, when the moment is right." Even she thought that sounded feeble.

"I doubt Charlotte's tramp stayed in the area, anyway," Beaumont said. "There have been no signs of poachers in these woods. But I'll have a hunt about, and I'll ask my uncle's gamekeeper to do the same."

"Thank you," Serena said.

"Miss Granville walks in the woods all the time." He meant Marianne, not Charlotte, she realized. "Her well-being is my primary concern."

"I would dearly love to believe that," Serena said. Could he have been telling the truth, when he'd hinted that his dishonorable days were behind him? That he'd repented?

"Have faith," he said, so lightly that she didn't know what to believe.

"Serena," Marianne called. "We really do need to hurry."

Beaumont left them at the edge of the wood, to Serena's relief and Marianne's well-concealed regret.

"Knight to F6," Marianne said, as they parted.

Beaumont lifted his hat. "Touché."

"He's such a nice man," she said, as soon as they were alone.

"We don't know him well," Serena said.

"You said yourself he's charming, the first day we met. And what could be more appealing than a man who listens in church and takes the message to heart?"

Serena made a noncommittal sound.

"You're as much of a Doubting Thomas as Dominic is," Marianne said. "Has he said something to you about Beaumont?"

"I know your brother worries about you," Serena evaded.

"He doesn't need to," Marianne said. "I'm twenty-five years old, not a young girl on her come-out. I don't for a moment think Mr. Beaumont is as pure as the driven snow, but I'm every bit as capable as Dominic of deciding who's a fortune hunter and who's not."

"I hope you're right," Serena said, "and that Mr. Beaumont is entirely trustworthy."

For her own sake, as well as Marianne's, now that Beaumont held her secret.

The next day, Sunday, clouds rolled in to cover skies that had been uniformly blue. Then the rain pelted down, and plans to row the boat out on the lake after early morning church were abandoned.

"We need some indoor entertainment," Marianne said. "Charades?"

The popular game met with nearly universal approval—Serena was fairly sure she heard a groan from Dominic—and occupied the better part of two hours. When that was finished, the ladies partook of their customary light luncheon. The men usually considered the meal unnecessary, but with the weather precluding everything else but billiards, which was already planned for later this afternoon, most of them ate something.

The discussion around the table centered on what should be the next entertainment. Various games were suggested and discarded.

"Hunt the Squirrel," Mrs. Evans suggested, after another round of charades had been vetoed.

Two of the mamas expressed the opinion that the game was a bit *fast*, but their daughters jumped on the suggestion. Serena had played Hunt the Squirrel once before, with her mother's permission, and thought it fun.

"Oh, let the young ones play," Lady Mary's father said. "We older people can always find a chessboard, or some other amusement."

Marianne looked momentarily tempted by the prospect of a game of chess played with a present opponent. Then she said, "I'll be the hunter first."

Serena guessed she was eager to postpone rushing about the house for the sake of her skin. The rules of the game were simple: the hunter would count slowly to one hundred while everyone else—the squirrels—went to hide. Dominic decreed the hiding places must be restricted to the two lower floors.

The moment Marianne started counting, the others scattered in all directions. Mrs. Evans set off up the main staircase behind Dominic. Serena took the servants' stairs at the western end of the house, planning to hide in the gallery, behind the Chinese screen procured by some long-dead Granville on his travels.

When she got there, Mr. Trent had beaten her to it.

"Do join me, dear lady," he urged. "There's plenty of room for two."

That was part of the fun of the game, several people squeezing into one hiding place, then trying not to give themselves away by laughing. Mr. Trent seemed a nice, amusing man, but Serena remembered Dominic's reaction when Trent had sat next to her while Lady Mary played the pianoforte.

To be on the safe side, she said, "Thank you, but I have another idea."

Marianne's voice floated up from the hallway below. "Seventy-one, seventy-two..."

Serena hurried back through the gallery and out the other end. Bedchambers were out-of-bounds, but there was a closet adjacent to the servant stairs. She slipped into the small, windowless room used to store sheets and bedding, and pulled the door so it was still slightly open. Without a window, there'd be no light at all if she shut it.

The room smelled of lavender and camphor and something else used to preserve linens from moths. It also smelled, intriguingly, of Dominic. Serena would not have imagined that he had a distinctive scent, but his sheets must be stored in here, because she could smell a citrus-and-spice blend, and somehow associated the fragrance with him.

The sliver of light admitted by the door revealed dust motes floating in the air. Her hasty entry must have disturbed them, because now her nose was starting to tickle. Serena sniffed, pressed a finger beneath her nose. Just her luck that Marianne would be right this moment standing outside.

Then, drat it, she couldn't contain her sneeze any longer. She screwed up her face in an attempt to make it as discreet as possible. "Ah-*choo!*"

That wasn't so bad. No one could possibly—

"Bless you," Dominic said, from the dark recesses.

Serena yelped.

"Tut, tut," he murmured. "We'll be discovered if you scream like that."

She pressed a hand to her wildly beating heart. Her eyes raked the darkness, but couldn't discern him. "Why didn't you say you were here?" she whispered.

"I was about to, but then you started fidgeting in your efforts not to sneeze, and it was so entertaining—" she almost *heard* him shrug "—I suppose I forgot."

"Extremely rude," she muttered, aware that he'd just revealed he could see her, thanks no doubt to that narrow beam of light, and thus had the advantage.

"My apologies," he said, with enough laughter to render it completely remorseless.

She heard a rustle. "Did you just bow?"

"I did. By way of apology."

"Just how big is this closet?" she asked.

"If you're asking is anyone else in here, no, I think it's just us."

She snickered. Then realized… "Perhaps I should leave, in case it's not proper."

"The door is open enough to meet the standards of any chaperone," he pointed out. "And the whole rationale for games like Hunt the Squirrel is…"

"For men and ladies to have a socially acceptable way of spending time alone," she agreed. They were talking in low voices now, loud enough to be heard by anyone outside. Marianne must still be hunting downstairs. "Even my papa has no objection to these games," Serena admitted, "as long as they're played during daylight hours."

"So you don't need to leave." Dominic's voice was deep, calm, sure. Somehow, it resonated inside her.

"I can't see you," Serena said.

"You already know what I look like."

True, she had no trouble at all picturing his handsome face, his strong physique.

"Whereas I do have the pleasure of being able to see you," he added.

There was a moment of frozen silence. Had he just said

that to look at her was a pleasure? Serena licked her lips, and wished more than ever that she could see him.

"I apologize," Dominic said, his voice strained. "I went beyond commonplace courtesy."

"I don't mind." Who would prefer a commonplace courtesy, when the alternative was that she was a pleasure to behold?

Far later than she should, she remembered why they were embroiled in this house party, why they were playing Hunt the Squirrel.

She cleared her throat. "The charades were fun, weren't they? Mrs. Evans seems very nice. As does Lady Mary."

He muttered something that might have been agreement. She had no idea to what. That he liked one of those women? Both of them?

"Lady Mary is rather young," Serena suggested.

"She's twenty-one," he said. "Like you."

Did he mean twenty-one was too young, or that it wasn't? In the ensuing silence, Serena thought of Marianne, who at twenty-five was dangerously close to old maid territory....

"Marianne and I encountered Mr. Beaumont on our walk yesterday," she said.

Dominic's hiss decided her against mentioning her suspicion that the rendezvous had been arranged.

"Did he behave himself?" Dominic asked.

"His manners were impeccable. If he's acting," Serena said, "he's very good at it. He gives every impression of an attachment to Marianne."

"That's what fortune hunters do, Serena."

She sighed. "I suppose. Did it occur to you that maybe he's reformed his fortune-hunting ways, now that he's Sir Charles's heir?"

"He is heir to a *small* fortune," Dominic said. "A man of his expensive habits will be interested in making it larger.

Also, he'll be hoping that a marriage would inspire me to look more favorably on parting with a piece of land my family acquired from his."

"How could Mr. Beaumont hope to buy any of your land?" Serena leaned against the back wall. "Surely the estate is entailed?"

"Not all of it. Early last century, one of my forebears purchased a hundred acres from Ramsay's forebear, including a pond that makes all the difference if you want to keep livestock." Dominic's voice shifted and eased, as if he, too, were leaning against a wall. "Ramsay has tried several times to buy the land back. I suspect Beaumont shares that objective."

"What if your friend the Marquess of Severn was merely reporting hearsay?" she asked.

"Even if Severn's knowledge of Beaumont is by reputation, those things are not usually formed out of thin air." Dominic paused. "Don't tell me his stories have fascinated you, too?"

"Of course not," she said. "But I do believe people can change. I do believe we should grant them a second chance."

"I share that belief. However, I believe such character reversals are not as common as idealists like yourself wish to think."

"If only there were some way to know for sure," she mused.

"There isn't," Dominic said flatly. "But I trust Severn. Which means I see no reason to believe that Beaumont's piety and charm aren't disguises intended to dupe my sister." Serena heard him shift in the darkness. "I hold my sister in the greatest esteem—"

"You mean you love her," she said, amused.

He pffed. "But I'm not blinded to the fact that her affliction renders her ineligible for a man-about-town such as Geoffrey Beaumont."

Serena feared he was right. But she persisted, "Have you not heard of the attraction of opposites?"

Silence.

"I've heard of it," he said, his voice clipped.

Four little words, but somehow they changed things. The air felt thick and heavy, as before a thunderstorm.

"Have *you* ever…" Serena began, then stopped. She couldn't ask him that!

"Been a victim of such an attraction?" he asked roughly.

She huffed a little laugh. "*Victim* isn't the word I would have chosen. But…yes." Her heart quickened, in an anticipation her mind wouldn't acknowledge.

"It seems…I have." His voice had deepened. "Quite recently, in fact."

She *knew* he meant her…and yet she couldn't believe it. Not when she'd irked him and provoked him and nagged him. And he'd done the same to her.

"What did you do about it?" she asked.

"My view of such an attraction," he said, "is that it can go nowhere. An attraction, even if mutual, is not a sufficient basis on which to found a relationship." His voice sounded closer…she could nearly make out his shape in the gloom. "Not when philosophical differences promise incompatibility."

The only insurmountable philosophical difference she could think of was that he intended to marry for convenience. Which she'd implied, if not outright stated, she would never do.

"Added to which," he said, "the very nature of an *opposite* attraction implies there would be differences, conflicts."

"Some might say it would be dull to be always in agreement."

"I wouldn't find it dull," he said firmly. "I would find it

peaceful. The spark of difference that would be kindled with a woman who is my opposite would be most…disturbing."

Serena had grown up in a home where disagreement was the norm, where healthy debate invigorated the participants. She would be entirely unsuited to the placid existence Dominic seemed to desire.

So why, now, did she take a half step in his direction? Yes, Dominic was the handsomest man she'd met. More importantly, he was a man of faith, loyal to the woman he'd loved, who protected his sister, who applauded his children when they gave quite simply the worst musical performance ever.

Dominic moved, too. He stepped forward, so she could see his face in the half-light: intent, serious, *ardent*. He reached for her, his hands cupping her elbows. Serena caught her breath.

"*Most* disturbing," he murmured.

Then his mouth came down on hers.

Chapter Ten

Serena's lips were soft, yielding beneath Dominic's. Yet he kept a distance between them with his grip on her arms, as if that would negate the intimacy of the kiss. In the dim light, her pale cheeks, the sweep of her lashes, were beautiful mysteries to behold.

The kiss did not feel *convenient.* Not like the kind of embrace he anticipated in his marriage.

It felt right. Perfect.

It can't be. Dominic's rational mind stepped in, pointing out the obvious. Yes, Serena was kind and giving and a young woman—emphasis on *young*—of admirable faith, but Dominic still loved Emily. His *wife.* The wife of his heart.

He didn't know Serena the way he'd known Emily. He didn't love her.

So now, even though his senses screamed to deepen the kiss, he pulled back.

Serena pressed her fingers to her lips, her eyes wide. She looked…innocent. She *was* innocent. He'd shocked her. Probably appalled her. Frightened her, even.

"Dominic," she said uncertainly.

Before he even knew what he intended, he blurted, "Will you marry me?"

She gasped. "Dominic!"

Dear heaven, what was he thinking?

He'd kissed her, that's what he was thinking.

But now, images of Serena from the past few weeks filled his mind, images of her with his children, his sister. *It's a good idea.*

"Serena...Miss Somerton—"

Her slightly wild laugh told him it was too late to revert to surnames. "Serena, I mean it, will you marry me?"

He'd shocked her into silence. He wondered with grim humor if anyone had ever done that before.

When she spoke, her voice was a whisper. "Are you saying...you *love* me?"

Right away, he knew he'd made a big mistake. Yet some stupid, stubborn part of him wouldn't let the idea drop.

"I won't deceive you," he said. "My reasons for wanting to marry haven't changed. But I hope you'll consider—you love my children, and they love you." As he began to enumerate the reasons she should accept his proposal, his conviction grew. He took both her hands in his, and was aware of a faint tremor, though he wasn't sure if it originated with him or with her. "Marianne relies on you, and already loves you like a sister," he continued. "You'll never lack for material comfort. You'll be mistress of your own home, and a mother."

"Dominic..." Serena found her voice. "This is crazy. You just said opposites cannot be happily wed."

He *had* said something like that. But not *exactly* that. "I expressed a view that to build a relationship on the attraction of opposites would be inherently unstable," he said carefully. "But I'm asking you to build our relationship on practical reasons. Despite the attraction, not because of it."

She pulled free. "I was under the impression you're asking because you kissed me."

He wanted to take her hands again, but "practical reasons"

didn't necessitate such contact. "I shouldn't have kissed you," he admitted. "And, yes, my proposal contained an element of wanting to put that right. But, Serena, the more I think about this, the more it makes sense."

"You said you wouldn't enjoy the conflict inherent in a union of opposites."

Confound it, she'd never listened to a word he said before! Now she seemed compelled to fling his every hastily spoken opinion back at him.

"No marriage is perfect," he said. "Both persons must commit to working toward harmony."

"Was your marriage to Emily perfect?" she demanded.

She had no right...no, she had *every* right, if she was considering marrying him. The very thought that she might accept his proposal filled him with excitement. And trepidation.

About to say that his marriage with Emily had been one of those rare, perfect unions, he realized that couldn't be true. No marriage was perfect.

"You know me well enough to know I'm not always easy to live with," he said.

"Very true." She sounded somewhat grim. Grimness didn't seem a particularly positive emotion in this situation.

"Emily and I almost never argued," he said. "Very little is important enough to be allowed to disrupt marital harmony. But I know my tendency to make decisions for the good of the family without consulting her rankled."

Serena gurgled a laugh.

"Yes," he said sheepishly, "I, too, am guilty of deciding what's best for others."

"So you were imperfect," Serena said. "Which I already knew."

"Emily was imperfect, too." He expected a shaft of guilt, but it didn't come. "She changed her mind often. She would choose one course of action, then a day later regret it.

Whether she changed course, or complained about the fact she couldn't do so, it was a source of irritation. *Mild* irritation," he clarified. "Our marriage flourished despite both our faults."

"You loved her," Serena pointed out, "and that covers over a multitude of sins. You wouldn't be bringing love into a marriage to me."

She spoke calmly of a fact they both knew, and he was in no way ashamed of his desire to marry for practical reasons. But, somehow his offer sounded mean-spirited.

Lord, help me to say this right.

"Nor do you love me," he pointed out carefully. "You said you don't wish to marry soon, but with your father's future uncertain and your reluctance to be beholden to the earl, your brother-in-law—" Marianne had told him these things "—maybe you should consider my proposal. Unless you wish to be a companion for the rest of your life."

He couldn't imagine that. If she said yes to his proposal, he could kiss her again. He quelled that thought.

"Will you have me?" he asked.

Serena pressed a hand to her chest, unable to explain the ache behind her ribs. Dominic was being logical. Practical. She could be mother to his children, never have to leave them. A part of her wanted to accept this man who made her laugh, who challenged her assumptions, whose touch produced butterflies in her stomach. But those were romantic notions, and his proposal had most certainly not been about romance.

In her heart, she knew what he was offering would never be enough for her.

"I would never marry for anything other than love," she said. "And by that I mean a love that fills my heart and my husband's." She was embarrassed to say such things, but if she didn't, he might try to convince her that some pale imitation of love, some "friendly fondness" was enough.

"Therefore, although I am honored by your proposal—" how ridiculous, to be employing the socially correct means of rejecting a marriage proposal in a linen closet! "—I must regretfully decline."

He seemed shocked, though surely he couldn't have imagined anything he'd said would persuade her.

"You may never find the kind of love you're talking about," he pointed out.

"You did."

"My love for Emily... I knew her all my life," he said. "I cannot see how that kind of *complete* love can grow between people who've known each other only a few weeks or months."

"*Complete* is exactly the right word," Serena declared. "Dominic, maybe you're right, maybe I expect too much. But I won't accept less. And if you feel that kiss obligated you to propose marriage...well, please don't. You—you're not the first man to kiss me."

It took Dominic a moment to absorb her meaning. Then it slammed into him, leaving him winded. *She's jesting.* The thought, the hope, burst into life. But, no, her face was serious in the dim light.

"You're too young to have given your heart," he said uncertainly. Though hadn't he and Emily loved each other from childhood?

"I was sixteen," she said. "Not too young to form an attachment."

"And to whom were you attached?" The harshness in his voice surprised him, and made her flinch.

But she didn't shrink from the question. "A young man from Piper's Mead, my village. A soldier."

"Did he return your feelings? How old was he?" Dominic sounded like a betrayed lover. *I don't love her.* There was nothing to betray.

"He was eighteen, and yes, he felt the same."

Dominic's fingers curled into his palms. "Did you kiss him?" Hadn't she already confessed as much?

"You have no right…" she said in a low voice.

"*Did* you?" He didn't care a fig about his *rights*. He wanted—*needed*—to know.

"We were betrothed," she said.

Despite the sudden coyness, her implication was clear.

Dominic was shocked to feel cheated. "But you didn't marry him." He felt as if he was clutching at straws. "Did he jilt you?"

Because if that young man—nameless, faceless, but he didn't want to know any of those details—had hurt her, Dominic would make sure he regretted it.

"His regiment, the 36th Foot, was fighting the French in Portugal, at Almeida," Serena said.

"The Siege of Almeida," Dominic said. "In 1811." Five years ago, but he remembered it because it had already gone down in history as one of Britain's less glorious wartime moments. Somehow the French troops they'd been attempting to starve out of their blockaded fortress had slipped out, blowing up the fortress behind them. Most of the French had got clean away, much to the Duke of Wellington's disgust.

"The 36th Foot was ambushed," Serena said. "They lost thirty-five men, including Alastair."

Alastair. Dominic hated the name instantly. Hated the man, even though he was dead. Which was surely the most reprehensible thought of his life.

"Alastair had only been gone from Piper's Mead six months when the army informed his family he was missing, presumed dead," Serena said. "For the longest time, I refused to believe he was gone." She shook her head. "Perhaps it would have been easier to relinquish my feelings if his body had been returned to his family."

Conflicting emotions assailed Dominic. Sympathy for her loss. Relief that no living rival had a claim to her affections, a claim that preceded his proposal—which she had, of course, turned down. Resentment that he hadn't been the first man to kiss her.

"This is why you're so fixated on second chances," he said. "You want one for yourself."

Her gaze slid away. "Naturally, I would."

"Do you still love him?" Dominic asked.

"I—don't know," Serena said. "I mourned him a long time. I believe I still mourn. Though now perhaps it's more regret than sorrow."

He didn't want to hear another word. "Miss Somerton," he said stiffly, "I thank you for your openness." Truthfully? He wished he'd never heard of *Alastair.* "It's quite clear my proposal of marriage wouldn't suit you. Indeed, I suspect you're right, it wouldn't suit me, either. I shan't trouble you further."

Something flashed across her face—he might have said it was hurt, if she hadn't just told him the tale of her great lost love. Then she inclined her head with a graciousness that made him feel like a jealous child.

Before he could apologize, Serena opened the door wide, flooding their hiding place with light, and stepped out.

Serena flitted from one group of ladies to the next, making sure that all had refreshments, that no one appeared in danger of being a wallflower.

It was the last night of the house party, the night of the supper dance. This was an informal, country occasion, carefully arranged for the dancing to look spontaneous so there would be no need for the rigorous protocols and rules of an official ball.

There was a strong possibility Dominic would propose tonight.

To someone else.

He'd already proposed to Serena.

And now, while a part of her was glad she'd refused, doubt had sprouted in a corner of her mind.

Serena cooled herself with her fan, an old one of her mother's, but still pretty. Goodness, it was warm in here. The doors between the drawing room and the blue salon had been folded back to form one enormous space, lit by hundreds of candles in the overhead chandeliers.

Marianne caught her arm. "Serena, stop rushing around. I'm going red just looking at you."

About to refuse, Serena recalled that she was here to support her friend. Not to endlessly replay in her mind the marriage proposal from Marianne's brother. Deliberately, she slowed her thoughts, checked her steps.

"Would you like me to get you another lemonade?" she asked.

"I would like for you to stand still for five minutes," Marianne said. She'd been moving at her usual decorous pace and her complexion, though flushed, wasn't outrageously red.

Serena let out a long breath. "Will you dance tonight?"

Ordinarily, Marianne wouldn't risk the exertion. But Mr. Beaumont was here, and the two had been engrossed in conversation earlier. Serena was relieved Beaumont hadn't attempted to monopolize Marianne, or done anything else that might start tongues wagging.

"I believe I may dance, as a matter of fact." Marianne sneaked a glance at Beaumont, currently dancing with Lady Shelton's niece. "What about you?"

"I have already had four dances," Serena said. "It's been fun."

She had enjoyed herself, truly. None of her dances had been with Dominic, who had avoided her since yesterday's kiss. The strategy was mutual—she had no wish to talk to him, either. Or to dance with him.

She'd given her full attention to each of her partners tonight, making sure to be vivacious and graceful. She almost hadn't noticed Dominic smiling and chatting with Mrs. Evans and Lady Mary.

The two ladies appeared to be his favored candidates. Now that Serena had removed herself from the running.

In the bright light of the drawing room, with all these beautiful women present, the episode during Hunt the Squirrel seemed like a dream. And yet...Dominic had proposed!

Only after he kissed me, she reminded herself. Something she should not have permitted, but all that talk of marriage and attraction had heightened her awareness of what a good, honorable man he was. It was because he was honorable that he'd felt obliged to ask her to marry him. And while in the end he'd agreed with her that a marriage between them would be the wrong thing—absolutely, it would—the whole conversation, not to mention the kiss, had been very unsettling.

Disturbing was Dominic's word.

She tsked at her own sudden pang of hunger for something she couldn't have. The sooner Dominic got on with proposing to Mrs. Evans or Lady Mary, the better. In fact, he was dancing with Lady Mary right now.

"Has Dominic told you which of your guests he intends to marry?" she asked Marianne.

"Hmm?" His sister's attention was on the other side of the room. "Oh. No. I don't think he would, do you? But Lady Mary and Mrs. Evans took tea in the nursery with me and Dominic yesterday while you were having your nap."

What? The one day when Serena had felt so exhausted that she needed an afternoon rest—oh, all right, she'd been hiding in her room after that kiss—Dominic sneaked off to see the children with his potential brides!

Maybe not sneaking, since Marianne had gone with them. But had their kiss meant so little that he could blithely flaunt his prospective wife to his children five minutes after proposing to Serena?

To think she'd been doubting the wisdom of refusing him! His kiss had stirred up all kinds of emotions. She felt... hungry. Hungry to be loved completely. She'd loved Alastair Givens with all her heart, just as he had loved her. As Dominic had loved Emily. Serena wouldn't accept less from her husband.

Dominic had made it plain he would never love her like that. She could almost appreciate his honesty, but now she'd learned he had so little respect for her that he'd hastened to introduce two other women to his children.... "I wash my hands of him," she muttered. *God loves me like that. He is enough for me.*

"What did you say, my dear?" Thankfully, Marianne was engrossed in ogling Beaumont. No, wait, that was a bad thing. At least, if Dominic was right about Beaumont's intentions, though at this moment Serena wasn't inclined to think he was right about anything at all.

"He's coming this way," Marianne hissed.

Serena's pulse leaped, but she refused to look. "Surely he didn't just abandon Lady Mary on the dance floor?"

"Not Dominic," Marianne said impatiently. "Mr. Beaumont."

Annoyingly deflated, Serena observed that their neighbor was indeed threading his way through the crowd to join them. She tried to muster disapproval, but her resentment of Dominic overshadowed Beaumont's reported crimes.

"Oh, confound it," Marianne said miserably, and Serena saw that her cheeks had fired crimson.

She squeezed Marianne's hand.

"Miss Granville, may I have the pleasure of this dance?" Mr. Beaumont asked. "I believe it's a waltz."

Marianne would have danced the waltz before, during her debut Season in London, but Serena was certain Dominic wouldn't want his sister engaging in such close contact with a scoundrel.

"Perhaps you shouldn't, Marianne," Serena suggested. "Your, er, health."

"I'll take good care of you," Beaumont said to Marianne.

She slipped her gloved hand in his. "I would love to dance, thank you."

As they left, Beaumont murmured to Serena, "Both my uncle's gamekeeper and I have searched your woods and ours, Miss Somerton, and have found no sign of any tramp or poacher. The fellow must have moved on."

"Thank you," she was obliged to say.

Please, Father, let his interest in Marianne be genuine, she prayed, as she watched the couple assume their place among the dancers. Beaumont certainly appeared to have eyes for no one else, and the smile that played around his mouth seemed affectionate.

Serena realized she was glaring at him as he led Marianne away. At this rate, she'd draw unwelcome attention. She forced herself to turn aside, to talk with Miss Peckham.

From across the room, Dominic caught Serena's eye. Before she could avert her gaze, he directed a speaking glance toward his sister, waltzing in Mr. Beaumont's arms.

"How was I supposed to stop them?" she muttered. Then had to assure Miss Peckham she'd said nothing at all worth listening to.

Half a minute later, Marianne joined her, her face the color of claret.

"Is your dance over?" Serena asked. The music was still playing.

She shook her head as she fanned herself. "Dominic came to ask some silly question about what time supper will be served." Serena guessed it was a cobbled-together plan to interrupt his sister's waltz with Beaumont. "Mr. Beaumont told him he was anxious to have a private conversation with him, and the next moment Dominic whisked him off to the library." Marianne grasped her hand. "Serena, dearest, do you think he plans to propose?"

Chapter Eleven

Dominic and Beaumont sat in the library, in armchairs on either side of the fire that a footman had hastily stoked. Molson had brought a tray of drinks. When Dominic offered him a brandy, Beaumont requested water instead. Dominic poured two glasses of water and handed one to the other man.

"I must thank you for your hospitality," Beaumont said.

Dominic nodded. He hadn't expected a direct approach just yet. What was the man up to?

"Or should I thank Miss Granville?" Beaumont asked.

Dominic forced himself not to stiffen at the mention of Marianne. "What are you trying to say, Beaumont?"

"I can't put my finger on it, but I'm under the impression you don't welcome me as a guest," he said with a faint smile. "I wish to remind you that the Ramsays—" his mother's family "—have always been friends of the Granvilles, and I hope that will remain the case."

"Thank you," Dominic said. "I have great respect for your uncle. If you're a man in his mold, then I don't doubt the friendship will continue." He limited himself to a subtle emphasis on the *if.* Because despite what he'd told Serena, one didn't accuse a man of ungentlemanly conduct without hard evidence.

"Might I ask what I've done to deserve such a guarded reception?"

The man was practically inviting the accusation!

"Since you ask," Dominic said, "I'm glad not to have to dance around the subject. I'd appreciate the opportunity, Beaumont, to hear your version of the stories that have reached me from London. I don't believe in condemning a man out of hand." Belief or no, he was uncomfortably aware he'd done just that.

"By stories, you mean gossip," Beaumont said.

"Let me be frank." He was starting to speak like Serena, Dominic realized. "You have a reputation as a drinker, and a gambler beyond your means. A womanizer."

Beaumont swirled the water in his glass. "I won't deny that in my younger days I did some wild things. Regretted most of 'em…but not all," he added, with an honesty that Dominic found both admirable and annoying.

He himself hadn't been entirely lily-white as a youth—who had?—but he'd been blessed to marry Emily at a young age. Before he could get into much trouble.

Which made him think about Serena, and the shocking news that she'd been betrothed to another man. The thought had kept him awake most of last night.

"You're hardly an old man now," Dominic pointed out. "How long ago were these younger days?"

Beaumont grinned. "I'm twenty-five. Perhaps I meant my spiritual youth."

Dominic had a vague recollection of Bible verses about infancy as Christians, and the like. Was that what he meant?

"I hear your father was a drunkard," he said.

Beaumont's smile twisted. "You're well-informed. The family tries to keep that information private. But yes, my father drank himself senseless every day for the first sixteen years of my life, at which point, having frittered away the family fortune, he had the decency to die and set my mother free." Beaumont leaned forward, elbows on his knees, and stared into the fire. "Too late, of course. By then my mother had a nervous condition that the doctors couldn't do much about. She died six months later."

"I'm sorry," Dominic said.

"If you're worried I have bad blood," Beaumont asked, "would it help if I told you I've given up strong drink? I find it impairs my judgment…leads to those gambling debts you mentioned." He took a drink of water, as if to prove his point.

Dominic didn't know whether to believe him. "If all you are to me and all you plan to remain is a neighbor, then I don't much care what you drink or how much you gamble. And I agree, youthful follies ought to be left behind as a man matures. My concern is for your friendship with my sister. Frankly, Beaumont, your more recent history of making up to heiresses is unpardonable." Even if his father *had* squandered the family's wealth.

Beaumont examined his perfectly manicured fingernails. "Unpardonable? Really? I was under the impression that God forgives all. And before you accuse me of hypocrisy, as Miss Somerton did…"

Serena had done that? Dominic could just imagine it; his heart warmed at the thought of such typical, outrageous impetuosity.

"…I'm far from perfect, but my faith is real, albeit recent." Beaumont drank again and grimaced. "This water is awful stuff. If there's anything that could drive a man back to brandy… Do you believe in second chances, Granville?"

Dominic groaned.

Beaumont eyed him strangely. "A few months back, I encountered a band of Methodists in Hyde Park early one morning. I was returning home from a night out, somewhat the worse for wear, and they were starting their day with a dawn worship service." He looked mildly revolted by the concept. "Somehow—I admit, my memory is indistinct—we ended up talking, and an hour later I'd given my life to the Lord."

It was the last thing Dominic expected. "You're telling me that since then you've been a reformed character?"

"Since then I've been one of God's works in progress," Beaumont corrected him. "The drinking I gave up easily enough. But total reform ain't that easy, Granville." He stared moodily at the fire. "I still like a wager, though I know I shouldn't."

"Which brings us to the fortune hunting," Dominic said.

Beaumont barked a laugh. "I won't deny that my financial circumstances will necessitate my marrying a lady with a decent dowry. Which makes me no different from half the ton. In return, I can offer my name, which is a respected one, if you overlook my late father, and a degree of personal charm that I'm told makes me pleasing company."

"But now you're Sir Charles's heir, not just the penniless Mr. Beaumont," Dominic said. Was it possible he'd been wrong? That though Beaumont was, by his own admission, far from perfect, he was on the right road?

Beaumont shifted in his chair. "Sir Charles's legacy means I can no longer be called a fortune hunter, at least not to my face. But the fact is, Granville, I'm not a man of simple tastes."

"A way of saying you're extravagant."

Beaumont lifted one exquisitely, expensively coated shoulder. "I spent my early life in seclusion, tucked away in the country with my drunken papa. It's fair to say that when at last I made it to town, I quickly grew to enjoy the pleasures of that society. Many of which are expensive."

"So Sir Charles's fortune isn't enough, and you still hope to marry for money."

"For *convenience*," Beaumont said. "Is it your view, Granville, that a convenient marriage is a wicked thing? If so, you'll be shocked to hear what people are saying about this house party of yours."

"I admit, sir, I desire a convenient marriage for myself," Dominic said through clenched teeth. "But I'll state that intention clearly to my bride. Although I have every intention of honoring my wife in accordance with biblical instructions, I won't be feigning a romantic attachment."

"Very noble," Beaumont said. "I only hope to discover a similar strength of character in myself."

"Tell me your intentions with regard to my sister," Dominic demanded. "Isn't that why we're here, in this room? So you can ask to court her?"

Beaumont shook his head. "I wanted to address, as best I can, the doubts I see on your face every time we meet. I accept that I may not have succeeded," he admitted. "But as for Miss Granville, at twenty-five she has no need of your permission to court. Or to marry."

"Have you told her you need to marry money?" Dominic demanded.

"Money is always a consideration in the ton," Beaumont said. "But it's not the only one."

"You can't tell me you pay so much attention to my sister because her appearance attracts you. That you haven't noticed her high color?" An understatement of description.

"Of course I have," Beaumont said. "I admit, at first I found it distracting. But then I saw past that and, well, I like her. She has a fine mind, a sweet disposition. If you ignore the redness, she's pretty."

Dominic wanted to believe him. "She blushes like that all the time, you know," he said, with a mental apology to his sister. "Apparently not when she's alone, but the rest of the time. I don't even know what she looks like in her pale state."

Beaumont's face was impassive. "I assume she has consulted doctors?"

"Many," Dominic admitted. "The condition is a combination of shyness and nerves and a physical response, each feeding the other. The doctors say there's nothing they can do."

"I presume these herbs she's forever gathering are an attempt at treatment," Beaumont said.

Dominic nodded. "They don't work." He downed the rest of his water and leaned forward. "If you think, Beaumont, that your marrying my sister will convince me to relinquish those hundred acres your family is so anxious to get back, I swear to you now, I'll never let you have them. And your family name is no greater than ours, nothing to attract my sister. So the *conveniences* you envisage won't come to pass."

Beaumont's mouth tightened. "I can live without the land, Granville—it's well known your sister has five thousand pounds a year. And though my name may not offer any advantage over yours, the fact is, Marianne—Miss Granville— has few prospects for marriage. She seems to me the sort of lady who would want to marry and to have children, and proximity to Woodbridge Hall would be a real attraction. I assure you I'd be a kind husband."

"Whenever you found your way home from the gaming tables," Dominic sneered.

Beaumont flushed slightly. "We'll see. I may yet get past that habit, with the Lord's help. But the biggest factor in my favor, Granville, is that your sister cares for me."

"She deserves better than anything you will ever be," Dominic growled. "If you care for her at all, stay away from her."

The other man dropped his gaze, and for a moment Dominic thought he'd gotten through.

Then Beaumont pushed himself out of his armchair and stood. "The fact that you have a handful of children in need of a mother doesn't make your marriage of convenience any more honorable than mine. So spare me the sermons, Granville. I intend to marry Marianne."

Chapter Twelve

The last house party guests left at noon the day after the supper dance, with, it seemed, no proposal of marriage being offered. At least, that's what Serena took from Mrs. Evans's and Lady Mary's determinedly cheerful farewells.

Dominic's glowering mood could have meant anything.

After his meeting with Beaumont, he'd gone back on his plan not to openly interfere between Marianne and her suitor. He'd been so shocked by the man's blatant admission that he was after Marianne's money, he'd had to tell her.

Serena hadn't been present during that conversation, but Marianne had reported it to her. She had accused Dominic of trying to ruin her chances of marriage, of exaggerating Beaumont's financial needs while downplaying the man's genuine liking for her.

"Beaumont is perfectly right," she'd told Serena. "Fortune is never irrelevant. It doesn't matter that he needs my money, if he truly cares for me. Dominic should appreciate his honesty."

"But has Mr. Beaumont been that honest with you?" Serena asked.

"No," Marianne admitted. "But he hasn't spoken of marriage to me, so the time for that honesty hasn't yet come. I trust him."

Her trust was stretched beyond comfort over the following days. Rain set in, making the children fidgety, and confining Marianne and Serena indoors. The showers weren't so heavy as to deter a determined suitor from paying a call, but Beaumont didn't arrive. Serena wasn't sure how her friend was taking his neglect, as Marianne spent much of her time in her room, pondering her chessboard.

On Friday morning, more than a week after the guests left, Serena walked into the breakfast room to find Dominic still eating.

He uttered a polite greeting. The one good thing about Beaumont's infamous behavior was that Serena and Dominic were united in their desire to protect Marianne from hurt, which meant they'd been able to put aside any embarrassment over that kiss they'd shared. At least, most of the time, in Serena's case.

Dominic didn't look up from the letter he was perusing as Serena helped herself to some ham and cheese, and a baked egg. She nodded her thanks to the footman who offered to pour coffee for her. The servant left the room as Dominic set down his letter and picked up the next one.

"From the Earl of Spenford," he said, surprised.

Serena set down her knife and fork. "If he's writing to say it's not acceptable for me to act as Marianne's companion, tell him to stay out of your business!"

Dominic greeted that instruction to be rude to a peer of the realm with the lift of an eyebrow, which somehow lightened the atmosphere. He broke the seal, unfolded the missive, began to read. "The earl and countess are to host a ball on June 6," he said. "Your parents and sisters are to attend."

"Constance mentioned the ball. I had a letter from her just two days ago," Serena said.

"Lord Spenford wishes to surprise his wife and her family with your presence," Dominic said. He frowned. "What a peculiar idea."

"To invite me to my own sister's ball?" Though in truth, she hadn't expected an invitation.

"The element of surprise," he explained.

"I think it's romantic," Serena said. "What a relief!" At Dominic's questioning glance, she explained, "The earl's marriage to Constance was one of convenience."

"You allowed your sister to enter into such a union?" he asked, feigning shock.

"She didn't ask my advice, so I forbore to give it."

"Very restrained of you," he murmured.

"Not to mention the wedding was too sudden for a letter from me to have reached her in time," Serena confessed. "Constance and Spenford didn't know each other well before they married, though Constance has long admired the earl." Serena wondered if she'd said too much, though she'd stopped short of the whole truth. Which was that Constance had been infatuated with the Earl of Spenford for years, for reasons Serena had never understood. She'd always found the man too proud.

But a husband who would arrange such a surprise for his wife… "I think perhaps he loves her," Serena said happily.

"You draw a long bow to reach that conclusion." Dominic held out the letter. "Spenford has invited me and Marianne to accompany you to the ball. A courtesy, since I haven't seen him in five years."

Since Emily died and Dominic withdrew from ton life, Serena guessed.

"A *generous* courtesy," he amended. "Would you like to attend?"

"Would I like to travel to London, one of the world's greatest cities, and attend a sparkling ball in the presence of all those who are dearest to me?" she asked.

He grinned. "I can see you'd hate it."

"If you think Marianne can spare me…"

"Maybe we can convince her to accept the earl's invitation," Dominic said. "I must say, I'd be pleased to remove her from the neighborhood while Beaumont is here."

"She's still undeterred by your revelation of his character," Serena said. "I'm afraid it's only a matter of time before he turns up at the door."

"The problem is, I suspect that in his own way, Beaumont is sincere," Dominic said. "She senses that. But I don't want my sister bankrupted and brokenhearted while he learns to live out his new faith."

"No," Serena agreed. "I know some people commence their Christian journey from a worse place than others," she mused, "but I don't think I've ever considered how difficult it might be for them to give up their old ways."

Dominic picked up the earl's letter and read it again.

"Do *you* want to attend the ball?" she asked him. Her mind became filled with an entrancing picture: herself, held in his arms, whirling to the strains of a waltz. He hadn't stood up for even a country dance with her at their own supper dance, so to assume he would waltz with her at the Spenford ball was, as he would say, drawing a long bow.

"I enjoy London," he said. "I'd be pleased of the excuse to visit. And I have business that would be more easily accomplished there than from here."

"And," Serena said, prompted by the need to inject some realism into the fanciful picture in her head, "you could continue your hunt for a wife. Surely there must be a lady in all of London…"

"The thought had occurred to me," he agreed.

Serena felt as if someone had doused her with cold water.

She picked up her coffee cup and held it to her mouth, letting the warm air rise over her suddenly chilled face. She took a sip.

"The young man you promised to marry," Dominic said. "What was his name?"

She choked on her coffee, grabbed her napkin and dabbed at her mouth. By the time she said, "Alastair Givens," she sounded perfectly calm.

Dominic had watched that little performance with what appeared to be detached interest. "Yours wouldn't have been a marriage of convenience?"

"No. Why do you ask?"

"He was a suitable match for you?"

"His father is a gentleman of comfortable means," Serena said. "Though Alastair was the second son." If they'd married, they wouldn't have been wealthy, but certainly wouldn't have lacked the necessities and a few luxuries.

"I suppose your parents approved the match at such a young age because he was going away to war?" Dominic asked.

Drat. Serena took her time cutting a morsel of ham. "Ah, no. My parents didn't give their approval." She popped the ham into her mouth.

Dominic frowned. "But you said you were betrothed."

Serena realized with a shock that she was about to confess her concealment to another person for the first time. And rather than finding a kind, gentle confessor, she'd chosen Dominic Granville. She swallowed. "My parents felt I was too young to accept a marriage proposal. Alastair and I agreed to keep our betrothal secret until such time as they would welcome the news."

Dominic was staring at her, open-mouthed.

Guilt needled her yet again. It was indeed quite shocking

for her to have agreed to marry a man without her parents' approval. In the face of their *dis*approval.

But it wasn't for Dominic to condemn her.

"I loved him," she said crossly.

"You were sixteen years old," he observed. "I suggest you weren't qualified to make that assessment. A view your parents obviously shared."

"They were wrong," Serena said. "Did Emily love you when she was sixteen?"

He waved the question away. "Our parents approved the match. Wished for it, even. I would never have considered a secret betrothal." He wiped his mouth with his napkin, and crumpled the linen square onto the table. "Serena, if your betrothal had become known, the world would have assumed you had serious reason to cut your father out of the decision to wed. Either that he was a cruel parent, or you were a girl of no morals. *Ruined,* even."

Tears smarted in her eyes. She'd worried for months that somehow the truth would come out and her family's reputation be destroyed. The worst of it was, a tiny amount of relief that they would never be discovered had seeped into her grief over Alastair's death.

"It makes no difference now," she said defiantly.

"Are you insane?" Dominic demanded. "You've said your father has a rocky relationship with his bishop. For his daughter to be branded a wanton could only make that worse."

Wonderful. Another awful consequence, one she hadn't thought of, so hadn't yet felt guilty about.

"I understand you might defend your own behavior on grounds of immaturity," Dominic said, "but surely you can't defend this Alastair Givens. That he would ask you to marry him when he himself wasn't of age suggests he planned to force your father's hand through compromising you."

Serena gasped at his bluntness. "I was never compro-

mised!" But Alastair had, on one occasion, used their betrothal in an attempt to persuade her to more intimacy. She
had resisted, but…

"And when your father did find out," Dominic went on
inexorably, "he would have had far less power in negotiat-
ing your pin money and widow's benefits. Not to mention
dowries for your daughters…"

"Stop!" Serena cried. "I was wrong, I know it! Are you
satisfied?" Those tears spilled over onto her cheeks, and she
scrubbed at them with her napkin.

In a trice, Dominic had left his seat and made his way
around to her. "Serena, I'm sorry." Crouching beside her, he
took the napkin she was balling, and offered her his handkerchief. He sounded almost distraught as he said, "I didn't
mean to upset you. Forgive me, my dear, please."

Serena caught her breath. *My dear.* "You're not the one
who needs forgiveness," she said shakily. "I've never told
my parents the truth because I see no point in hurting them
so long after the fact. But this has been on my conscience."

"You've confessed to God, though," he said.

"Yes, of course." She gave a watery chuckle and met
Dominic's expectant gaze. "So I'm already forgiven," she
acknowledged.

"Exactly. 'As far as the east is from the west, so far hath
He removed our transgressions from us,'" he quoted from
the Psalms.

Something inside her shifted, lightened.

He stood. "You're free of guilt, Serena."

"Ye-es." The weight settled again.

Dominic narrowed his gaze, just as Marianne entered the
breakfast room.

"Good morning, my dear," he said to her, as he returned
to his seat.

My dear. It meant nothing…nothing that Serena might

wish it to mean, at least. She stuffed his handkerchief into her pocket.

"I overslept," Marianne said. "My queen was in a particularly thorny position last night, and I couldn't go to bed until I had her safe." Her eyes sharpened as she sensed the charged atmosphere. "What's the matter?"

"The Earl of Spenford has invited us to a ball in London," Dominic said heartily. "He wants to surprise his wife with Serena's attendance, and has done the courtesy of inviting you and me to accompany her."

Marianne took a slice of bread and added an apple from the bowl in the middle of the table. "That was kind of him." She began peeling the apple with her knife.

"Serena, the earl has offered to hire a chaise for you," Dominic said. "Though if I attend, you could travel in our own chaise while I ride alongside."

Technically, it wasn't improper for a gentleman to travel unchaperoned in a closed carriage with a governess or lady's companion, both positions being glorified servants. But Serena hadn't acted like a servant, or even much like an employee, in the past few weeks, and Dominic hadn't treated her like one.

"If I come with you, we could all travel in the chaise," Marianne mused.

"Really?" Serena said. "You would come to London?"

"You wouldn't have to attend the ball," Dominic assured his sister. "But you've always said you'd like to view the Summer Exhibition at the Royal Academy, and to visit the British Museum."

"I'd love to see both of those," Marianne agreed. "And lots of other places. But, Dominic, I may also attend the Spenfords' ball."

His cup clattered back into its saucer. Serena was equally

shocked. A hot ballroom, crowded with strangers…it was a recipe for a complexion disaster.

"Are you sure?" Dominic asked.

"I'm turning into a hermit, Dom!" Marianne stirred sugar into her coffee with excessive force. "I'll end up a lunatic old lady gathering herbs by the light of the full moon and talking to my chess pieces." She stopped. "I already talk to my chess pieces!" she said, dismayed.

Dominic chuckled, despite his obvious worry.

"I need to do this," Marianne said. "Who knows, Dom, maybe I'll decide being part of society isn't so miserable. In which case, I can chaperone the girls for you in years to come, and you won't need to marry, after all."

"Now that," Dominic said, "is the best news I've heard in weeks."

His glance clashed with Serena's. Then he said, "But just in case you continue to prefer to avoid the bustle of the ton, I'll take the opportunity to call on Miss Lacey when we're in town, if she's recovered from the influenza."

Miss Lacey. His wife's best friend. The most eligible woman on his list.

His calm announcement was like a slap to Serena's face. The kind of slap you administer to someone hysterical, who's lost touch with reality.

Just the kind of slap she needed.

Serena took a forkful of egg. Dominic wasn't the only one who would have *opportunities* in London. Attending a ball full of gentlemen of the ton would be a useful reminder that the sun didn't rise and set on Dominic Granville.

Doubtless, in their midst, he would look entirely ordinary. She couldn't wait.

Lord Spenford's plan to surprise his wife had come at short notice; Serena and the Granvilles left for London just two days later. Marianne had already written ahead to one of London's top modistes, Madame Louvier, to say they would each require a dress for the Spenford ball. The woman would be busy, so they needed to secure her services in advance.

"Talented though our own Mrs. Fletcher is," Marianne had told Serena, "we can't be sure she's up with the London fashions. It would be a disaster to look provincial."

Serena suspected she herself had never looked anything else, but it was impossible not to get caught up in Marianne's excitement. Besides, a new dress was a new dress. And it was wonderful to see Marianne looking forward to a ball…though Serena still couldn't quite believe she would go through with it.

Mr. Beaumont hadn't visited Woodbridge since the supper dance, and they hadn't met him in the woods. Which Serena assumed meant he'd heeded Dominic's appeal to his better nature.

They'd seen him in church, though. He'd attended with Sir Charles, taking the arm of his uncle, who walked with the aid of a cane. Beaumont had greeted them after the service, very properly, and they'd responded with equal civility. Serena wasn't sure if the urge to be nicer to people in church than one might be elsewhere was a sign of hypocrisy, or of the improving effect of being among one's fellow Christians.

Marianne seemed cheerful enough, before and after that encounter. Hopefully, the prospect of a trip to London would distract her from thoughts of Beaumont.

They reached London on the Monday evening ten days before the ball, having stayed overnight on the way. Dominic hadn't considered it worthwhile opening Granville House for just a short visit, so they stayed with his very elderly aunt in Brook Street. On the Friday, Serena's parents arrived in town.

After a joyous reunion with her parents and her young sisters, Serena continued to stay in Brook Street. Marianne needed her—she couldn't go out alone while Dominic was in his meetings, and preferred not to have the company of a maid—and the arrangement had the advantage of keeping Serena's presence at the ball a surprise for Constance.

Serena went out with Marianne each morning, while it was cooler, then in the afternoons she went with her family to one of London's many attractions.

On Monday, her father sent a note informing her that he and her mother would arrive at Brook Street at two o'clock.

Just before two, Serena heard the knocker and hurried downstairs. The butler opened the door to her parents.

"Hello, my dear." Her father kissed her cheek. "Have you just come in?" The sweep of his hand indicated her bonnet and pelisse.

"I'm just going out," Serena said, confused. "With you."

"Adrian, it sounds as if you wrote one of your too-hasty notes," Serena's mother scolded. "Did your father not explain that we're to take tea with Mr. Granville?"

Serena's jaw dropped. "No!"

"Naturally, your mother and I wish to meet your employer while we're all in London," he said.

"Papa, it's not necessary." Instinct told her it was a bad idea for a man as observant as her father to meet Dominic, though why, she couldn't explain.

"I wrote him a letter, and he kindly invited your mother and me to visit," the reverend stated. "We will most certainly meet him, Serena."

She didn't remember him ever raising his voice, but there were times when he employed a certain inflexion and no one argued. This was one of those times.

The butler, obviously as capable of reading that tone as she was, cleared his throat. "Mr. Granville is in the salon. May I take your hat, Miss Somerton?"

Dominic rose as her parents entered the salon. He shook

their hands, his greeting courteous. More than courteous, Serena realized. Friendly.

"It's a pleasure to meet you both," he said. "Reverend Somerton, I've heard a lot about you."

"You mean, you've heard a lot of my advice," her father suggested, his blue eyes as keen as Serena had feared they would be.

"That, too," Dominic agreed, with a smile. "I'm sorry my sister can't meet you. She's not feeling well this afternoon. Since my aunt no longer comes downstairs, it's just us."

In Marianne's absence, Serena poured the tea. Which, with Dominic next to her and her parents opposite, felt alarmingly as if she were Dominic's wife. Oh, gracious, now *her* cheeks were warming. She glanced up to find her father watching her, his feet crossed at the ankles as he thumbed the distinctive cleft in his chin.

She handed the cups around with a thankfully steady hand. And why not? There was no reason to feel the way she had the day Alastair had called on her father to ask permission to court her.

After a few minutes spent comparing their views on London's attractions, the two men fell into a discussion of the recent repeal of the income tax imposed during the war years. Both men believed the repeal would disadvantage the poor, who would be subject to more indirect taxation.

"I'm pleased to find my daughter living in the household of a man of such good sense," the reverend said as the discussion drew to a close.

"No more pleased than I am to find you so reasonable, sir," Dominic replied with a laugh.

Her father raised an eyebrow.

"I often fall into disagreement with Serena," Dominic said, "and she usually supports her position by quoting you."

Her parents exchanged glances as they registered Dominic's use of her Christian name.

Quickly, Serena said, "Marianne enjoys a spirited discussion, too." An exaggeration as far as her friend was concerned, but it conveyed to her parents that the use of Christian names applied to both Granvilles, and wasn't a sign of anything beyond friendship.

"A good debate aids the digestion," her father said.

"Even when the words are hard to swallow?" Dominic countered.

"Especially then." He sipped his tea, his big hand awkward around the fine china. "I've enjoyed hearing of your children from Serena, Mr. Granville."

"They sound adorable," Margaret Somerton said. "Especially little Charlotte."

Serena eyed her parents in consternation. She'd told them a lot about the children in her letters, and had been honest as she sought her mother's advice. If they repeated her words back to Dominic...

Dominic blinked at the mention of "Charlotte" and "adorable" in the same sentence. "I love all my children," he said, "and in some ways Charlotte most of all."

Serena stared. He did?

"She's so easily hurt," he explained, with a half smile at Serena. "How can I not cherish her? But I wouldn't describe her as adorable, unless you'd also say a bramble bush is adorable."

Margaret Somerton laughed. "All families have one of those, Mr. Granville. My daughter Amanda—" she sent a look to Serena that told her these words were not to be repeated "—is always an inch away from making a mistake that could ruin her, yet though she drives me to distraction, I just want to hold her close."

"Amanda's a very pretty girl," Reverend Somerton said.

"Which, unfortunately, has a lot of men making cakes of themselves."

"We can only hope they'll grow out of it," Margaret said. "Since it doesn't seem likely *she* will."

"Mama," Serena asked, "how can one tell if a man has moved past his cake-making days? There's a gentleman, a neighbor to Woodbridge Hall, whose past is checkered. He vows his dark days are behind him, but if they are, it's only recently."

"This man hasn't made advances to you, has he?" Her mother sounded suddenly most unforgiving, devoid of Christian grace.

"Not at all," Serena said. "But he has to another young lady."

"I hope, Mr. Granville, I can rely on your protection for Serena," Reverend Somerton said. "She's still very young, and lacks experience of the opposite sex."

Serena winced. Dominic knew far more than her father about her *experience*. He looked awkward in the extreme.

"I— Certainly I will protect your daughter as far as I can, sir," he said. He would be conscious that in kissing her, he could be said to have taken advantage of a young woman living in his house.

It wasn't like that. Dominic and I talk as equals.

Her father's piercing gaze seemed to bore into her thoughts. He began thumbing his chin again. "This young man you mentioned…"

To her relief, she realized he'd returned to Mr. Beaumont.

"…I suppose eventually his behavior will reveal his character. Unfortunately, not always as soon as we'd like." He removed his spectacles and polished them with his handkerchief.

"On a related subject," Dominic said, "what do you think about marriages of convenience?"

Serena supposed there was a connection, given that was Beaumont's aim…but was Dominic asking on his sister's behalf, or his own?

"I have nothing against them, as long as both parties have their eyes open," her father said. "The Bible is full of arranged marriages, many of which prospered. But there's one thing all marriages, convenient or not, require. And that's courage."

"Courage, sir?" Dominic asked.

"Marriage is never unadulterated ease," the reverend said, "so my advice is to marry to the level of one's courage. If you're brave enough to risk your heart, then your choice will be different from that of a man, or woman, who prefers a safer, more measured existence. So, this neighbor of yours and the woman he's pursuing—"

Serena had forgotten about Beaumont. She was too busy thinking about whether Dominic would ever be brave enough to marry for love. Whether she would ever be brave enough to marry without it.

I don't think I'm so brave that I could marry in the hope love would come one day. I'm not as brave as Constance.

"—it will come down to whether the lady has the courage to marry him without knowing for certain whether he has reformed," Reverend Somerton said. "And the courage to live with the consequences."

Chapter Thirteen

After Reverend and Mrs. Somerton left, Dominic decided to walk to the home of Mrs. Lacey and her daughter, Hester. He needed to think, to clear his head of Serena, the woman who occupied his thoughts beyond all that was reasonable.

Her father's wise words had leveled Dominic. Had shone a light on his decision to marry for convenience, and revealed it for what it was. A lack of courage.

Serena had once accused him of being too cowardly to risk losing a woman he loved again. She was right.

But why should he put himself through that? Confound it, he had enough to worry about with his children! To marry a woman who would demand the love and intimacy he'd sensibly turned his back on, a woman like Serena…that would require a braver man than he.

As he traversed the southwest corner of Berkeley Square, Dominic thanked the Lord he hadn't done anything so stupid as to fall in love with her, despite the considerable attraction she held for him.

All he had to do now was stop thinking about her. That should be much easier in London, in the society of people who thought the way he did.

A few minutes later, Dominic arrived at the Laceys' house

in Half Moon Street. After checking that the ladies were at home to visitors, the butler showed Dominic to an upstairs salon where Hester and her mother were sewing.

"Mr. Granville, how kind of you to call." Mrs. Lacey extended a hand for the old-fashioned courtesy of a kiss.

Hester dropped a small curtsy as she shook his hand. "How are you, Mr. Granville?"

When Emily was alive, Hester had called him Dominic. The two women had been best friends, so there'd been no formality. But he wouldn't expect such familiarity now.

"Miss Lacey, I trust you're recovered from your illness?"

"Completely," Hester said.

Her mother contradicted her with a fond glance. "She's still very pale, poor dear, and weak as a kitten."

Hester's eyes gleamed with humor. "Luckily, I still have the energy to mend the sheets." She set her sewing aside. Emily had been like that, as well. Susceptible to illness, but never wallowing in it, always at peace with her situation.

Dominic smiled and took the seat she indicated. "Marianne and I missed you at our house party."

"No doubt it was a great success." There was the faintest hint of a question in her tone.

She knew, of course, the reason for the house party. Doubtless the whole of London knew. Was she asking if he had found a bride?

"Marianne tells me it was so," he said carefully. Was that enough to convey that he was still unspoken for?

Judging by her mama's quickly quelled look of delight, it was. "We were sorry to miss it," the older lady said. "I remember Woodbridge Hall has the most exquisite rose garden."

"Mama has a great passion for roses," Hester said. She wasn't exactly pretty, but a fine-looking woman, her features having perhaps a little too much character to be universally admired. Looking at her now, Dominic could see she was attractive. He recalled from their earlier acquaintance that she was sensible and kind. The Laceys were a very respectable family, well-to-do; Dominic imagined her settlement must be more than adequate. It seemed odd that she wasn't married, when she must be thirty years old.

A footman arrived with tea and macaroons. Mrs. Lacey poured, then passed the cups around.

"What brings you to London, Mr. Granville?" she asked.

"Several reasons," he said, "but primarily the Countess of Spenford's ball on Thursday. Marianne's companion is a sister of the countess, so Lord Spenford invited us all to attend."

"The earl's sister a companion? How unusual," Mrs. Lacey said. Which proved exactly why Serena couldn't have remained a governess, even lower on the ladder. "We also have been invited to the ball—the dowager countess and I came out together in 1775 and have been friends ever since—so I daresay we shall see you there."

"I shall hope to secure a dance or two with you, Miss Lacey," Dominic said.

"Of course," Hester said calmly. "Mr. Granville, how are the children? I think of them often—most especially of my namesake, of course."

"They're all well...and were grateful for the gifts you sent last Christmas." Just in time, he remembered she'd done so. Small trinkets, but thoughtful nonetheless. He hoped Serena had overseen the writing of suitable thank-you letters.

"They all wrote beautiful notes of thanks," Miss Lacey said. "I could picture them sitting in the nursery, bent over their pencils."

He smiled at the idyllic image. The reality might well have been different, and involved more coercion, but Hester certainly had a knack for putting a man at his ease.

"They don't sit for very long," he said ruefully. "Thomas

is forever bringing insects and rodents into the house, and Charlotte's most recent escapade saw her running after a beggar with a leg of lamb." With the distance of time, the image amused him, and he chuckled.

Hester's smile was more hesitant, for which he couldn't fault her.

"It's lovely to see children showing some enterprise," she said. "I remember my governess was very good at diverting energy that might otherwise be disruptive into activities that were still fun, but a bit more disciplined."

"Exactly what the children need," Dominic said. She'd said precisely what he thought himself, only she'd couched it in words that wouldn't rile even a free spirit like Serena. "It's too long since you've seen them," he said. "You and Mrs. Lacey must visit us soon."

He spoke impulsively, full of fond memories of what Hester's friendship had meant to Emily, and appreciation for her delicately expressed views. But of course, it was a silly thing to say. Neither she nor her mother would know how to take such an invitation. "Marianne is all talk of another house party," he said quickly. It wasn't true, but the release of tension was palpable.

Did courtship have to be such an awkward thing? And was that what this visit was…the start of a courtship?

It could be. Marrying Hester Lacey would require no courage at all.

The Spenford ball was an enormous success, if the number of people crammed into the spacious Spenford town house was anything to go by.

Dominic and Marianne arrived at nine-thirty—the ball had started at nine—and had to wait several minutes to greet the earl and countess. Serena wasn't with them. She'd been invited to dinner beforehand, the big surprise for her sister.

The countess looked nothing like Serena, Dominic observed. Though beautifully dressed, she was plain, with brown hair and a rather pointy chin. But she possessed a quiet strength that Dominic imagined might enable her to hold her own in a society that admired dazzle.

He escorted Marianne to greet the dowager countess, whose poor health prevented her staying on her feet for long. Then, at last, he could look for Serena—for Marianne's sake, of course. He hadn't spent more than a few minutes in Serena's company over the past couple of days; he'd taken her father's words to heart and spent much of the time with Hester. At the level of his courage.

He found Serena immediately, over by the French doors to the terrace. She would expect Marianne to head for the cooling breeze.

"Serena, hello, what a crush!" Marianne had turned bright red during the greeting process, and now turned redder as she kissed Serena's cheek.

Dominic couldn't say a word.

Serena was a vision in a pale gold dress with a sheer white overskirt. Matching satin slippers peeped from beneath her skirt, and at her neck, a string of pearls. Her hair had been swept into a style that looked too simple to have been easy.

"It's wonderful, isn't it?" she said. Excitement rippled through her voice. "Good evening, Dominic."

"Serena." He felt compelled to bow. "You look enchanting."

She smiled. "There are so many lovely dresses here, but I think Madame Louvier did a particularly good job for me and Marianne."

Marianne's dress, like most of her clothing, was too fussy, designed to draw attention from her face. But the blue color suited her, so Dominic was able to agree without resorting to untruth.

"I've never seen so many people in one room," Marianne said. "So many beautiful women."

Serena agreed. Dominic wondered if she knew she was one them. Several gentlemen were staring, speculating about who she was. Any moment now, one of them would— Even as Dominic watched, he saw three or four start in their direction.

"Miss Somerton, may I have the honor of the next dance?" he asked quickly. It would be the height of rudeness not to dance with her at some stage during the evening.

He took her hand and led her to the dance floor, where they lined up with the other couples for a cotillion. Her gloved hand in his was strong, yet delicate. The feel of it did the oddest things to Dominic. Made him want to keep her to himself, to protect her, yet also to show her off to the world and claim her as his own.

No. Dash it all, he'd spent days acquainting himself with Miss Lacey, and enjoying it most tolerably. So why did he still hanker for something he knew was impossible?

The opening bars of the dance required them both to concentrate on memorizing the steps of the chorus, which would be repeated between the changes. Serena put all her effort into looking as if she wasn't on such tenterhooks with this proximity to Dominic that she might fall over her own feet. She caught sight of her father, dancing with her sister Amanda—forbidden to dance with anyone except Papa— and just the thought of what he would say if he could read her mind cooled her fevered thoughts.

The dance lasted half an hour. When the music ended Serena felt a pang of dismay at the thought of having to relinquish Dominic's hand. But another gentleman was waiting to take his place. Besides, they couldn't dance twice in a row without the world assuming a relationship that didn't exist.

She chatted inconsequentially with her next partner, trying not to watch Dominic. After that, she danced a minuet with her father, and was careful to give him the respectful attention he merited. When that dance was over, she sought Marianne, and found her once again at the French doors next to the terrace. They'd been chatting for a few minutes when her friend grabbed Serena's arm. Serena turned to follow the direction of her gaze.

Mr. Beaumont was here.

He must have felt their eyes on him, for he turned. When he saw Marianne, he jerked backward. Serena would have said he was shocked.

But a moment later, he walked toward them, all smiles.

"Miss Granville, Miss Somerton, what a delightful surprise."

One look at Marianne's face told Serena that though he might be surprised, she wasn't. Serena came to her friend's rescue. "Mr. Beaumont," she said. "We didn't know you were in London." She and Dominic hadn't, at least.

A deepening of Marianne's flush, despite the lotions she'd applied to her skin today, confirmed that she had in fact been aware of Beaumont's whereabouts. Which explained why she'd been so keen to come to town. She and Beaumont must have been corresponding. And yet she'd not warned him of her presence tonight.

"I hope to dance with both of you." Beaumont cast a quick glance over his shoulder. "Perhaps, Miss Granville, you could dance this next quadrille with me."

Marianne's color deepened. "Not just now, thank you. Serena, why don't you dance with Geoff—Mr. Beaumont."

"Please do, Miss Somerton." He extended a hand. "The quadrille is the most enjoyable of dances, I always think."

Serena enjoyed it herself, with its four different movements that kept one literally on one's toes. *If I dance with Beaumont, I'll be keeping him away from Marianne.*

The dancers assembled in sets of four couples. The music began immediately.

"How did you and the Granvilles come to be at tonight's ball?" Beaumont asked casually, as they began to move.

He seemed distracted as she explained the connection.

"Perhaps it's just as well you're here," he said, when they'd completed the first set. "I was wondering how I might discreetly inform you of some news from my uncle. He mentioned in a letter I received yesterday that his gamekeeper found the remains of a recent fire in the woods, along with enough feathers to suggest one of your hens or ours met an untimely end."

"He didn't see the tramp?" she asked, alarmed.

He shook his head. "But there's definitely someone about. Probably not the same fellow, as they tend to move around. And he's most likely harmless. But my uncle has asked the gamekeeper to watch out for him and to get rid of him."

Serena bit her lip. She agreed that after all this time, it was unlikely to be "Albert," Charlotte's tramp. Still, if they were going to have a steady stream of vagrants, it was beyond time she spoke to Dominic.

At the end of the dance, Beaumont returned Serena to Marianne, then chatted with them for a few minutes before excusing himself. Marianne struggled to hide her disappointment as he walked off.

"Where's Dominic?" Serena asked her. "There's something I must tell him."

His sister craned her neck. "I saw him a moment ago… ah, there he is. Dancing with Miss Lacey."

Miss Lacey? *The* Miss Lacey? Serena's palms were damp as she turned to look.

To see Dominic waltzing—waltzing!—with a lady whose hair was an attractive, rich shade of brown. Her plum-colored dress proclaimed her a spinster; young ladies hoping to attract a husband were required to wear more demure, pale colors. The plum suited Miss Lacey very well. Dominic was smiling down at her as they danced.

"She looks nice," Serena said, and was embarrassed to find her voice sounded thin.

"I'd forgotten how much I like her," Marianne admitted. "She and Dominic have been inseparable these past few days."

"Really?" Serena heard dismay in her own voice. "I mean, I didn't know." She'd spent most of her time with her family, and had assumed Dominic's absences were related to the business he'd mentioned. "You obviously have met with her, too." She hoped that didn't sound accusing.

"She came shopping with me yesterday," Marianne said, "when you went with your parents to see the Elgin Marbles. That's when I bought this." She held up her dark blue velvet reticule. "Miss Lacey chose it."

Serena knew a stab of something that could only be jealousy. *Forgive me, Lord. What's wrong with me?*

When the music stopped, Dominic released Miss Lacey immediately, as he should. Some small consolation. But of course, he would behave as he ought. He was a gentleman.

And yet...he kissed me.

When Lord Spenford announced that supper was served, it was clear Dominic planned to lead Miss Lacey in. At the last second, Beaumont turned up to escort Marianne. Serena felt suddenly and utterly miserable. Even being invited in to supper by a handsome gentleman with a nicely trimmed mustache didn't improve her mood.

The food was probably exquisite, but Serena barely tasted it as she conversed with her companion, and then with her parents and her sister Isabel. The two younger girls, Amanda and Charity, had already been sent to bed. Constance was so busy with her other guests Serena had hardly seen her tonight.

She nibbled on an eclair, then accepted an ice—such delicious extravagance—from her dinner escort. Dominic didn't seem to have noticed Beaumont's presence; he was busy entertaining Miss Lacey.

When they'd finished eating, Mr. Beaumont excused himself on the grounds that he'd engaged for the next dance with Miss Deverell, not having known Marianne would be here. Serena and Marianne visited the retiring room to wash their hands and refresh their appearance.

As they stepped out again, Serena said, "It's so much cooler away from the ballroom. Why don't we spend a few minutes relaxing somewhere quiet?" She didn't think she could bear to watch Dominic dance with Miss Lacey again, and Marianne never turned down the chance to restore calm to her complexion. "If we find the library, we might even be able to sit."

Truth be told, her feet ached and she had a tickle in her throat. She felt as if she was sickening for something.

The library, when they found it, was deserted, with most of the guests still at supper. Serena and Marianne settled on a high-backed sofa facing the hearth. There was no fire, but none was needed. Above the mantelpiece hung a rather gruesome painting of a hunting scene, a deer cornered by dogs while two huntsmen dressed in pinks approached. The nameplate set into the frame titled it *The Kill*.

Marianne shut her eyes. "Ah, this is better."

Serena followed suit, closing her eyes, and they stayed like that for a few minutes.

Serena was jolted back to awareness by a male voice. "...so many people I want to avoid."

The owner of the voice was Mr. Beaumont, and the increasing volume said he'd advanced into the room. Marianne perked up, her flush almost pretty. She smoothed her skirt, ready to stand.

Then another man spoke. "Is the red-faced Granville girl one of those you're avoiding?" His voice and familiarity of tone suggested he was around the same age as Beaumont, and well acquainted.

Marianne froze. Serena recalled her mother's homily about eavesdroppers never hearing any good about themselves, and was suddenly afraid. Before she could reveal their presence, Marianne's hand closed about her wrist in an iron grip.

"Not avoiding, no," Beaumont said. "But I wasn't expecting to see her in town. She doesn't usually leave her place up at Melton Mowbray. I had other fish to fry tonight."

"The Deverell girl," his friend said sagely. "Saw her watching you earlier. Keen as mustard. She'll look a jolly sight nicer on your arm than Miss Granville, too. A girl like that isn't right for a man of style like yourself."

There was a pause.

"Miss Granville has five thousand a year," Beaumont said.

Marianne's face crumpled.

His companion gave a low whistle. "That ought to buy her a decent husband. Poor girl, cursed with that complexion." He didn't speak unkindly, but still, Marianne pressed her lips together. She and Serena both knew this was how people thought of her, spoke of her—if not with malice, then with pity. But to hear it firsthand was difficult.

Next came the sound of a decanter being unstopped, and liquid gurgling into a glass.

"Brandy?" the stranger asked.

Marianne closed her eyes.

"I'm abstaining," Beaumont said. "Stuff's not good for me."

She relaxed a fraction.

"So you'll take her for the five thousand?" the stranger asked. "Miss Granville, I mean?"

Lord, let Beaumont say he doesn't care, Serena prayed.

But everyone cared about fortune, everyone in that ballroom tonight. With the exception of her parents. *Very well, so he'll care. But let him make it plain it's not the most important thing.*

"Nice girl, too," Beaumont said, briefly raising hopes on the sofa. Then he chuckled, and the sound grated on Serena's ears. "But, yes, it's a pretty sum. Not to mention the brother owns a parcel of land my family would very much like to see restored."

Marianne's fingers curled tighter around Serena's wrist.

"Ah," said his companion, as if that explained everything. "But a word of advice, my friend. Before you make her an offer, ask yourself if you can stare at that face across the dinner table every night for the rest of your life."

Silence.

Then Beaumont said abruptly, "I wouldn't be the only gentleman to leave his wife in the country while he partakes of the city's pleasures."

"But would she stay in the country? She's here tonight, isn't she?" the friend pointed out.

Beaumont ignored that. "With the Season, and then Brighton, and then hunting parties, a man could contrive to be away half the year."

Serena wished with all desperation that Dominic was present. He would surely kill Beaumont, a fate far too good for the scoundrel, but satisfying nonetheless.

Marianne stared down at her lap, her famous shade of scarlet spreading up from the neckline of her dress.

The second man laughed. "Very true. I wish you luck, my friend."

They heard the thud of a glass hitting the desk.

"Shall we return to the ballroom?" Beaumont said. "I have some wooing to do."

Chapter Fourteen

"Marianne, I'm so sorry," Serena said, knowing it was inadequate.

Marianne sat stiffly on the sofa, as pale as Serena had ever seen her, her color concentrated in two bright spots on her cheeks. "I suppose we were fortunate to hear the truth," she said shakily.

Serena pulled her friend into her arms, hugged her close. But Marianne didn't allow the connection for long. She drew back, fumbled in her reticule for a handkerchief and blew her nose.

"You knew he'd be here tonight, didn't you?" Serena asked.

"We've been corresponding." Marianne reached into her reticule again. She pulled out a folded piece of paper and handed it over.

"You don't have to—" Serena began.

"Read it," Marianne ordered.

Serena unfolded the note. And found a coded message: "BxE7."

"It's the chess move I planned to give him tonight," she said. "My bishop to E7 would capture his queen. He hasn't seen it coming."

"So, you've been writing chess notes to him?"

"It started that way," Marianne said. "At home, we were corresponding sometimes once or twice a day by messenger."

"Once or twice a day!" Serena was shocked.

"Depending how quickly each of us could decide on our next move, of course," Marianne said. "We got into the habit of sending a note back with the messenger. Sometimes about chess, but sometimes about other things. I think I would have won this game," she said wistfully, "but I can't be sure."

"This isn't the same game you started that day in the woods?" Serena demanded.

Marianne nodded. "We both like a long game. We're both what I'd call wary players. Geoffrey wrote to me when he arrived in London, and we continued the game," she said. "He had his housekeeper address the letters, as no one would suspect a letter written in a woman's hand. Then he mentioned that everyone was talking about the Spenford ball, so when we were invited..." The memory of the past few minutes seemed to rush back at her and she gave a convulsive sob.

"Serena, Beaumont always talks of how much he loves the Season, and London. I thought, if I proved to him my willingness to attend such events... I didn't realize he'd be embarrassed to be seen with me!"

"He didn't say that," Serena argued, without much conviction.

"He didn't need to," Marianne retorted. "His friend said it for him, and Beaumont didn't disagree."

"My dear, I wish I could do something to lessen your pain."

Marianne squeezed her hand. "I know Beaumont isn't the most upright of gentlemen—his faith has required him to change his ways, and that doesn't happen instantly. But I love him with all my heart. I was prepared to accept his liking and his respect, and to take a chance that we could build a strong marriage. That one day he would realize he loved me. But a man who plans to abandon me at every opportunity..."

"Impossible," Serena agreed. She stood and almost fell, thanks to her left foot having gone to sleep. She pressed hard into her dance slipper, flexing her ankle until sensation returned. "You wait here. I'll tell Dominic we need to leave."

Marianne stood in turn. "Serena, I'm not leaving. I've been a fool, but I'm not going to be chickenhearted, too. Mr. Beaumont needs to see that while he might find me an embarrassment, I know that I am more than my complexion."

Back in the ballroom, Serena led Marianne over to talk to her sister Isabel, who'd just finished dancing with the Marquess of Severn, the friend of Dominic's who'd written to him about Beaumont. There was something about Isabel that drew men in droves. She had a classic beauty, almost flawless features and a calm, kind intelligence that never made anyone feel inferior.

"Quite the handsomest man in the room," she agreed blandly, when Serena congratulated her on her dance partner. "But he's the most frippery fellow. I couldn't engage him on anything serious."

Since Isabel took life rather seriously, that was far from a compliment. As for the Marquess of Severn being the handsomest man here...Serena considered Dominic far better looking. She murmured polite but unenthusiastic agreement. As did Marianne, who was doubtless thinking that good looks had little to say about a man's character.

As Isabel chatted with them, she turned down at least a dozen requests to dance.

"Don't feel you have to talk to us," Marianne assured her. "This could be your best chance at falling in love with an eligible bachelor."

"They're few and far between in Piper's Mead," Isabel

agreed. "But I'm not looking to fall in love. If I marry it will be for more practical considerations."

Serena and Marianne exchanged a glance. Serena chose not to inform Isabel they were both heartily weary of practical considerations. Beaumont with his land and his money, Dominic with his aspirations for a "convenient" marriage. Instead, she said, "You've turned very unromantic at the tender age of eighteen, Izzy."

Her sister snickered. "I hope I *am* unromantic. With the exception of our parents, romance causes a great deal of trouble, from what I've observed. Couples who marry on the basis of respect and mutual support stand a greater chance of contentment."

"You think that should be our ambition? Contentment?" Serena asked. "Where does that leave joy? Contentment sounds dreadfully..."

She was going to say "dull," but she saw Dominic approaching, and her heart set up such a ridiculous thumping, every beat proclaiming this man to be the exact opposite of dull, she half expected Isabel to ask what the noise was.

"Will you dance with me, Serena?" he asked. "I believe there's to be a waltz."

"Thank you, but Marianne needs—"

Her friend gave her a little shove. "Go, you goose. I want to talk to your sister some more about her fascinating views on marriage."

"I haven't waltzed at Almack's yet—I'm not sure I can do so here," Serena said. What a blow! The rules of the waltz for young, unmarried ladies were strict. While it might be acceptable to waltz at an impromptu dance at a country house, to waltz in London without having been granted permission by the venerable patronesses of Almack's assembly rooms would be social suicide.

"Lady Jersey—" one of the patronesses "—is here tonight," Dominic said. "I've spoken to her and she says that since this is your sister's home, you may waltz."

A few seconds later, Serena found herself in Dominic's arms, closer than she'd been even when he'd kissed her. His right hand slid around her waist to rest lightly against her back. His left hand clasped her fingers, strong but gentle. And when he swept her along to the tempo of the music, Serena wanted to weep.

Which made no sense at all. Except that it felt as if everything was upside down. Bitter and sweet.

She'd dreamed of this, of waltzing with Dominic, and now she couldn't enjoy it. He seemed equally preoccupied. Probably with thoughts of Miss Lacey.

"Serena, is there a problem?" he asked.

She found herself blinking away tears.

"Tell me who's hurt your feelings," he demanded.

No one. But you could, so easily. "It's Marianne's feelings that are the issue," she said. She didn't want to tell him, but he needed to know. "We overheard Beaumont talking to a friend.... He made it plain he's after Marianne's fortune and cares nothing for her. He's not, after all, a reformed character." That was an understatement. Time enough later to give Dominic the details.

He bit off an imprecation. "Is Marianne all right? Perhaps we should leave."

"She won't go." Serena explained his sister's resolution.

Dominic was momentarily speechless. "I admire her courage," he said at last.

Which had the absurd effect of bringing a lump to Serena's throat.

Unwittingly, she'd tightened her grip on his shoulder. In response, his hand moved farther across her back, drawing her closer. She wanted to burrow into the shelter of his arms.

Miss Lacey might have something to say about that. Serena eased away.

The sounds of a commotion reached them from the doorway, where a small crowd had gathered.

"What's going on?" Serena asked, glad of the distraction.

"Probably some young man who's drunk too much."

"I hope it's not Beaumont," she said. "He seemed to be drinking only water, but it's not as if he can be trusted."

Dominic twirled her in the direction of the doorway. As they approached, they could hear a young man engaged in heated discussion with the butler. The voice wasn't Beaumont's...but it was familiar. Then a gap in the crowd gave them a clear view.

Serena cried out.

Startled, Dominic released her. "Serena?"

With a sense of dreaming, of past and present colliding in a way that simply wasn't possible, she walked toward the doorway. The young man trying to gain entry wore regimental colors; his red coat with green facings emphasized shoulders considerably broader than when she'd last seen him. Above them was a face thinner and more mature than the one she'd known.

He saw her. Joy burst across his face. "Serena!"

"Alastair?" she whispered.

Then she sank in a slow, swaying motion to the floor.

Chapter Fifteen

Serena became aware of the buzz of anxious voices around her. Hard on the heels of that awareness came a strong desire not to open her eyes. She couldn't remember why, but she knew it was a bad idea.

Then her mother mentioned summoning a doctor, in tones of great urgency, and the bliss of oblivion was no longer an option. Serena didn't intend to utter a groan as she tried to open her eyes, but somehow one slipped out, silencing her audience.

She was in the library, where she'd sat so recently with Marianne. As her vision cleared she saw Dominic standing at the end of the sofa—yes, the same sofa. His face was pale, almost ashen, and his mouth grim.

"Darling, you're awake," her mother said, squeezing her fingers. Serena turned her head to see her. "Thank you, Mr. Granville, for having the presence of mind to send that footman to fetch me. Serena, dear, I've sent him to find your father."

Serena tried to move, but not only did her mother have a firm grip on her left hand, someone else was holding her right. She looked in that direction.

Oh, gracious. The swoon came over her again, but she fought it off.

"Alastair? Is that really you?" Silly question, when he stood right there, leaning over the back of the sofa, clutching her hand. In the flesh, not a romantic dream or memory.

Back from the dead.

"It is I, my love." His voice throbbed with emotion. "Serena, I—"

"That's enough, sir." Her father spoke from the doorway. "I don't know who you are, but you may not talk to my daughter in that familiar manner."

Serena had never heard such iron in her father's voice.

Alastair sprang back. "Reverend Somerton, sir, I beg your pardon. But don't you remember me?" He bowed. "Lieutenant Alastair Givens, at your service."

"Givens?" Reverend Somerton advanced into the room, pulling off his glasses. "Adam Givens's youngest? The one who…?"

Alastair smiled. "Indeed, sir, the one long ago given up for dead. Lost, but now found."

The two men shook hands, then her father trained his gaze on Serena. "My dear, you're as white as chalk."

"Yes, Papa, but it was just a faint." She struggled to sit up, and her mother helped her. "The shock of seeing Al—Lieutenant Givens." And now? Now she was terrified of what Alastair might say. She sent a pleading glance to Dominic, not even sure what she was asking. His expression was achingly distant.

Her father greeted Dominic. Dominic and Alastair exchanged cool glances. Serena could see her father taking it all in. She wondered which of the two men had carried her in here. Dominic?

"No doubt there's a long and interesting story behind your miraculous reappearance, Lieutenant Givens," her father said.

"But that must wait for another day and another place. My daughter is unwell." He walked around the sofa to stand in front of the empty fireplace. "Serena, is there a reason for this excess of sensibility in a girl I know to be levelheaded and not prone to swooning? And is there also a reason that Lieutenant Givens should consider he has the right to hold your hand?"

Just the question she didn't want to answer.

Dominic looked away from her, past her father, to that awful painting. *The Kill.*

Nausea surged in Serena's throat. She considered a relapse, but if Marianne could walk back into that ballroom to face Beaumont, then she herself couldn't be so craven. "Papa, perhaps Mama and I could talk privately."

"Sir, please don't reprimand your daughter for my own presumption." Alastair jumped in. "I'm afraid I owe you and Mrs. Somerton both a confession and an apology."

Identical expressions of apprehension settled over her parents' faces.

"Perhaps," her father said, "Mr. Granville could leave us."

No matter that Dominic knew everything already, Serena didn't want him to hear it again. So why this urge to beg him to stay within her sight?

"I intend to remain, Reverend Somerton," he said. "Nothing Lieutenant Givens says will be news to me." One eyebrow rose slightly in inquiry as Dominic at last looked directly at her. She shook her head. No, there was nothing else.

Once again her parents exchanged glances. It now appeared their eldest daughter had reached undesirable levels of intimacy with not one man, but two.

Alastair looked shocked. "Who *are* you, sir?"

Dominic's gaze held Serena's.

A simple question…no easy answer.

She licked her dry lips. "Mr. Granville is my employer."

Was it her imagination, or did Dominic's eyes grow shuttered? "I'm companion to his sister, Miss Marianne Granville."

"Miss Somerton lives at my home near Melton Mowbray," Dominic said, almost as if staking a claim.

Reverend Somerton rolled his eyes, showing a rare lack of patience. "Let us get back to the matter at hand. Lieutenant Givens, proceed."

"You're aware that Miss Somerton and I were, er, friends before I left to join my regiment," Alastair said.

"Call a spade a spade, please, Lieutenant," her father said. "You asked my permission to court my daughter."

"Yes, sir," Alastair said.

"I refused that permission."

Shame washed over Serena.

Alastair cleared his throat. "I don't doubt, Reverend Somerton, that you and Mrs. Somerton will be disappointed to know I didn't heed your refusal. I asked your daughter to marry me. She said yes. We were betrothed." He rushed out those last three words.

But there was no skimming over them.

Her mother turned so reproachful a gaze on Serena, she wanted to sink through the sofa, through the floor.

"Serena, is this true?" her father asked. "Did you act in a manner that went beyond everything you were taught about what is proper and right?" He held himself very still, in a way she'd never seen before.

"It's true," she muttered. "At the time, I—I couldn't wait."

Her father's face whitened. "Did Lieutenant Givens compromise you?"

"No!" she said, at the same time as Alastair. "Papa, I promise he didn't." Thank God she hadn't allowed him to do more than kiss her chastely on the lips. If she had, she'd be walking down the aisle on a special license before the week was out.

Her mother gave a sob of relief. Her father's shoulders eased slightly. Oh, this was awful, every bit as bad as Dominic had said. She couldn't read his expression. He wouldn't be shocked, having heard it before, but surely he must think her the worst kind of girl.

"It obviously didn't occur to you that you were putting not only your reputation at risk, but the security that would underpin any future marriage," her father said.

"It has occurred to me since," she said.

"Reverend Somerton, neither I nor my father would have used the betrothal to force your hand in a marriage settlement," Alastair protested.

"Quiet," her father ordered. "You were…how old at the time?"

"Eighteen, sir."

"You were in no position to commit to anything on your father's behalf, and his concern would rightly have been all for you, rather than for the girl he would consider had lured his son into a secret betrothal. There would have been very little I could do to ensure Serena's material comfort, and she would always have been seen by your parents as an encroacher."

Alastair looked as if he wanted to argue, but he didn't.

"I am appalled, miss," her father said.

"Reverend Somerton," Dominic interjected. "Please speak to your daughter with more kindness."

Her mother made a tiny sound.

Serena had never seen her father at a loss for words. Now, if only for a second, Dominic had rendered him speechless.

"I beg your pardon?" the reverend said.

"We all have things in our past of which we're ashamed," Dominic said. "Few of us experience the misfortune of having our sins come back to confront us. I don't know about you, but if I were in Serena's situation I'd hope for kindness. For compassion." He slanted her a small smile, acknowledging his use of a word he'd accused her of bandying about too freely.

Her father thumbed his chin, and for a moment looked as if he might smile. Then he said to Serena, "What do you have to say for yourself?"

"Only..." A convulsive sob almost escaped, but she swallowed it. "Only that I'm sorry, Papa. Please forgive me."

He sighed. "And of course, that's exactly what I must do. In fact, if I'm to do the thing properly, I must act as if this never happened."

She pushed herself up off the sofa, rubbing damp palms against her ball dress. "Could you, Papa, do you think? Please?"

When her father seemed momentarily lost in thought, Dominic cleared his throat expectantly.

"You're forgiven," the reverend said, with a wry glance at Dominic.

Serena hugged him, and then her mother.

"Reverend Somerton, please accept my humble apology, too," Alastair said. "I behaved dishonorably five years ago out of youthful foolishness, but let me assure you my feelings were genuine then, and they haven't changed." He took an impulsive step forward. "Serena, tell me I still have your heart."

Serena's stomach hollowed. "I— Of course you do." Because she wouldn't have risked her reputation, her family, her future children's stability for a love that couldn't stand the test of time. That would surely be unforgivable.

Dominic made a strangled sound. He crossed to the window, stared out.

"Reverend Somerton," Alastair said, "with your permission, Serena and I can announce our betrothal tonight. This is our chance to put right the sins of the past."

Whatever it was that struck Serena's heart, it wasn't the joy of love rediscovered. But Alastair's words made sense. If they were betrothed now, everything would be right. She wished Dominic would turn around, so she could… She didn't know what she wanted from him. But she hated that he was looking out into the street, his shoulders relaxed, as if her future was of no account to him.

She took an involuntary half step toward him.

Then her mother said, "Sit down, my dear," and pushed forcibly on Serena's shoulders, until she was back on the sofa.

"Young man," her father said, "I have no intention of approving a betrothal tonight, and I don't care that Serena is of age and doesn't need my permission. I certainly don't care if you still *have her heart*. I hope by now she's wise enough to know I wouldn't withhold permission without good reason."

"Yes, Papa," Serena murmured. Relief made her lightheaded.

"How old are you now?" the reverend asked Alastair.

"Twenty-three, sir."

"Still young," her father said, "but not too young. If you and my daughter still feel the same way in three months' time, when you've paid your attentions to her in an aboveboard manner, then I will countenance a betrothal."

Alastair looked as if he would argue. Serena said quickly, "Thank you, Papa."

Dominic turned from the window. He bowed. "Miss Somerton, allow me to offer my felicitations on your newly rediscovered connection."

Her father held up a hand. "There is no connection yet, Mr. Granville."

Dominic acknowledged that with a skeptical nod. "I assume you'll wish to relinquish your post in my household immediately, in order to return home," he said to Serena.

"Very decent of you, sir," Alastair said.

"No!" Serena blurted. And found herself the target of several stares.

Dominic would let her go, just like that? But then, why wouldn't he?

"Miss Granville has particular need of a loyal companion just now," she told her parents, with a beseeching glance at Dominic. "It would be quite wrong of me to leave her."

After a pause, Dominic said, "It's true, my sister has suffered a recent shock, and is in some distress."

Margaret Somerton clucked in sympathy. "Of course you mustn't leave her, Serena."

"Of course," Alastair muttered, with obvious disappointment. Not that anyone had asked him, Serena thought crossly.

"Then you will remain at Woodbridge Hall," Dominic said, with about as much interest as he would use to read the mail coach schedule. "If you're sufficiently recovered from your faint, I propose we return to Brook Street. I'll have the carriage brought round and will tell Marianne we are to leave. Excuse me, Mrs. Somerton, Reverend Somerton."

Margaret Somerton spent the time neatening her daughter's hair, disheveled by her faint, while the reverend and Alastair talked quietly over by the window. Alastair didn't seem comfortable, and Serena imagined her father was lecturing him.

Dominic returned a few minutes later to report that the carriage would be here any moment, and that Marianne was saying their goodbyes to the Spenfords. Margaret Somerton stood. "I'll leave you now, Serena—Isabel's too young to be alone in a ballroom this long."

"Of course you must go, Mama." Serena kissed her.

With her father and Alastair still engrossed in their discussion, she and Dominic were left standing awkwardly near the door.

"It's kind of you to put Marianne's needs first, in deciding to stay in your post," Dominic said formally.

Serena shook her head, denying any kindness.

He glanced at the other man. "Serena…" he lowered his voice "…did you mean what you said, that Lieutenant Givens still has your heart?"

How could he ask her that? And why?

She pressed her hands to her cheeks. "You know you have no right…"

"I've been thinking," he said. "When God gives us a second chance, we don't always have to start from where we left off. It can be brand-new."

"What do you mean?" She sensed movement behind her, as if her father and Alastair had finished their discussion.

"Just tell me this," Dominic said urgently. "Is my sister the only reason you chose to stay at Woodbridge Hall?"

His hazel eyes locked on her face with an intensity that cut through to her soul.

What did he expect her to say?

There was nothing she *could* say, not without making a hideous situation worse.

She'd just announced that she still cared for Alastair. What kind of woman would then tell another man she couldn't bear the thought of leaving him?

A man who had never professed to love her. Who had vowed, in fact, that he would never marry her.

"To leave immediately would be too sudden," she said. "It would upset the children."

"The children," he murmured. As if he'd forgotten they existed. "Of course." His mouth twisted, too bleak to be a smile.

Alastair and her father approached. The possessive glint in her suitor's eye made Serena want to bolt.

Thankfully, a servant entered to report that the carriage was ready. Serena could have kissed him.

"I shall miss you, Serena," Alastair said, a public declaration of affection that embarrassed her.

The poor man has been a prisoner in France or some such place. Naturally, he's overwhelmed with emotion. Equally natural that he'd forgotten the manners expected of an English gentleman.

"Though I wouldn't have been in Piper's Mead the first week or two, anyway," Alastair continued. "General Blake of the 3rd Foot is currently at his home in York and has requested I visit him there to report on various observations I made while in prison." *Yes, he's been a prisoner, poor Alastair.* "I travel to see my parents tomorrow, then north to Yorkshire on Monday."

"Lieutenant Givens, if Reverend Somerton approves, you're most welcome to visit us at Woodbridge Hall on your way back south," Dominic said.

Serena stared at him. *No!*

"If you wish to stay a night or two, we have fishing and some nice walks," Dominic continued. "My sister will chaperone Miss Somerton."

Alastair turned to Serena's father with barely checked enthusiasm. "Reverend Somerton, would you object to such a visit?"

Say no, Serena willed him.

Her father looked from Serena to Alastair, then to Dominic. He thumbed the cleft in his chin and said with the driest of smiles, "I don't object."

Serena felt as if the last sandbag holding back a flood of complications had given way. Three men—her father, Alastair, Dominic—waited for her response.

"Thank you," she murmured.

It seemed the thing to say.

Chapter Sixteen

Dominic collected Hester Lacey from her home at ten o'clock the next morning with the promise of a walk in Hyde Park.

"Not the fashionable hour," he apologized, as they alighted from the hackney at the park's Curzon Gate, "but tranquil."

"Just what I like." Hester smiled as she took his arm.

So did he. Right now, he craved tranquility, craved an end to the storm of thoughts and doubts that had buffeted him through the night.

Serena's lost love had returned to her.

Alastair Givens was not only alive, but he still loved her. And Dominic had a sinking feeling the lieutenant's tale of survival, when revealed, would focus heavily on how his love for Serena had sustained him under harrowing conditions, inspiring him to heroism.

Serena had said she loved him, too.

More accurately, she'd said Givens still had her heart. If there was a difference between the two, Dominic couldn't see it.

None of that should mean anything to him, he knew. Indeed, if this pain—always a dull, numbing presence, but sometimes so piercing he lost his breath—meant there was a danger he might be falling in love with her, then he wanted no part of it.

My jealousy is perhaps more because Serena has her love back, whereas I won't see Emily again in this lifetime.

Jealousy was a base emotion. He couldn't allow it to gain a foothold.

Hence his need for tranquility. Hence his visit to Hester, for she was indeed a tranquil person.

"Did you enjoy last night's ball?" he asked.

"It was lovely." She adjusted her bonnet against the glare of the sun. "I didn't see you when we left."

"Miss Somerton, Marianne's companion, was unwell, so we returned to Brook Street early."

He steered her around a bed of primroses to a seat. "Shall we rest awhile?"

The bench's wooden slats and wrought-iron back looked clean enough, but he gave them a wipe with his handkerchief before Hester sat. She moved along to make room for him.

An accommodating lady. Just what a man needed in a wife.

They sat in silence—Dominic told himself he enjoyed silence, rather than the steady flow of conversation Serena would have subjected him to. He hadn't seen her this morning. Both she and his sister had slept in.

"We leave for home tomorrow," he said at last.

"I'm sorry we shan't see more of you and Marianne," Hester said. "It's been too long."

This was the moment he was here to seize.

"Miss Lacey—Hester." Dominic turned to face her. "My sudden departure from London forces me to speak sooner than I might otherwise have."

He saw the dawning comprehension in her face as to the

purpose of this walk. Even so, it was impossible to read her reaction.

"I desire to marry again, to find a mother for my children, and a life's companion for myself."

"That's…understandable," Hester said, when the pause grew too long.

"While you and I haven't spent much time together since Emily died—not before this week—I've always thought of you with the utmost liking and respect. As a dear friend of the family."

"Thank you," she murmured.

Dash it, this was difficult. He and Emily had reached an understanding at such a young age, there'd never been a scene such as this. He wished Hester would give him some indication of her feelings. But that was not in her nature.

"I'm not in a position to offer any lady my heart," he said. "I gave that to Emily in its entirety." A vision of Serena crossed his mind. He expunged it, shocked that he would let the thought of another woman intrude at such a moment. He was making a hash of this; it would serve him right if Hester pulled off her gloves and slapped him with them.

"I know how much you loved Emily, Dominic," Hester said.

Her use of his Christian name seemed a positive sign. Even if they *were* talking about how much he'd loved his wife.

Lord, help me. He really should have enlisted divine assistance *before* he reached this point.

"Hester, I like you very much." He'd already said that. "You're kind, caring, and you're soothing company. You deserve the unqualified love and affection of a man far worthier than myself. But I'm hoping you'll accept— Hester, will you do me the honor of becoming my wife?"

Her lips parted with shock, as if despite seeing his proposal coming, she hadn't quite believed he would get it out.

Hastily, Dominic took her gloved hands in his. He refused to compare them with Serena's shorter fingers, instead focusing on their steadiness.

Hester was breathing a little heavily. "Let us be quite clear, Dominic, about what you're offering. I will be your wife, the mother of your children. As well as—" she blushed "—any other children that may result."

He found himself reddening, too. "That's right." He hadn't thought that far ahead, but of course, they would have a marriage in every sense of the word. Other than the romantic love sense.

Some might accuse her of indelicacy with her mention of procreation, but she was hardly a schoolroom miss. Or a twenty-one-year-old likely to have her head turned by every dashing soldier who returned from the dead....

Stop that.

"We would live at Woodbridge Hall," she said. It wasn't a question.

"It's my home," he said. "My visits to London have been sporadic in recent years, but I would be happy to spend the Season in town each year, if that suited you."

She nodded, still noncommittal.

"There's one thing I must tell you, Hester," he said. "Marianne would continue to live with us. Likely for the rest of her life."

"She could hardly set up home on her own," Hester agreed. "I don't know your sister well, but I like her, and I know Emily was very fond of her."

"You're not recently acquainted with the children," Dominic began. It felt as if they were discussing an offer of employment, rather than a marriage. But this was exactly what he'd planned. "They can be a trifle unruly, but for the most part are—" he meant to say *well-behaved,* but somehow ended up with "—dear."

"I would always love Emily's children," Hester said with a smile. "No doubt they need the disciplined loving of a mother and the loving discipline of a governess."

"You've said it perfectly," Dominic said. Relief filled him—he'd made the right decision. "In fact, we need a new governess. I've delayed the appointment, feeling that my wife would choose best."

She nodded again.

"Your face," he said ruefully, "reflects the level of enthusiasm my poorly worded proposal deserves. It must sound as if I'm offering you a life of service to my family, with nothing in return. But I promise I will be a good, faithful, affectionate husband." He lifted her gloved hand to his lips, kissed it. "Hester, I'd be delighted if you'd do me the honor of becoming my wife. Will you marry me?"

"It's the most romantic thing." Marianne adjusted the enormous pink straw bonnet she was trying on. In her spirit of determined resilience, she'd refused to leave London without a new hat. She signaled to the milliner to hold up a mirror behind her, so she could see the reflection of the back of the bonnet in the larger mirror in front of her. "Five years away, and all that time Lieutenant Givens's love for you hasn't wavered."

"I'm truly fortunate," Serena agreed, conscious of a lack of gratitude in her heart. Oh, she was grateful Alastair was alive, of course. But overwhelmingly, she felt guilt at her indiscretion so many years ago. Strange to think that at the time, her youthful besottedness had convinced her it would be a crime *not* to be secretly betrothed!

She'd been kept awake by the thought that to marry Alastair now, to do everything properly, would be a chance to atone for that error.

"But enough about me," Serena said. "Are you recovered

from last night?" She stepped back to let the milliner adjust the set of one of the bonnet's feathers.

"Ah." Marianne's color deepened. She waited until the milliner had moved away, then said quietly, "Serena, last night I was so angry, I didn't feel embarrassed, but this morning I feel like the world's biggest fool. How could I have imagined a man like Mr. Beaumont would have a real interest in me?"

"Mr. Beaumont quoted enough scripture for me to feel he had more depth to him than preoccupation with appearances, too," Serena said. "Part of me still wants to think there's hope for him. But if, as my father says, we should know a man by his deeds…"

Marianne retied the ribbon of the bonnet, then turned to her left to examine it in profile. "I'm looking forward to going home. I hope I never have to see Beaumont again."

The tinkle of the bell above the shop door drew their attention.

The new arrival turned out to be Dominic. He nodded to the milliner, then approached Serena and Marianne. More specifically, Marianne—he hadn't spoken to Serena since they'd left the ball last night. He'd demanded kindness for her from her father, but stayed distant himself.

"Dom, how did you know we were here?" Marianne asked.

"I didn't. I was picking up some gloves I'd ordered in Savile Row, and thought I'd walk back to Brook Street. I saw you through the window." He stood, slightly nervous, hat in hand.

Dominic was *never* nervous.

"I've just dropped Miss Lacey back at her mother's house after a walk in Hyde Park," he said.

"You must have dragged her out at the crack of dawn," Marianne said. "What do you think of this bonnet, Dom? Is it big enough? The feathers are certainly prominent."

"It's…feathery." He sounded distracted.

"Maybe one with a bigger brim," Marianne mused.

If she bought a bigger bonnet, she wouldn't be visible at all. Inside Serena, something snapped. "Excuse me," she called to the milliner. "Do you have a smaller bonnet Miss Granville could try? In the same pink, but *much* smaller?"

"Serena, what are you talking about?" Marianne asked. "You know I don't—"

"Do you even believe what you told me last night? What you wanted Beaumont to see?" Serena demanded. "That you're more than your complexion?"

"Of course I do," Marianne said, her cheeks like two tomatoes.

"Then why do you persist in buying hats and dresses that render your face near invisible?"

"You know how people stare…." Marianne began.

"Do you think they talk about you any less when you hide your face?" Serena asked. "Because I assure you, whatever you think they're saying, they certainly are."

"Serena!" Marianne glanced at Dominic for support.

"Go on," he said to Serena, and his confidence in her felt like a gift, especially after the silence he'd preserved since last night.

"Your sense of inferiority, your lack of confidence—those are what allowed Beaumont to take advantage of you."

Dominic's face turned thunderous. "He *what?*"

"Not that kind of advantage," Marianne quickly assured him.

"No, not that kind," Serena said. "But you're *more* worthy of admiration than Beaumont, Marianne, not less. I'm sick of you feeling you have to make your appearance less offensive, when it's people like Beaumont who offend beyond measure."

"Hear, hear," Dominic said. "Bravo, Serena." The chasm

that seemed to have been carved between them last night was suddenly less intimidating.

She lost her way for a moment. Recalling it, she said, "Marianne, you've asked God to take away this thorn in your flesh. Instead, He loves you as you are. If that's good enough for Him, then it should be good enough for you."

There was a moment's stunned silence.

"Easy for you to say," Marianne grumbled. "You're flawless."

Dominic burst out laughing. "Serena is *not* flawless."

"Dominic…" Serena said. Surely he wouldn't tell Marianne her sins?

"Her appearance is fine," Dominic admitted. "Very fine. But five minutes is all it takes to discover she lacks tact, she's interfering and she's forever pushing her romantic notions forward."

"Dominic!" Marianne glanced from him to Serena in shocked bemusement.

"The point is, appearance isn't the sum of the person, whether you're red in the face or—" he eyed Serena "—a blue-eyed, flaxen-haired beauty."

Serena's pulse quickened. Suddenly, the gap between them didn't seem that wide at all.

"Thank you, Dominic," Marianne said. "I feel so much better now." She let out a peal of laughter.

Serena found herself in the unusual position of being the one trying to restore propriety as the milliner returned with three new bonnets.

"You win, Serena." Marianne wiped her eyes with her gloved fingers. "I have no idea why God made me this way, and I daresay I'll continue to complain about it as long as I live, but I have nothing to be ashamed of." She pointed to the smallest bonnet on offer, which, compared with the feathery one, was positively minuscule. "That one," she told the milliner. "I won't try it on. I might scare myself."

When the woman went to wrap her purchase, Marianne sat down heavily. "What have I done?"

"You've taken an important step," Dominic told her. "Thank you, Serena, for saying what I should have said years ago."

"I had the advantage of coming in from outside," Serena said. "Sometimes it enables one to see more clearly."

"Which explains why you lecture me about my children."

"Exactly." She smiled. He'd been so much better with the children lately. Though his manner and his speech were far from effusive, the children had noticed and responded to his increasing warmth. "And why I felt qualified to make recommendations about your remarriage."

Her words fell into an awkward silence.

What had possessed her to bring up a topic that had become a source of sleepless nights?

Dominic folded his arms across his chest. "Marianne, if you have recovered your strength, there's something I need to tell you."

She snapped her fan shut. "What's wrong?"

He did indeed sound grave. Serena tensed.

"Nothing's wrong," he said. "On the contrary, I have good news." His gaze didn't stray from his sister's face. "I asked Hester to marry me."

Marianne's squeal of excitement, her rush from the chair into her brother's arms, all provided cover for Serena, who clutched the back of the chair on the pretext of steadying it.

Dominic proposed to Miss Lacey.

Had she accepted?

Marianne pulled back from her brother. "I assume she accepted?"

"She did," he agreed.

Of course she did. A lead weight settled on Serena's heart. Now, his eyes met hers. She couldn't decipher their expression. Certainly not the joy of a man in love, but then, that wasn't what he wanted.

"Congratulations," she said woodenly. "I wish you both every happiness."

"Thank you," he said stiffly.

"Tell me, Dom, was it romantic?" Marianne demanded. "Did you go down on bended knee?"

"You know me better than that," he said. "Hester is a woman of great good sense. We shall suit each other very well."

"I can't believe it wasn't at least a little romantic," Marianne scolded. "But I won't make you tell me."

"I don't suppose you *could,*" he said, with a lightness that seemed forced.

His reticence left Serena's imagination to run riot. What had happened *after* he'd proposed and Hester accepted? He may not have declared his love to his betrothed, but he had surely kissed her.

"I invited Hester and her mother to visit us at Woodbridge Hall next week," Dominic announced.

"How lovely," Marianne said. "The children will be eager to see her—I'm sure they scarcely remember her."

"I have no doubt they'll like her," he said.

"I look forward to getting to know my new sister, too...." Marianne trailed off.

"Hester is insistent that you must continue to live with us," Dominic said quickly.

How like him to have ensured his sister was protected, Serena thought.

"We'll have quite the house party again," Marianne said, with a determined cheerfulness that told Serena she was thinking about the loss of her own prospects last night. "With

Hester and her mother, and Serena's Lieutenant Givens—did you not think him very dashing, Dominic?"

His gaze brushed against Serena's. "I'm no judge of dashing, I'm afraid," he said. "I've never had much dash myself."

Serena opened her mouth to protest that he had as much dash as any man could…then realized she would be defending another woman's affianced husband ahead of the man who wanted to be her own.

She held her tongue. Whatever she had hoped, imagined, conjectured…it was over.

There were some things that couldn't be undone.

Dominic was getting married.

Chapter Seventeen

"But why must Papa marry again?" Charlotte demanded.

"It's not that he *must*." Serena tucked a curl of Charlotte's hair behind her ear. The children had been lined up in the entrance hall since one of the grooms had ridden up to report that the Laceys had turned through the gates and would be here in mere minutes. "But remember how God created Eve because it wasn't good for Adam to be alone? Your father will have a wife, and you children will have a new mother."

"I think it's nice," Hetty said. "She and I have the same name."

"Oh, shut up about the stupid name," Thomas said, in a rare moment of impatience with his twin. With his hair slicked back, he looked just like his father. "We don't even know her. We don't need her."

"You remember her perfectly well, Thomas Granville, so don't try telling me otherwise," Hetty said. "It's just the babies who don't."

"I'm not a baby," Charlotte said. "I remember Mama and I don't need a new mother."

"I want her if she's pretty," Louisa said.

"Louisa, you know that what matters is who a person is on the inside," Serena said.

"I just don't know." William sounded about fifty years old, not seven. "I don't know what to think."

"You'll meet her in a few minutes, and you can make up your own mind," Serena said. "But I assure you, Miss Lacey is a very nice lady and was a dear friend of your mother's. You'll all—you children and your father—be very happy." If Serena kept telling herself that, maybe she wouldn't feel so depressed.

"I wanted *you* to marry Papa," Charlotte said. "When he's with you, he likes me."

Serena caught her breath. "Charlotte, your father loves you always." How sad that she still doubted Dominic's feelings. Though Serena might have guessed it would take longer for Charlotte than it would for the others to trust his changing attitude. "Sometimes, two people are so alike, they find it hard to get along," Serena said. "You and your papa are like that."

"I'm not like Papa," Charlotte objected.

"You're both determined to have your way. And you're both kind. But neither of you likes to depend on another person."

"That's not true," Charlotte said halfheartedly. "Besides, I still don't see why you can't—"

"You need to understand this, my girl," Serena said sternly. "I am *not* going to marry your father."

"I'm delighted to hear it," said a voice from the open front door.

Serena whirled around. Miss Lacey stood there, parasol in hand.

Serena curtsied. "Miss Lacey, I'm so sorry. Charlotte is caught up in a—a silly fantasy."

Charlotte gave an angry sob and ran toward the kitchen. Serena hesitated, then gave the new arrival her full attention. "Did you come alone?" Her solo appearance was very odd.

"Mama is a fanatical rose grower," Miss Lacey said. "One

look at the rose garden as we passed, and she demanded the carriage stop immediately. Not being a rose enthusiast myself, I chose to walk the last hundred yards."

Just what Serena would have done. She cast an urgent glance around. "Where is Molson?" Dash it, why couldn't the butler materialize when she actually wanted him to? "He needs to fetch Dom—Mr. Granville."

A flicker of Miss Lacey's eyes registered her near-use of his Christian name.

Serena ran a hand across her forehead. This was all turning out wrong. "Marianne is on her way downstairs," she said. "Oh, dear, I'm so sorry for this appalling welcome."

Just as she finished speaking, she heard the crunch of carriage wheels on gravel. The sound brought Molson—too late, of course!—and Dominic, who emerged from the library. No sixth sense to tell him when his betrothed was on the premises, Serena thought crossly.

Molson was plainly chagrined not to have heard Miss Lacey's arrival. Dominic, on the other hand, was all pleasure.

"Hester," he said warmly, as he approached. She held out both her hands, and he took them as he kissed her cheek.

By the time that sentimental interlude was over, Mrs. Lacey had stepped through the doorway. Dominic introduced the two women to the children. Any hope that he might not notice he was a child short evaporated when he asked, "Where's Charlotte?"

In an almost eerie answer to his question, Charlotte came running from the direction of the kitchen. She had something tucked under her arm. It looked like... Serena groaned. It looked remarkably like a roast chicken.

"Charlotte," Dominic rapped out. "Slow down. Come and greet Miss Lacey."

She slowed, momentarily. Just long enough for him to

register the chicken legs protruding from the towel wrapped around her loot.

"Charlotte…" he growled.

She took off out the front door, still open from the Laceys' arrival.

"Hester, Mrs. Lacey, I do apologize," Dominic said.

"We need to go after her," Serena said.

Dominic barely looked at her. "I'm not about to go running after my daughter."

"She's taking that chicken to a tramp," Serena said.

Now she had his full attention. "*What* did you say?"

"At least, that's what I'm guessing. There's been one other incident since the leg of lamb." At last, she'd confessed.

"Are you saying that, right now, little Charlotte is off befriending a tramp?" Miss Lacey asked.

Not helpful.

"I'm not sure how friendly he is," Serena said cautiously.

Even less helpful, but it had to be said.

"Excuse me, ladies. Molson will serve you tea." Dominic wheeled on the heel of one Hessian boot and strode to the door.

"Dominic," Serena called from the porch. "The Ramsay gamekeeper found signs of a poacher in the East Wood last week. He'll be able to tell you where."

Dominic was heading for the stables. Serena picked up her skirt and sped after him.

"You will be kind to Charlotte when you find her, won't you?" she asked.

"I'll do whatever's necessary," he called over his shoulder.

"She's worried you won't love her once you have a wife," Serena said.

His stride faltered.

"She needs reassurance," Serena said.

"She *needs* to stop stealing food," Dominic said grimly.

Before he reached the stables, Mr. Beaumont rounded the building, mounted on his black horse. He pulled up next to them and dismounted. "Good afternoon. Is Miss Granville in?"

This was the first they'd seen of him since leaving London. He had no idea Marianne had overheard him at the ball. That his scheme was at an end.

"Not to you," Dominic said.

"Mr. Beaumont, did you see Charlotte as you rode through the woods?" Serena asked.

"No." He shook his head. "Has she been feeding tramps again?"

Dominic turned rigid. "What does he know about this?" he asked Serena.

She ignored that. "Mr. Beaumont, would you be able to search the East Wood?"

"Of course." He remounted the horse and left at a gallop.

When Serena turned around, Dominic was gone, too. He soon reappeared, perched on his bay mare.

"Beaumont?" he demanded.

Serena swallowed. "He told me he'd seen Charlotte walking alone in the woods. He offered to keep an eye open for poachers."

"And you didn't tell me?" he demanded. "This is my estate, my daughter."

"Charlotte didn't want you to be angry with her...."

"So you allowed *Beaumont* to get involved? A man without decency?"

Serena didn't believe Beaumont was entirely without decency—witness the way he'd charged off to look for Charlotte. But now wasn't the time to say so.

Dominic left before she could say anything at all.

* * *

Dominic arrived back an hour later to find Serena still pacing on the front steps.

"Marianne is entertaining the Laceys," she said. "I wanted to keep watch for Charlotte."

Beaumont rode up a moment later. He hadn't seen any sign of Charlotte.

Dominic started to pray silently, grimly aware of the approaching dusk.

"If she plans to be outside for a long time, she'll have found somewhere comfortable," Serena said. "She hates to be cold."

Dominic didn't know that.

"Why didn't you say so?" Beaumont asked. "In that case, she'll be in the same place I used to go when I was a child. Check your hayloft, Granville."

Five minutes later, the three of them crept into the barn. Their stealth enabled them to hear Charlotte's voice almost as soon as they entered.

"My papa is Mr. Dominic Granville," she was saying. "He gets very cross—" Dominic bristled…then realized he was indeed getting very cross "—but he's kind," Charlotte said. "He'll help you."

"She has the cursed tramp up there with her," Beaumont hissed.

Dominic signaled for him and Serena to stay where they were. Then, silently, he climbed the ladder. He hadn't been sure what he'd find when he stuck his head over the top, but it certainly wasn't what met his eyes. The small, high window at the back of the loft illuminated Charlotte, lying on her stomach, legs kicked up behind her. Next to her, his face almost touching hers, was a boy. About the same size as Charlotte, but probably older, Dominic decided, if that world-weary look on his face was anything to go by. In front of them, half unwrapped from its cloth, sat what was left of the chicken.

"Charlotte," Dominic said sharply.

She squawked, and the boy scampered backward into a dark corner.

Dominic wanted to shout at her. But Serena's comment about her being worried about his remarriage had stuck in his mind.

"It's dinnertime," he said, as mildly as he could. "If you come down now, you may bring your friend with you."

"You won't summon the magistrate?" she asked.

Did his daughter really think he would have a child jailed? "I won't."

"It's all right, Albert," she said. "Papa says you may eat with us—"

"He'll eat in the kitchen," Dominic said firmly.

Soon, they were walking back to the house. All except Beaumont, whom Dominic had thanked for his help—it went against the grain, but someone had to be the gentleman around here—and sent on his way.

As they headed inside, Dominic heard the convoluted story of how the orphaned Albert had ended up sleeping rough. The boy seemed a lawless brat, but Dominic supposed that in the absence of someone like Charlotte to feed him, stealing might seem the only way to obtain food.

"We can find you a place here," he told Albert. "You'll need to work. Not all the time, because you'll need to learn to read, too. And—" he slid a glance at Serena "—I daresay you should play occasionally."

She beamed.

"One of the tenants might be willing to foster you," Dominic continued. Sarah Mullins in Ivy Cottage would be just the woman—she was kind, but she didn't take any nonsense. If Dominic paid for the boy's upkeep…

He was surprised, and touched, when Charlotte's hand stole into his.

"Papa," she said, as they walked in the front door, "who's that man?"

Everyone—everything—came to a halt.

Waiting in the entrance hall was Lieutenant Alastair Givens.

Marvelous.

Miss Lacey was kind, well-dressed, God-fearing, beautifully mannered, affectionate toward the children and respectfully fond of Dominic. She had a wry sense of humor, she liked things done in an orderly fashion and she believed women should generally not argue with the man of the house, nor engage in noisy dinner table conversation.

She was perfect for Dominic.

Serena had the most unchristian impulse to provoke her into shouting, maybe by upsetting one of Miss Lacey's charming flower arrangements.

But what would that achieve? Even if Miss Lacey turned into a harridan, a gentleman could no more jilt a lady than he could fly to the moon.

Not that Serena should want Dominic to jilt the woman, she reminded herself as she sat sewing in the blue salon with Hester and Mrs. Lacey and Marianne during a restful afternoon. Dominic and Alastair had gone fishing.

The salon door opened, and Molson made his usual silent entrance. "Mr. Beaumont is here, Miss Granville."

Marianne's color flared, she'd given up on all her creams and potions, but her complexion was no worse. Or better. "I'm not at home," she reminded the butler.

Molson had been instructed that Miss Granville was "not at home" to Mr. Beaumont whenever he might appear.

"I've told him, Miss Granville, but Mr. Beaumont refuses to accept the excuse. He insists on seeing you."

Miss Lacey and her mother were politely pretending deafness. Serena said tentatively, "Marianne, if you wish me to speak to him…"

She shook her head. "Show Mr. Beaumont into the red salon, please, Molson. I'll be there shortly." She turned to their guests. "Will you excuse me? Serena, could you come with me?"

They went upstairs, where Marianne's maid tidied her hair.

"I don't want to see him alone," Marianne said, watching the maid's progress in the mirror. "Serena, would you mind attending our interview?"

"If that's what you wish, of course."

Marianne made a last adjustment to the neckline of her dress. She sighed as she looked in the mirror—her color had risen noticeably in the past few minutes—then squared her shoulders. "I'm as ready as ever I'll be."

Disappointment flashed across Mr. Beaumont's face when he saw Serena. He masked it quickly and stepped toward Marianne, effectively shutting Serena out of his line of sight.

"It's been so long," he said to Marianne. "I'm worried that I've offended you in some way."

"We have guests, the Laceys, occupying our time," she replied. "You may have heard that my brother is to marry Miss Lacey?"

"I did hear," he said. "I haven't seen you since you disappeared from the Spenford ball. I was reminded of Cinderella's vanishing act."

"Cinderella was fleeing a prince," Marianne pointed out.

He blinked, disconcerted. Then he laughed. "I meant more that you were the mysterious, vanished beauty than that I was a prize catch," he said ruefully. "I wanted to waltz with you, but I got cornered by some parson chappie, couldn't get away."

Serena straightened. "Do you mean my father?"

"Does your father keep rubbing his chin?" he asked, acknowledging her at last. At her nod, he said, "That explains a lot. Fellow read me a couple of sermons, though he could see I wanted to get back to the dancing. Like father, like daughter."

He sounded so disgusted, Serena had an improper urge to laugh.

"Mr. Beaumont, how dare you be rude about my friend," Marianne said coldly. "Or her father, a most admirable man." Her tone said *unlike you*.

"I didn't—I just meant he was a bit long-winded—I'm sorry." Beaumont ran a hand around the back of his neck. "Marianne—Miss Granville, I can tell I've done something wrong, and I'm not just talking about Miss Somerton's father. Let me make it up to you. Would you and Miss Somerton care to visit Farley Hall one day this week? I have discovered a plant that may be your lemon balm."

Marianne hesitated. "Thank you, but I no longer have need of it."

It seemed that was Beaumont's best offer. Silence fell.

Marianne hadn't ordered refreshments, so there was nothing to fill the conversational void. "Thank you for your visit," she said in dismissal, as she stood.

Beaumont seemed perplexed, but he couldn't refuse such an obvious cue to leave. "May I call on you after church tomorrow?"

"Miss Lacey and I will be practicing music," she said.

"On Monday, then?"

"I'm sorry, we have plans."

"I'm having trouble deciding on my next move," he said.

Did he mean in chess, or in courtship? Serena wondered.

"Please don't tax yourself," Marianne said. "It's only a game."

At last even Beaumont could no longer avoid the conclusion that he was out of favor. His bow was stiff. "I will leave you, then."

"Good day, Mr. Beaumont," Marianne said. Momentarily, she looked as if she would run from the room and burst into tears. Instead, she stood there, face crimson but head held high, until Beaumont left.

Chapter Eighteen

On Monday, Serena and Marianne drove into Melton Mowbray with Hester, escorted by Lieutenant Givens. Instead of enjoying the peace, Dominic found himself bored in his library. He knew a sudden hankering to spend time with his children.

Up in the nursery, he received a rapturous welcome, its warmth fueled by his offer to play dominoes.

Thomas fetched the game from the cupboard. Dominic shuffled the dominoes, moving them around facedown on the nursery table. "Would you like to draw first, Charlotte?"

"Yes, please, Papa," she said. As was her way, the words were correct, but her action—she snatched the first tile with an eagerness that seemed mostly about preventing anyone else from having it—was graceless and hasty.

On the verge of scolding her as the draw moved around the table, Dominic checked himself. Now that he'd made the effort to come up here, best not to add a sour note. He reached out and ruffled Charlotte's hair. "You're a curious miss."

She stared at him.

"What?" he asked.

She ducked her head and began to help Louisa draw her tiles.

What was bothering her now? he wondered. Then he realized she was smiling. He supposed he didn't often touch Charlotte—she was so prickly it felt like reaching out to a hedgehog.

Beside him, William yawned, stretching his mouth impossibly wide, as he inspected his tiles.

"Put your hand over your mouth," Dominic reminded him. William complied.

"Why are you so tired?" Dominic asked.

"No reason," he muttered.

Hetty was giving Dominic a significant look. So was Thomas. William must have had an attack of his fear of the dark. On closer inspection, Dominic could see his face was pale with exhaustion, and his thin shoulders seemed to carry the weight of the world.

Dominic pushed back his chair. "Come with me," he told his son.

"What about our game?" Charlotte asked.

"Play one round without us. I'm leaving you in charge."

That drew immediate protest from Hetty and Thomas, but he told them to mind Charlotte. Then he walked up to the attic with William.

"Why are we here, Papa?" William held his father's hand, demonstrating complete trust in him. Dominic thought of Mrs. Gordon, and her suggestion his son be locked in a cupboard, and felt sick.

"There's something I wish to give you." He saw his target, the old toy chest that had sat in the nursery when he was a child. "Over here."

He brushed dust off the chest, and opened it. William coughed at the dust, but then dug into the box and was soon laughing at some of the antiquated toys. Of course, many of the things Dominic had played with were used by his children today. These were the oldest and most dilapidated, things his sentimental nurse hadn't been able to throw away.

Dominic found what he wanted near the bottom. "Here it is." He pulled out a tattered, knitted dog stuffed with rags.

Hmm, he didn't remember it looking quite this disreputable.

"What is it?" William asked.

Dominic began stowing the other things back in the trunk. "When I was your age, William, or in fact a little older, I was terrified of dogs."

The boy gave an uncertain chuckle.

"You mock my fear?" Dominic teased.

William smiled. "You have two dogs, Papa, and you're not afraid. You're brave."

"I'm not afraid now, at least not of dogs. And it's easy to be brave when we don't have to face our fears," Dominic said. Which made him think of losing Emily. Of his children. Of marrying again and the fact one could never be certain that the people one loved would always be safe.

He drew a deep breath. "My fear wasn't a problem when I was very young, because my family didn't keep dogs. *You* have to face your fear every night."

William's smile vanished. He scuffed the floor with his slipper.

"When I was ten years old," Dominic said, "my father took a sudden fancy to have a dog. He was having his portrait painted and thought a dog in the scene would be just the thing."

"That portrait that hangs in the gallery?" William asked, intrigued. "That's a gigantic dog!" He darted a glance of sympathy at Dominic. "Were you afraid?"

"Terrified," Dominic admitted. "When I first saw it, I ran upstairs and cried like Louisa."

William's peal of laughter warmed his heart.

"I didn't let anyone see me, of course," he confided.

William, no stranger to attempting to conceal his fear, nodded.

"My father doted on the dog," Dominic said. "He let it have the run of the house. Every time I stepped outside the nursery I was convinced it would tear me limb from limb. I couldn't stop thinking about the monster, even when it was nowhere about."

"What did you do?" William appeared to be holding his breath.

"I used this." Dominic showed him the stuffed animal. "My nurse knitted it for me and stuffed it with old stockings. Every time I got that sick, terrified feeling, I hung on to this for dear life. And I prayed."

"I've prayed that God will take away my fear," William said. "But He hasn't."

"Sometimes He takes away our troubles. Other times, He gives us the strength to live with them." Again, Dominic thought about losing Emily.

"I don't want to live with my trouble," William protested.

"No one does," he agreed. "But a man knows life doesn't always go exactly the way he wants. To have Someone who'll never leave us, whatever befalls—that's a true blessing."

"So did God stay with you when you were afraid of the dog?" William asked.

"The monster," Dominic corrected him, and William giggled. "He did stay with me. I was still afraid, but I could bear it." Dominic suddenly remembered something. "I had a song I used to sing."

His son's mouth gaped. "What song?"

Dominic was already regretting the admission. But in for a penny... "It went like this." The tune was unsophisticated, but easily memorized, and he sang confidently. "He is with me, He is with me, my Lord will never leave me. He is with me, He is with me, and with Him I will overcome."

The words didn't say much…and yet they said it all.

"He is with me…" William started to sing, off-key, of course, but trailed off as he forgot the words.

"Let's sing it together," Dominic suggested.

After half a dozen practices, William had committed the words, if not the tune, to memory.

Dominic stood, brushing dust from his pantaloons. Trimble would huff with disapproval when he caught sight of them. William finished packing the last toys back into the chest.

"Would you like to take the dog?" Dominic asked, seeing the knitted toy disappearing into the depths.

"Thank you very much, Papa, but I'm too old for that," seven-year-old William said, with a scrupulous politeness that put the once ten-year-old Dominic firmly in his place.

As they walked back downstairs, hand in hand, they sang the song again, at the tops of their voices, hands swinging. When they reached the servants' floor landing, Serena was waiting, one hand on the newel post, watching them descend.

Her smile was so wide Dominic could have gotten lost in it.

"Dominic," she scolded, "I can't believe it."

He checked William's pants, brushed at his son's backside. "We're only a little dusty," he said defensively. Which made William giggle.

"Not that." Of course, she was the last person to object to a little dust-raising.

"Off you go, William." Dominic patted his son's shoulder.

"Yes, Papa. Excuse me, Miss Somerton." He scampered away.

"Now." Dominic smiled at Serena, and felt the kick of

pleasure at looking into her sparkling eyes. "What have I done that's so reprehensible?"

"You blamed *me* for your children's appalling musical performance," she said severely.

"You were their teacher," he said. "Who else— Oh." He drew himself up. "Miss Somerton, are you saying I can't sing?"

"Let's just say it's clear the children, with the exception of Charlotte, inherited their musical abilities from you."

He pressed a fist to his chest. "I'm wounded!"

She laughed, and it sounded like music itself. "They do say the truth hurts."

He chuckled. "And Thomas Gray's poem says ignorance is bliss. I'm glad William doesn't know he can't hold a tune. It might put him off using that song."

"Using it?" She leaned against the banister, her face turned up to his in inquiry.

"An old ditty I employed to overcome my childhood fear of dogs."

"I had no idea you were afraid of dogs."

"I was forced to deal with it when my father acquired an animal that wanted to kill me."

She pressed her lips together, but her eyes brimmed with merriment.

"Ha! I should have known better than to expect sympathy. William took my story to heart," he said, "even if you mock me."

"I heard the words of your song," she said, serious now. "Simple but perfect."

"You're speaking to the composer," he said with pride.

"No!" Her eyes danced. "Dominic, is there no end to your talents?"

"Apparently there is, since you say singing isn't one of them."

"Which makes it all the more admirable that you were able to compose a song while completely tone deaf," she pointed out.

He found himself laughing, as he so often did with her. "Is that your idea of a compliment, Miss Somerton?"

"Of course."

"Only you could find a positive aspect to tone deafness," he said. "I daresay if I were to fall down these stairs now you'd extol the joys of a broken neck to me."

For an instant, fear and horror chased across her features, as if the prospect of him sustaining such an injury was more than she could bear. Then she said, "The time spent recovering would give you ample time to read. Your children would see so much more of you, and I would have the chance to lecture you about the changes I think you should make to your way of life, thus fulfilling my insatiable desire to order you around."

He laughed. "You see what I mean? I dread to think how gloomy we'll be without you."

He spoke lightly, but the moment the words left his mouth, he knew they were true.

Serena brought light and laughter…and love…to his home. To his heart.

No, his heart wasn't relevant here.

She broke the tense silence to say, "I know that's not true. Marianne has come through her failed romance with Mr. Beaumont a much stronger person. And the children are excited about having a new mother. And—and you will be a husband again, with a helpmeet and a life companion." She smiled so brightly, it seemed beyond natural.

None of her assurances meant anything. Realization slammed Dominic.

I love Serena.

But that couldn't be true. Emily…

Loving Emily hadn't stopped Dominic from falling in love with the woman in front of him.

With Serena.

The concept was dizzying. Even more dizzying was the fact that loving Serena didn't diminish his love for Emily.

He loved her flushed cheeks and her bright eyes, her kind nature, her tender heart. The employee who dared tell him he couldn't sing a note and that he neglected his children. The parson's daughter who dealt out sermons without hesitation, and tortured herself over her own youthful failings. Her mischievous sense of humor that had him worrying what she might do next. Her tender love for his children. Her deep and true faith. *I love her.*

"Dominic? Are you all right?" Serena stretched out a hand toward him, but let it drop before it reached his arm.

She couldn't touch him, nor he her.

Because he was promised to another.

Chapter Nineteen

When Alastair invited Serena to take a turn about the rose garden with him on Tuesday morning, she suggested instead that they walk down to the lake. The rose garden… Dominic had touched her chin there.

So the lake it was. A longer walk, but she needed the invigoration. She'd felt so oppressed since they'd returned from London.

With her arm tucked in Alastair's, she strolled the edge of the lake beneath cloudless skies. Serena pointed out the water lilies that guests usually admired.

"Delightful," Alastair said. He closed his free hand over hers where it rested in the crook of his elbow. "I wish I didn't need to leave today."

He was such a nice young man. In so many ways he was the Alastair she remembered. In other ways, he wasn't. Her heart no longer beat faster at the sight of him. Which Dominic would doubtless consider far more sensible than the absurd tattoo her heart set up whenever she thought of— *I won't think about him.*

"Your parents will be longing for you to return home," Serena said. "You've only had, what, one night with them so far?"

"That couldn't be helped. When one's general summons, one obeys."

"Your mother will be desperate to fatten you up." Over the past few days, she'd heard the full story of Alastair's survival. How he'd been injured in battle, left for dead when his regiment retreated. A Portuguese baker and his wife had nursed him until he was well enough to start back for England. But he'd been caught en route, charged with spying and left to molder in a prison cell for four years. During which time he'd gathered from his fellow prisoners some intelligence of considerable use to his general, even now that the war was over. Then he'd escaped, and made his way back to England.

"I've missed Mother's cooking," he admitted.

"Your mother has always been very pleasant to me," Serena said. "I hope she won't despise me after learning of our secret betrothal." She'd urged him to confess the truth to his parents.

"Of course she won't." He squeezed her fingertips. "Serena, I must ask your forgiveness."

She stilled. "Have you changed your mind? You no longer wish to marry me?"

"As if that could ever be the case!" He stopped walking. "It was wrong of me to ask you to marry me, knowing your parents disapproved."

"No more wrong than it was of me to accept," she said.

"I was older than you, I should have known better."

"You were eighteen to my sixteen." She removed her hand from his arm and took a step back. "Alastair, we both erred."

"But you were the one forced to see your parents every day while keeping our secret. No doubt you saw my parents in church every Sunday, too."

She smiled ruefully. "They're very regular attendees."

"You must have felt the burden every time you saw them," he said.

She nodded. "I did feel awful, but then…well, it was less than a year before we learned you were missing, presumed dead." Her voice caught at the memory of that dismal time. Of his mother's sobs and his father's ashen stoicism. Of her own tears, wept into her pillow so no one else would hear. "The worst thing was, I couldn't even wear mourning," she said. "Your parents wore black the entire twelve months afterward… How I wished I could make public my loss."

He took her hands. "I'm sorry, my love. I thought of you every day, it's what got me through. I prayed you'd wait for me—that sounds selfish, I know."

"No," she said. Although it did, a little. "You needed to hold out hope."

"Most people don't get a second chance, the way we have," he said.

Serena knew what was coming next.

Alastair tugged her closer. "Serena, we haven't talked of our feelings since that night at the ball—I don't blame you after I made such a hash of things." For an awful moment, she thought he would go down on one knee; mercifully, he stayed upright. "I know your father insists we wait three months before we're betrothed, and we will. But my love for you is as strong as ever. Before I leave for Piper's Mead, it would mean the world to me to know you feel the same. That when the time comes, you'll agree to be my wife."

He carried her right hand to his lips, kissed her palm. "I love you," he declared.

And waited.

"Alastair, I…" Explanations hovered on her lips. *It's too soon. I still feel guilty. My feelings are confused.*

All those were true. But none were The Truth that would stop her ever saying yes to his proposal.

"Serena?" He tugged at her hand.

"Alastair, I'm so sorry." She withdrew from his clasp. "I can't."

"You think it's improper for us to discuss this before the three months are up."

"No, we're both of age, it's not that." She drew a deep breath of lake-scented air. "I'm no longer in love with you."

He stumbled backward. "What?"

"Love needs to be nurtured," she said. "Nourished by each other's company. My love for you didn't survive our separation, though I never realized that."

He ran a shaking hand over his face, and turned away.

"I'm so sorry," she said again. "I only just now understood, else I never would have encouraged you to hope."

"You said I still had your heart!" His voice was muffled.

"I believed it. Indeed, I wished it, after we'd behaved so improperly. But when you left, you were just a boy, I a mere girl."

"Soldiers have been away longer and come home to wives who haven't tired of them," he accused.

"I thought you were dead," Serena protested. "I didn't decide not to love you—it was a natural consequence that eventually my heart moved on."

"Are you in love with Granville?" he demanded.

Her chest constricted. "No!" She didn't deny Dominic was the kind of man who— But he wasn't for her.

"Then why can't we start again?" Alastair asked.

"Because..." All of a sudden the words came to her. Dominic's words. "Because I'm free of my guilt." Dominic had told her that, when he'd first learned of her betrothal. "Because a second chance doesn't have to mean reworking old mistakes. It can be brand-new." He'd told her that the night Alastair returned.

At last she understood.

* * *

When Dominic entered the drawing room after dinner, he found Marianne and Hester playing a hand of whist. Mrs. Lacey was engrossed in a large and rather ugly, in his inexpert opinion, embroidery project. His eye was drawn to a far more pleasant sight: Serena, seated at the escritoire over by the window, writing.

"Dominic, you're here. I'll order tea," Marianne said.

"I'll do it," he replied. "Finish your game."

He crossed the room to pull the bell, then walked over to Serena. She'd been pale and quiet during dinner, but now her cheeks were flushed, her eyes bright. As if—his heart clenched—as if she might have been sitting here with her back to the other ladies, crying.

When she realized he was nearby, she moved, as if to shield her writing from him.

"Writing letters?" he asked.

She nodded.

"To Lieutenant Givens, I presume." It must be the lieutenant's departure this afternoon that had upset her. Though to start writing when the man would barely be thirty miles away by now seemed excessive.

She cleared her throat. "I'm writing to my parents."

Relief he wasn't entitled to surged through him. "They'll be glad to have you near them when you marry." He paced away from her a few steps, then turned back. "No doubt you're already missing Lieutenant Givens."

It sounded like an accusation. Serena turned a shocked expression on him.

"That was impertinent," he said stiffly. "Forgive me."

"There's nothing to forgive." She glanced over at the ladies. "But…perhaps I should tell you…to avoid any awkwardness that might result from unconscious comments…" She glanced down at her letter.

"What is it?" he asked.

"I'm writing to inform my parents that Lieutenant Givens and I…" She drew a breath. "I've told him I won't marry him."

Blood rushed in Dominic's ears. "You *what?*" he barked.

The other ladies' heads turned in their direction.

Serena pressed her lips together. He'd heard her correctly.

"Since when?" he asked more quietly, but with no less urgency. "Why?" He realized he was being impertinent again, and he didn't care a fig.

Her cheeks turned pink, but she held his gaze. "My feelings had undergone a change," she said. "I could no longer marry him."

Serena was not to be betrothed. Her affections were unengaged.

"You told him he still had your heart." Confound it, Dominic had interrogated her on that very subject!

"I made a mistake." She busied herself folding her letter.

"Blast it, Serena…" He wanted to shake her for not coming to this realization sooner; he wanted to shout for joy.

He could do neither.

It's too late.

The knowledge hit him. Joy drained away, leaving him empty.

Serena might be free, but *he* wasn't. He was to marry Hester.

Dominic spun away, before Serena could see the despair in his eyes.

While he was composing himself, the tea tray arrived. Hester stacked the playing cards into a neat pile, then moved to the sofa. She smiled at Dominic, expecting him to join her there.

He would do so, of course. Just as he would marry her next month. A gentleman couldn't jilt a lady without ruining her reputation forever. A gentleman always did his duty, always took care of those entitled to his protection.

He walked to the sofa and sat down.

The mood in the drawing room started subdued and turned downright depressing, in Serena's view. She suspected her parents wouldn't be too upset at the news she didn't plan to marry Alastair, but she hadn't enjoyed telling them. Nor had she enjoyed telling Dominic, who'd then gone to sit with Hester, and not so much as looked at Serena again. Did he feel she should have done more to atone for her past? Had he not meant those things he'd said, that she'd quoted to Alastair?

Marianne pleaded a headache soon after the tea arrived, and that served as a cue for the ladies to retire.

Serena changed into her nightdress, then donned her dressing gown. She found what she wanted in her chest of drawers, then walked along the candlelit hallway to Marianne's room. In response to her tap on the door, her friend called her in.

"I brought you some powdered cinchona bark," Serena said. "My mother swears by it for a headache."

"Thank you." Marianne took the screw of paper. "My own remedy—a ginger inhalation—doesn't seem to be working." She indicated the steaming bowl on her dressing table.

Serena poured her a cup of cold water from the jug the maid had left. Marianne tipped in the powder, then downed it. She grimaced. "Ugh."

A rattle against her window startled them both.

"Could it be hail?" Serena wondered.

"There was no sign of bad weather—the sunset was gorgeous," Marianne said. "And there's almost a full moon, no cloud."

Another rattle came, this one louder.

"Someone's throwing stones at your window," Serena realized.

Marianne crossed the room and peered through the glass. "There's a man on the lawn... Oh, my!" She turned back to Serena, her fingers pressed to her lips. "It's Beaumont."

"Close the curtains," Serena advised.

Yet another rattle made Marianne jump. "I'd better open this before he breaks the glass. Or worse, brings everyone in here to see what's happening." She struggled to raise the sash. Serena didn't move to help.

"Marianne, how does Mr. Beaumont know which is your window?" she asked.

Her friend spun around. "Serena, I swear, this hasn't happened before. But he did ask me one day when we were walking across the lawn, and I pointed out this room."

Serena nodded, believing her, but disapproving.

"Could you help me, please?" Marianne demanded. "I need to send him away before he wakes everyone."

That did seem the best plan. With Serena's assistance, the window slid up. Marianne leaned out. Before she should speak, Beaumont called, "Marianne, I need to talk to you."

"It's Miss Granville to you."

Oh, for goodness sake! Serena ranged herself alongside her friend and stuck her head out. "Go home, Mr. Beaumont, before I call Mr. Granville."

"Ah, Miss Somerton. How delightful."

Marianne giggled. The sound must have reached Beaumont, because in the light of the moon, his face filled with hope. "Marianne, tell me what I've done wrong. How else will I know how to put it right?"

"You can't put it right," she said, her own face flooding with color as remembered hurt rushed back.

"I miss you," he said. "I miss your letters. The game isn't as compelling without them."

"Marianne, are you still playing chess with him?" Serena demanded.

Marianne pulled her head back inside. "It's the best game of my life, and it's not finished. But I swear, all we're exchanging is chess moves, just as I would with a stranger."

She did, too, through the Grosvenor Chess Club, the more remote members of which thrived on their games played through the mail. Still, it didn't seem right.

Marianne stuck her head out the window once more in response to a call from Beaumont. "What did you say?"

"Bishop to F3."

Serena rolled her eyes as Marianne abandoned the window and went to move the black bishop. "That's my knight," she grumbled, removing one of the white chess pieces from the board. She returned to the window. "I've made the move— I'll let you know mine tomorrow by messenger. Now, go."

"I'm not leaving until you tell me what I've done to deserve this coldness." Beaumont folded his arms.

"*Deserve* this…" Words failed Marianne. "Fine," she flared. "You want to know? I'll tell you."

If this was to turn into a full debate, Serena wasn't about to perch in the window throughout. It was enough that Beaumont knew her friend was chaperoned.

She went to sit on the bed, from where she couldn't see outside unless she sat up straight and craned her neck. She would still hear their conversation, but wasn't quite so intrusive.

"Is Miss Somerton still there?" Beaumont called.

"Yes, she is, and she's staying."

"Some things should be said privately," Beaumont stated. "Not shouted for all to hear. Will you come down and meet me?"

"Of course not!"

"I meant, with Miss Somerton watching from the window. You couldn't come down otherwise."

Marianne exchanged a confused look with Serena. Surely Beaumont would prefer she come down unchaperoned. Compromising her would guarantee that he could marry her.

Serena shrugged, she didn't know what to make of the man. "You may go down if you wish. You're twenty-five years old, so I can't stop you. It's not exactly regular, but if I'm watching from the window... You'll need to put your dress back on, however."

"As if I'd go outside in my dressing gown," Marianne said. She thought for a moment, then called to Beaumont, "I've discovered that the words you utter in my company are very different from what you say about me to others. I won't open myself to that deception again. I'm staying here."

"What do you mean, my words are different?"

She told him how she and Serena had overheard him talking at the Spenford ball, reminded him of the atrocious things he'd said in verbatim detail, though it obviously pained her.

Serena expected him to concoct some story about how he'd been trying to protect her from his friend, who had villainous intentions, or some such nonsense.

When Marianne finished, there was a long silence.

Marianne shivered when a breeze gusted in the window.

Serena craned to see. Beaumont was standing in the same place, clutching his head.

Giving himself time to think of a story?

"Marianne, I've been an ass," he called. "The world's biggest fool."

"What, for blabbing your true intentions where I might overhear? For ruining your shot at my five thousand a year?"

Serena nodded in approval, but Marianne wasn't looking at her.

He groaned. "Yes, for all that! And for being so weak,

for caring what people might think to see me married to a woman with—with your affliction."

Marianne gasped, hurt.

"Babcock—that's the friend I was with—his words cut me at a place where I'm vulnerable," he said. "You've heard from your brother, no doubt, about my father. His drunkenness."

"Yes."

"Because of his addiction, our family was forced to live in seclusion," Beaumont said. "There was always the fear that others would find out how bad he was, and there was no money left to live a town life, in any case. When my mother died and I found myself with a small inheritance, I went straight to London, as I'd always dreamed of doing."

"He loves the city," Marianne reminded Serena.

"I discovered my—my appearance was considered pleasing, and I had an instinct for dressing well and getting on with people," Beaumont said. "I wasn't cooped up alone at home—I had friends, pastimes. I was happy for the first time in my life."

"Drinking and gambling," Marianne said.

"And other activities. Hang it, Marianne, it was fun. If it hadn't got out of hand, if I'd been able to afford the life that suited me..."

"He looks upset," Marianne commented.

Serena stretched to see again. Beaumont was pacing beneath the window. "I feel like I'm the Nurse in *Romeo and Juliet*," she muttered.

"But it did get out of hand," Beaumont admitted, "and although I came to faith and was able to deal with some of my problems, I realized marriage to an heiress would be the best way to preserve my way of life."

"So you chose me," Marianne said bitterly.

"Only because my first two attempts failed," he said, with a candor that shocked Serena. "You seemed an easier mark, out here in the country with no competition for me. And your insecurity about your appearance."

"You're shameless." Marianne's voice shook with anger.

"That's where you're wrong, more fool me." Beaumont sounded bitter. "With Miss Somerton hinting at my lack of Christian virtues and your brother appealing to a better nature we all know I don't have...I lost my nerve."

"That's why you didn't come back after the house party supper dance?" Marianne asked.

"I'm a slightly better matrimonial prospect now that I'm my uncle's heir, so I decided the best thing—for you—would be if I returned to London, to have another crack at Miss Deverell."

"Who has not as much money as I do, but a very nice complexion," Marianne said tartly.

Beaumont said nothing.

"Ask him what happened with Miss Deverell," Serena said. The way Beaumont's mind worked was oddly compelling.

Marianne rolled her eyes, but asked the question.

"I think I could still have her," Beaumont said carelessly. "But, hang it, Marianne, since you've stopped writing to me—the letters, not the chess moves—I've realized...I care for you."

What, exactly, did that mean?

Marianne drew a shuddery breath. "You can't *care* for me, yet want to leave me at home while you gallivant around enjoying yourself."

"I wouldn't do that! I admit, when Babcock talked about your looks, and how we would appear together, I panicked. I'm only recently accepted into society, and I've had enough of rustication to last me several lifetimes. I don't want to lose what's been so hard-won."

"You're crazy," Marianne said.

"But even more, I don't want to lose you," Beaumont said. "Marianne, if you'll marry me, there'll be no talk of leaving you behind. I'd want you with me."

"With you while you spend my five thousand a year?" she said sweetly.

Beaumont uttered a word no Christian should say.

But then, Beaumont wasn't your regular Christian. He was, as he called it, a work in progress. *Which we all are,* Serena reminded herself.

"Marianne, I love you!" He sounded so wretched, Serena could almost believe it.

Almost.

Marianne was crying quietly. She drew a deep breath to steady her voice, then said, "I don't believe you, Geoffrey. I don't trust you. Even if you think you mean it—"

"I know I mean it, woman!"

"—you don't have the—the steadiness of character I admire." She paused. "Goodbye, Mr. Beaumont."

She stepped back, tugged on the window. It crashed down with no help from Serena. Marianne pulled the curtains across, then turned, leaning against them, breathing heavily.

"He's a very unusual man," Serena said. "Very persuasive. But, Marianne, I think you did the right thing."

"Did I?" Her smile was bleak. "I don't know about that. But I do know that Geoffrey Beaumont is a powerful temptation for me. And the best cure for temptation is to remove oneself from its path."

Chapter Twenty

❧

At breakfast, Dominic learned from Serena that his sister had had a late-night visitor.

"So you think it's all over between them?" he asked at the end of her long, complicated report.

Before she could reply, Marianne walked into the breakfast room. She had circles beneath her eyes.

"I took his bishop, the one that took my knight," she announced with dark satisfaction as she poured her coffee.

"You're still playing chess with him?" Serena asked. "What happened to removing yourself from temptation?"

Marianne let out a hiss. "I won't see him again, I won't write him a letter. But this game is nearly over, and I need to finish it." She added two lumps of sugar to her coffee. "I sent a groom to Farley Hall with my move."

"You look as if you've been contemplating the chessboard all night," Dominic said.

Beaumont's move came by return messenger, along with a terse note informing Marianne he was leaving for London today, and she should send her next move to his lodgings in Curzon Street.

The Laceys left that day, too. As Mrs. Lacey said, the wedding wouldn't organize itself, and she needed to be back in

London. Dominic told himself that the unmistakable lightness that came over him as soon as they'd left was from the departure of his mother-in-law, not his bride.

A week later, he received a letter from his friend Severn, mentioning that Geoffrey Beaumont had once more been seen driving in Hyde Park with the pretty Miss Deverell.

Marianne clamped her lips together at the news.

Dominic raised his eyebrows at Serena across the breakfast table, to ask if his sister was all right. But she'd already told him Marianne wasn't confiding her feelings at the moment. Serena could only shrug in response.

The other letter he'd opened was a suggested list of wedding guests from Mrs. Lacey. Dominic handed it to Marianne. "Could you deal with this, my dear?"

"Of course. Serena, will you help me?"

Dominic pushed back his chair and left the room, intending to finish the rest of his correspondence in the library.

He'd been there only a few minutes when Serena tapped on the open door.

"Dominic, may I come in?"

"Of course." He sat back in his chair, but didn't put down the paper he was reading. He maintained what he'd decided was the safest demeanor toward her: polite distance. Much as it had been before all this had started. Before he'd fired her as governess; before she'd decided to tell him what he'd now realized were a few home truths about his children and his skills as a father. "Don't close the door," he told her, as she was about to do just that.

"I wanted to talk privately."

"No one will come by at this hour," he said. "Leave it open."

Dominic wasn't prepared to negotiate on that point. He'd met with Serena in here with the door closed before, as was entirely acceptable for an employer with an employee. But now…now that he was in love with her, a state of heart from which he was determined to extricate himself…well, he would rather not—he *should* not—be alone with her at all.

"Will this take long?" he asked curtly. "I have things to do." Such as get her out of his library as fast as possible. He gestured her to a seat, but she remained standing.

"Not long at all," she said coolly. "I wish to resign my position."

She might as well have pulled the chair out from beneath him.

With his right hand, he fumbled for the edge of the desk. "May I ask why?"

"I miss my family." Her gaze slid away from his. "I've spoken to Marianne, and she feels she won't need my companionship once you are married. I'd like to leave as soon as possible."

"There are still four weeks before…" He couldn't say *my wedding*. "And then another three weeks afterward…" He would be on a honeymoon—Hester had an old longing to see Scotland that he'd promised to indulge. Some small compensation for not having a husband who loved her.

The thought of a honeymoon, and all it entailed… He felt slightly ill. Which couldn't be a good sign.

"I must finish here now," Serena snapped.

"Well, you can't," he snapped back.

"Excuse me, sir." Molson had materialized next to the desk.

Serena squawked.

"Blast it, Molson," Dominic roared, "could you stop doing that?"

The butler showed not a flicker of remorse. It wasn't until Serena glared at him that his lips pursed ever so slightly. "Mr. Beaumont is here, sir. He stormed the staircase, shoving young Gregory—" the lizard-hating footman "—out of the way, and is right now in the blue salon, saying he won't budge until he sees Miss Granville." Molson cleared his throat. "Miss Granville's maid overheard this, and has gone to fetch her mistress."

Dominic rounded on Serena. "You'd leave Woodbridge Hall, leave Marianne, with all this drama going on?"

"At the rate these two play chess, this or something like it could be going on forever," Serena said. "And if you think I'm going to stay here when…"

"When what?" he demanded.

She swept out of the room, saying over her shoulder, "Consider my notice given, Mr. Granville. One more week, and I'll be on the mail coach to Hampshire."

Serena walked as quickly as she could, but Dominic's long stride soon caught her up. They arrived at the door to the blue salon together, at the same time as Marianne. She pushed past them to enter first.

Beaumont stood by the window, his usual immaculate, polished self. When he saw Marianne, he strolled toward her, a picture of elegance.

"What do you want?" she asked, with an absence of good manners that made Serena raise her eyebrows.

Beaumont's mouth curled in a cat-got-the-cream smile. He glanced down, adjusted his already perfect shirt cuffs, then met Marianne's eyes.

"Knight to E3," he said.

Dominic groaned.

Marianne actually paled. "Isn't that…"

"Yes, it is, madam," he said. "Checkmate."

Serena gasped. Had anyone beaten Marianne in recent years?

Her friend rallied, though she seemed shaken. "If you think this changes anything…"

"I'm not here to argue, I'm here to claim my prize." Beaumont swept her into his arms and caught her up in a kiss that was most definitely not for public viewing.

Dominic dragged the man away from his sister. "How dare you, sir! If you don't want me to call you out—"

"Hang it," Beaumont said, as he tore free of Dominic's hold, "what is it with you Christian fellows and your determination to break the sixth commandment? I've already fought two duels this week, and I have no interest in a third." As he adjusted his cuffs again, he added piously, "Besides, dueling's against the law."

Marianne, who'd been standing frozen since he'd kissed her, her hand to her lips, said, "*Two* duels? Geoffrey, what on earth…"

He grinned, and his elegant air fell away. "I exaggerate, sweetest. In one of them we both fired in the air. It was only Anthony Deverell who was determined to put a bullet through me."

Marianne swayed, and didn't object when Beaumont chafed her hand between his.

"And why did Miss Deverell's brother call you out?" Dominic demanded grimly.

"The usual reason," Beaumont said. "I insulted his sister's honor—no, not in that way." He held up a palm to ward off the suspicions of every person in the room. "It's all Miss Somerton's fault, actually." He jerked his head toward Serena.

"Mine?"

"Your father's, anyway." Beaumont had somehow managed to catch hold of Marianne's other hand and was running his thumb over her knuckles. "I got talking to him at that ball about the problem of a man's past sins being held over him, and he said that men find it harder to forgive than God does. That sometimes confessing our sins to each other is important."

"He has been known to say that," Serena admitted.

"I told him it was twaddle. If I blabbed my transgressions I'd lose everything I value—my standing in the ton, my friends. If God had forgiven me, that was good enough."

"Then how did you end up dueling?" Marianne asked.

He grimaced. "After I spoke to you the other night, I realized you didn't believe I could change. And as long as no one else knew quite how bad I'd been, I could get away with staying the way I am. So I thought I'd try Reverend Somerton's trick—I apologized to the two young ladies I'd pursued for their fortunes, and left in their hands whether or not to expose me as a self-declared fortune hunter."

"And they did?" Marianne asked, with a kind of horrified outrage.

He nodded. "I must admit, I'd hoped they'd be more forgiving. But no, they both had to have their brothers try to shoot me."

Serena looked at Dominic and found him stifling a laugh. Which meant she could stop holding in her own smile.

"But, Mr. Beaumont, are you saying you've now lost those things that are so important to you?" she asked. "Your friends, your standing?"

"I hope not," he said. "But there's a good chance I have. Though I did meet another relative of yours, Miss Somerton—your aunt, Miss Jane Somerton."

"You know Aunt Jane?"

"Met her in church on Sunday, after my duel with Deverell," he said. "Told her a little of my woes—she's like your father, a deuced good listener. She said if I manage to convince Marianne to marry me, she might invite us to a dinner or two, if it'll help reestablish me. If it doesn't work—" he lifted one shoulder "—we can spend the Season at Harrogate or somewhere else a bit less particular than London."

Since Aunt Jane was the niece of the Duke of Medway, her support would certainly help.

Beaumont turned his back on Serena and Dominic, and looked only at Marianne.

"Marianne, my love, can you find it in you to forgive my abominable behavior? I'm so ashamed of what I said to Babcock, words spoken from fear of losing things that really don't matter—not compared with losing you." He pressed her palm to his lips. "I do love you, sweetest, and I want you at my side, always. I think we can safely say I'll never be the most decent man you've known—though I'm working on it—but I promise I'll be the best husband you could have."

Marianne threw her arms around him. "Geoffrey, I love you."

No one who saw the joy that burst over Beaumont's face could doubt the genuineness of his feelings. His voice was choked as he said over his shoulder to Dominic, "By the way, Granville, I want nothing to do with that confounded hundred acres my uncle's so set on. In fact, I insist the marriage contract should specify you'll never let me have them."

"Oh, it will," Dominic promised. But he was grinning at his sister's obvious happiness.

Having dealt with the last of the details, Beaumont applied himself to sealing the bargain with a kiss. Marianne broke away first. "Geoffrey Beaumont," she said, cupping his face in her hands, "you are, quite simply, the best, most beautiful man I know."

And to the delight of everyone in the room, Geoffrey Beaumont blushed a deep, tomato red.

Chapter Twenty-One

Dominic waited long enough to agree on settlement details with Beaumont—not that he was responsible for Marianne at her age, but she asked him to get involved—then set off for London three days after Beaumont's unorthodox proposal.

Leaving before dawn, he completed the whole journey in a day, arriving at his aunt's house in Brook Street at nine o'clock Saturday night. He was so tired from the ride, he fell asleep before he had time to reflect on the irony that Geoffrey Beaumont had given him a lesson in how to grab a second chance with both hands, no matter how undeserved it was.

Knowing he was at last on the right track didn't make Sunday any easier. He sent a note around to Hester at breakfast time, asking to see her that afternoon. Her reply said she would expect him at three o'clock.

Dominic spent most of the intervening time in prayer. He arrived in Half Moon Street at three on the dot, and was shown into the drawing room, where Hester waited.

"Dominic, this is a nice surprise." She accepted his kiss on the cheek, then surveyed him. "You look tired."

"There's been a lot going on." He sat next to her on the sofa then told her about Beaumont and Marianne. He didn't blame her for not being a wholehearted supporter of the match.

To anyone who hadn't been present at the proposal, it all sounded very odd.

"Will they marry soon?" Hester asked. "It seems as if we won't have Marianne living with us for long. But how nice to have her as a neighbor."

Which was the obvious opportunity for him to state his business.

"It's you and I that I'm here to talk about," he said. "Hester, there's something you need to know."

She straightened, folded her hands in her lap.

"I've made it clear to you that, much as I like you, this marriage is primarily one of convenience," he said.

She nodded.

"Since I proposed to you, I've realized that I— My heart is with someone else."

She turned pale. "You're *in love* with someone?"

"I should have realized it sooner, much sooner. If I had, I'd never have been so rude as to propose marriage to you."

She pulled a handkerchief from her pocket and began twisting it through her fingers. "Are you jilting me, Dominic?" Her voice quavered.

"No, of course not. I could never do something that would ruin you. If you wish our marriage to go ahead, it will. But it won't go ahead with you in ignorance. If we do marry, I assure you I will be everything I promised—faithful, affectionate."

"But never in love with me."

"No, but that wasn't to be the case, anyway, Hester."

She pinched the bridge of her nose. "Does this other lady return your feelings?"

"Naturally, I haven't spoken to her on the subject," he said. "Please believe that. I really don't know her feelings." He could only hope.

She nodded. "Are you asking me to jilt you, Dominic?"

Although a gentleman couldn't jilt a lady, it was acceptable for the lady to change her mind. So long as she didn't do it too often.

"I think it would be best," he said. For him, certainly. "But I'm aware it's not that simple."

"You're aware you're likely my last hope for marriage," she said grimly. "What Mama would say if I had to tell her I jilted you…"

"I would support you in any way I can," he assured her.

Her smile was ironic. "You undertake to spare me a lifetime of recrimination from my mother? There's only one way to do that, Dominic."

Marry her.

"Then that's what I'll do," he said. "Hester, I wouldn't want you to suffer in any way." He wouldn't be so crass as to offer her money for a breach of promise now, but she must know it was there if she needed it.

She stood, paced to the window. Out of courtesy, Dominic stood, too.

"I understand that you had to tell me of your feelings," she said. "It would be shabby for you to marry me without mentioning your heart is engaged elsewhere."

He nodded, unsure if this was heading toward an agreement to release him, or an insistence that the wedding go ahead. This was where his situation differed from Beaumont's. He'd confessed his fault to someone he hoped would be more forgiving than the women Beaumont had deceived. But who knew, with a spurned woman…

Hester turned around, her back to the glass. "Dominic, I have a confession, too."

He gulped. "You do?"

"You see, when you asked me to marry you—" she paused "—my heart was already engaged, too."

He walked around the couch, over toward her. "Why didn't you say?"

Her smile was woeful. "I was sure you wouldn't want to hear it."

"I wouldn't have been in a position to object," he said, "given I wasn't offering a love match."

"The thing is, Dominic, the person who has my heart... is you."

The words fell into the silence.

For a moment he thought he'd misheard. Then he registered that she'd pulled her handkerchief almost to shreds.

"Hester?" He took a step nearer, but she held up a hand.

"Please don't think I've been pining for you for years, because I haven't. But you always seemed the best of men to me, Dominic, and when I thought of marrying, it was always you—or someone exactly like you—that came to my mind. So when you offered for me...you might have offered for convenient reasons, but that's not why I accepted."

He felt like a complete brute. "Hester, I'm sorry, my words today must have hurt you doubly."

"They did, but there's not much we can do about that," she said, with a return to the practicality he'd always admired. "But the fact is, I might have contemplated going ahead with our wedding knowing you cared for someone else, if I didn't lov—care for you. But I do have those feelings, and I think it would really be too—" her voice caught "—too painful to proceed. So, Dominic, if it's all the same to you, I think I'll jilt you."

Grimes, Marianne's maid, packed the last of Serena's new dresses into her trunk and closed it. "There, miss, you're all set."

"Wonderful," Serena said brightly. As if leaving Woodbridge Hall tomorrow morning was the summit of her ambitions.

Perhaps it was. Certainly "removing herself from temptation," as Marianne put it, was the key to her happiness, if the unhappiness she felt now was any indication. She had to get away from Dominic. From the imminent danger of falling completely, utterly in love with another woman's betrothed.

There, she'd admitted it. Her ability to deny the strength of her feelings for Dominic hung by a thread. She blamed Marianne and Beaumont, who were so ridiculously happy that no one could help thinking about love in their presence.

Serena was only thankful Dominic had been in London the past few days...even though that meant he'd been with Hester Lacey. Serena might be tormented with repeated visions of the kiss Dominic and Hester had parted with two weeks ago—how could a mere kiss on the cheek be so unbearable to watch?—but at least she'd been spared the sight of his increasingly lovable face, the sound of his more frequent laughter, the awareness of his growing tenderness for his children.

But he was back.

He'd returned late last night, breakfasted early, then stayed closeted in the library for hours. A little while ago, he'd asked for the children to be sent in.

"I'll have Gregory take this downstairs." Grimes patted the trunk. "Can I help you with anything else?"

"No, thank you, Grimes," Serena said. "I'll pack my last few things in my valise in the morning."

She went upstairs to the nursery, where she'd requested a special tea for the children tonight. A goodbye tea. The nursery maid was setting it up, and assured Serena there was nothing she could do to help.

Serena hiccuped a sob as she gazed around the airy room,

still bright with the late-afternoon sun streaming in through large windows.

She heard the pounding of young feet, and pulled herself together before the children arrived.

Not just the children. Dominic filled the doorway behind them, the perfect mix of tall and broad and handsome....

She tore her gaze away. "Tea's nearly ready, darlings."

The maid slipped past her to go and bring more food from the kitchen.

"Miss Somerton, now I can tell you my secret." William had been bursting with news this morning, but he'd said he wanted to tell his father first.

"About time," she joked. "Tell me quickly."

"You know how last night there was no moon, and it was dark and scary?"

She nodded.

"I sang the song Papa taught me, and I went to sleep!" the boy crowed.

"Really?" she said. Behind him, Dominic was grinning like an idiot.

"I was still afraid," William confided, "so I sang it twenty-seven times...."

"That many?" Serena asked, impressed.

"Yes, or maybe it was twenty-eight. I kept falling asleep, so it was hard to count." William screwed up his face in concentration.

"Don't worry about the numbers, just tell your story." Dominic scooped William up into his arms and tucked him against his hip. "Oof, you're growing far too big for me to carry."

William grinned at the compliment. "Anyway, I sang it and sang it and sang it...."

"Twenty-seven or twenty-eight times," Dominic told Serena.

"So I hear." His smile was so irresistible, she couldn't help grinning back at him in a way that she feared looked sappy.

"Yes! And then it was morning," William said simply. He pulled back, almost making Dominic overbalance, and grinned.

"Congratulations," Serena said warmly. "It may not be the last time you're kept awake by your fears, William, but now you know you can get past them. I'm convinced it will only get easier."

"That's what Papa said."

Dominic lowered him to the floor. "Now that's out of the way, the children have something to say to you."

She expected short speeches of thanks; she strongly hoped they weren't intending to sing. When they lined up in age order, she suffered a qualm, but pinned an appreciative smile on her face.

"I know what you're thinking," Dominic said. "But don't worry."

No song, then. She didn't feel as relieved as she expected.

Hetty stepped forward. "Miss Somerton, please stay."

Chapter Twenty-Two

Serena's eyes flew to Dominic. She knew he hadn't wanted her to leave before his wedding, but to use his children to convince her to stay was underhanded.

"We have six reasons you should stay," Hetty continued. "Number one, you love all of us children and we love you."

Nods from her siblings.

"I do love you," Serena said over a lump in her throat. "So much. But I'm afraid I can't—"

"Number two." Thomas stepped forward. "You know a lot about lizards. Papa didn't even know they're called vert—invert—inverbrates."

"Invertebrates." Relieved at his more pragmatic reasoning, Serena leveled an accusatory glance at Dominic. "Is that so?"

He hung his head. "My ignorance is woeful."

"Disgraceful, I should say. Did your governess teach you nothing?"

The children giggled.

"If you leave," Dominic said, "Thomas's plan to turn this house into a wildlife refuge will be severely undermined."

"That would be a great shame," she admitted. "But—"

"Reason number three." Charlotte raised her voice. "And I'm not shouting, it's my turn to talk, only Thomas is taking too long. But I'm not blaming him," she assured Serena quickly.

"I hope not," she replied. "Reason number three?"

"Well, I'm not certain I should say this," Charlotte confided, "but Papa says I may if I'm very quiet." She leaned forward, and Serena offered her an ear. Charlotte whispered, "Papa says that if you leave, evil will prevail."

Serena gurgled a laugh. "Dominic, that's too bad! I hope you're not referring to Cook."

"You're the one who decided she's evil," he pointed out.

"It's my turn." William jiggled on the spot. "Miss Somerton, Papa says you can teach me to sing my 'He Is With Me' song so it sounds nicer. That's number four reason to stay."

"I'm a governess, not a miracle worker," she told his father severely. "William, I believe God loves to hear your song sung just the way you do it."

Dominic bestowed on her a smile so filled with tenderness that she had to put a hand to the nursery table to steady herself.

"You've heard four reasons, Miss Somerton," he said. "Are you convinced yet?"

"Dominic, Mr. Granville, I can't stay. I *won't*."

He looked shocked...then he smacked his hand to his forehead. "I'm an idiot."

The children found that rather enjoyable.

"In the excitement of William sharing his news, I forgot to tell you one very important piece of information I meant to divulge at the very start." A rueful smile curved Dominic's lips. "I omitted to mention that Miss Lacey has ended our betrothal."

"I—I'm sorry," Serena said mechanically, her mind racing.

"I hope you're not," he retorted, in a way that encouraged her imagination into all kinds of forbidden paths. "It's a long story, one I will tell you in full later. But now, reason number five, the most compelling."

He glanced around, found Louisa, pushed her forward. "My secret weapon," he said smugly. "I saved her for last. She's irresistible."

"Very clever," Serena murmured.

Louisa handed her a piece of paper. "Look what I made." Serena unfolded it.

A painting. Written across the top, in Charlotte's hand, since Louisa didn't yet write, was the title: My Family.

Serena made out five childlike figures. Two much bigger ones. A man with dark hair...

"You'll notice I have only two eyes," Dominic said. "A vast improvement on my looks, some would say."

Serena examined the mess of colors and shapes. "Is this me?" She pointed to the figure of a yellow-haired woman, who, if she wasn't mistaken, happened to be holding Dominic's hand.

"Miss Somerton, we need you for our family," Louisa said.

Serena nearly burst into tears.

"Children, this is so sweet," she said. "And so monstrously unfair." The fact that Miss Lacey had broken things off didn't mean Serena could stay. She shot a glare at him; he had the nerve to smile lovingly.

Lovingly.

Serena's breath flew out of her.

"You've done a wonderful job, children," Dominic said. "But the last part of this is down to me."

Five pairs of eyes watched him expectantly.

"You're supposed to leave now," he prompted.

Their disappointment obvious, the children filed out. As they left, Dominic clapped the boys on the shoulder, kissed the girls.

"That really was unfair," Serena said when they were gone. "Who could resist?"

"Not you, I hope," he said.

"Dominic…" She laughed shakily. "I don't quite understand."

"Of all the woolly-headed women," he groaned, then laughed at her outrage. "Isn't it perfectly clear that the children love you and want you to stay?"

"That much is clear," she agreed. "And it's clear to me," she said softly, "that you love your children and they know it."

He emitted an embarrassed kind of sound that made her heart swell. While the blaze in his eyes made her pulse race.

"What I haven't made clear, my dear—" he began.

"You called me that once before," she interrupted. "It's what you call your sister."

"Ah." He reached for Serena's hands. "Yours was more of a 'my darling.'"

"Better," she approved, drinking in the warmth in his eyes, knowing she would never have enough of it.

"My feelings for you, Serena—my darling—are such that I never thought to know again," he said. "Yet also different from what I've felt before."

She squeezed his fingers.

"I love you, Serena, with all my heart. Which brings me both joy and terror, as I know that love can be lost."

Confident now, she could afford to tease. "I wouldn't want you to live in terror."

"Oh, I shan't, not most of the time," he said. "I know I have One to whom I can hand over all my fears, and I'm determined to get better at doing that. The real terror now, my sweet Serena, is that you might refuse my proposal of marriage."

He waited, expectant.

"*What* proposal?" she said.

"Ah." He smacked his forehead again. "I knew I'd forget something else."

He went down on one knee before her, the way he'd assured his sister he would never do. "Serena, my darling, I love you. I can scarcely hope that you return my affections, but if you do have even a crumb of regard for me…will you marry me?"

"No, I won't marry you for a crumb," she said.

He paled.

"You know perfectly well that I require wholehearted love on both sides," she said. "I won't marry for less."

"Then tell me you love me wholeheartedly," he ordered. "Either that, or shoot me, but one way or another, put me out of misery."

"I would hardly want to orphan five children," she said. "So I have no choice but to comply with your first request." She tugged on his hands. "Please stand up, Dominic, and kiss me."

Who knew that Dominic Granville could be so obliging?

Some time later, Serena snuggled into his arms. "I love you, Dominic," she said. "You're the finest man and the best father in the world."

He kissed her again. "I hate to quibble over the details, my darling, but you haven't yet said that you'll marry me."

"Ah." She kissed his chin. "Dominic, I love you, and I know I'm of age so I don't need permission, but I feel compelled to ask my parents before I accept. You understand, don't you?"

"No," he said calmly. "But I knew you'd come up with some such woolly-headed objection. I'm afraid I won't allow it, Serena."

"Oh, you won't?" she said, indignation sparking.

"Don't give me that look, my adorable one." He dropped a kiss on her mouth. "Before I left London yesterday, I wrote to your father and told him I'll agree to any terms he cares to name, but he can't stop me proposing to you. Your settlement can bleed me for every last penny—he has my assurance in writing. Serena, I admire your father and the way you care for your parents' good opinion, but your past is behind you. I am your future, and the sooner that future starts, the better."

She began to smile. "Dominic Granville, you're a man of excellent sense."

"The kind of man," he pointed out helpfully, "that you should marry."

"Yes," she said. "Oh, yes, Dominic." A laugh of pure joy burst from her as she went up on tiptoe to kiss him again.

His arms closed around her with an eagerness that said he felt as she did: they had their second chance, both of them, and they would savor every moment.

* * * * *

COMING NEXT MONTH
from Love Inspired® Historical
AVAILABLE OCTOBER 2, 2012

THE GIFT OF FAMILY
Cowboys of Eden Valley
Linda Ford and Karen Kirst

Surprise visitors and warm welcomes bring holiday hearts together in these two stories that show that home and family are the greatest Christmas gift of all.

A GROOM FOR GRETA
Amish Brides of Celery Fields
Anna Schmidt

When Greta Goodloe is jilted by her longtime sweetheart, love starts to seem like an impossible dream...until Luke Starns comes calling.

THE PREACHER'S BRIDE
Brides of Simpson Creek
Laurie Kingery

The new preacher in town is certainly handsome and kind—and he seems quite interested in Faith Bennett. But will his feelings for her fade when he learns her secret?

MARRIAGE OF INCONVENIENCE
Cheryl Bolen

Marriage to the Earl of Aynsley seems so sensible to Miss Rebecca Peabody that she does the proposing herself! It's up to the earl to convince her that true marriage is based on love.

REQUEST YOUR FREE BOOKS!

2 FREE INSPIRATIONAL NOVELS
PLUS 2
FREE
MYSTERY GIFTS

Love Inspired.
HISTORICAL
INSPIRATIONAL HISTORICAL ROMANCE

YES! Please send me 2 FREE Love Inspired® Historical novels and my 2 FREE mystery gifts (gifts are worth about $10). After receiving them, if I don't wish to receive any more books, I can return the shipping statement marked "cancel". If I don't cancel, I will receive 4 brand-new novels every month and be billed just $4.49 per book in the U.S. or $4.99 per book in Canada. That's a saving of at least 22% off the cover price. It's quite a bargain! Shipping and handling is just 50¢ per book in the U.S. and 75¢ per book in Canada.* I understand that accepting the 2 free books and gifts places me under no obligation to buy anything. I can always return a shipment and cancel at any time. Even if I never buy another book, the two free books and gifts are mine to keep forever.

102/302 IDN FEHF

Name	(PLEASE PRINT)	
Address		Apt. #
City	State/Prov.	Zip/Postal Code

Signature (if under 18, a parent or guardian must sign)

Mail to the **Reader Service:**
IN U.S.A.: P.O. Box 1867, Buffalo, NY 14240-1867
IN CANADA: P.O. Box 609, Fort Erie, Ontario L2A 5X3

Not valid for current subscribers to Love Inspired Historical books.

Want to try two free books from another series?
Call 1-800-873-8635 or visit www.ReaderService.com

* Terms and prices subject to change without notice. Prices do not include applicable taxes. Sales tax applicable in N.Y. Canadian residents will be charged applicable taxes. Offer not valid in Quebec. This offer is limited to one order per household. All orders subject to credit approval. Credit or debit balances in a customer's account(s) may be offset by any other outstanding balance owed by or to the customer. Please allow 4 to 6 weeks for delivery. Offer available while quantities last.

Your Privacy—The Reader Service is committed to protecting your privacy. Our Privacy Policy is available online at www.ReaderService.com or upon request from the Reader Service.

We make a portion of our mailing list available to reputable third parties that offer products we believe may interest you. If you prefer that we not exchange your name with third parties, or if you wish to clarify or modify your communication preferences, please visit us at www.ReaderService.com/consumerschoice or write to us at Reader Service Preference Service, P.O. Box 9062, Buffalo, NY 14269. Include your complete name and address.

LIH11B

When Greta Goodloe is jilted by her longtime sweetheart, she takes comfort in matchmaking between newcomer Luke Starns and her schoolmarm sister. Yet the more Greta tries to throw them together, the more Luke fascinates her.

Read on for a sneak peek of A GROOM FOR GRETA by Anna Schmidt, available October 2012 from Love Inspired® Historical.

***

"So what do you intend to do about this turn of events, Luke?"

"Do? Your sister made her feelings plain last evening. She does not wish to spend her time with me."

Greta sighed heavily. "She does not know what she wants. The question is, are you serious about finding a wife for yourself or not?"

"I am quite serious."

"Then—"

"What I will not do," Luke interrupted, "is go after a woman who has declared openly that she has no interest in making a home with me."

"And what of her idea that you and I should…" She let the sentence trail off.

"That depends," he said slowly.

"On what?"

"On whether or not you are able to put aside your feelings for Josef Bontrager. Your sister believes that your feelings for him were not as strong as they should be for two people planning a life together. Do you agree?"

"Lydia is…I mean…oh, I don't know," Greta replied.

"How can either of you expect me to know what it is that I'm feeling these days? It's too soon."

"If Josef came to you and asked for your forgiveness and pleaded with you to reconsider, would you?"

"No," she finally whispered. "I would not."

Luke felt his heart pounding, and he realized that over the months he had been in Celery Fields, he had taken more notice of the beautiful Greta Goodloe than he had allowed himself to admit. He had learned a hard lesson back in Ontario and he had been determined not to make the same mistake twice.

But if Greta had come to realize that Josef was not for her…

On the other hand, surely the idea that she might be firm in her decision to be rid of Josef did not mean that she was ready for someone new.

***

Don't miss A GROOM FOR GRETA by Anna Schmidt, the next heartwarming book in the AMISH BRIDES OF CELERY FIELDS series, on sale October 2012 wherever Love Inspired® Historical books are sold!

SHLIHEXP1012

Love Inspired HISTORICAL

celebrating
15
YEARS

A touching tale of new beginnings from author

LAURIE KINGERY

The Preacher's Bride

When her little brother died, Faith Bennett lost her trust in God. She's kept this secret from the good people of Simpson Creek, yet she can't deceive Gil Chadwick. Though Gil cherishes Faith's friendship, he wants a wife. And in kind, upright Faith, he's convinced he's found her. The secret heartaches of his past fade as he watches her nurse his father. And when danger finds her, he'll risk everything to save her. For where there's Faith, there's love...and the promise of a new beginning together.

Small-town Texas spinsters
find love with mail-order grooms!

Available October 2012 wherever books are sold!

www.LoveInspiredBooks.com

LIH82937

celebrating **15 YEARS**

Love Inspired™

Another heartwarming installment of

← **TEXAS TWINS** →

**Two sets of twins, torn apart by family secrets,
find their way home**

When big-city cop Grayson Wallace visits an elementary
school for career day, he finds his heartstrings
unexpectedly tugged by a six-year-old fatherless boy and
his widowed mother, Elise Lopez. Now he can't get the
struggling Lopezes off his mind. All he can think about
is what family means—especially after discovering
the identical twin brother he hadn't known he had
in Grasslands. Maybe a trip to ranch country is just
what he, Elise and little Cory need.

Look-Alike Lawman
by **Glynna Kaye**

*Available October 2012
wherever books are sold.*

www.LoveInspiredBooks.com

LI87770